the FlipSide

the Flip Side

SHAWN JOHNSON

with Amy Sonnichsen

SIMON & SCHUSTER BFYR

NEW YORK   LONDON   TORONTO   SYDNEY   NEW DELHI

An imprint of Simon & Schuster Children's Publishing Division
1230 Avenue of the Americas, New York, New York 10020

For information about special discounts for bulk purchases, please contact Simon & Schuster Special Sales at 1-866-506-1949 or business@simonandschuster.com.
The Simon & Schuster Speakers Bureau can bring authors to your live event. For more information or to book an event, contact the Simon & Schuster Speakers Bureau at 1-866-248-3049 or visit our website at www.simonspeakers.com.
Also available in a SIMON & SCHUSTER BFYR hardcover edition
Cover design by Krista Vossen
Interior design by Hilary Zarycky
The text for this book was set in Electra.
Manufactured in the United States of America
First SIMON & SCHUSTER BFYR paperback edition June 2017
2 4 6 8 10 9 7 5 3 1
The Library of Congress has cataloged the hardcover edition as follows:
Names: Johnson, Shawn, 1992- author. | Sonnichsen, A. L., author.
Title: The flip side / Shawn Johnson with Amy Sonnichsen.
Description: First edition. | New York : SSBFYR, [2016] | Summary: An elite teenaged gymnast with Olympic dreams finds it hard to train when a irresistible guy comes along and threatens to throw her whole world off balance.
Identifiers: LCCN 2016004893 (print) | LCCN 2016020689 (ebook) | ISBN 9781481460217 (hardback) | ISBN 9781481460224 (trade paper) | ISBN 9781481460231 (eBook)
Subjects: | CYAC: Gymnastics—Fiction. | Dating (Social customs)—Fiction. | BISAC: JUVENILE FICTION / Sports & Recreation / General. | JUVENILE FICTION / Social Issues / Adolescence. | JUVENILE FICTION / Social Issues / Friendship.
Classification: LCC PZ7.1.J63 Fl 2016 (print) | LCC PZ7.1.J63 (ebook) | DDC [Fic]—dc23
LC record available at https://lccn.loc.gov/2016004893

To my other half, for always believing in me and for giving me the courage to pursue my crazy ideas

—S. J.

Acknowledgments

A thank-you to the dream team behind the cover: Kyell Thomas, Jennifer Keene, and Octagon Entertainment.

And a reminder to everyone reading: Your wildest dreams are never out of reach.

Chapter One

"She stuck that series as if it were a floor pass. Amazing! One thing Charlie Ryland always brings to the table is consistency on beam."

A female commentator's voice chimes in. "That's right, Doug. She has both the grace of a ballerina and the fighting spirit of a warrior. It's a joy to watch her."

"Yes, an absolute joy. Here comes her dismount. Look at that focused concentration!"

I raise my arms. My mind, my muscles, know precisely what to do. Tight. Control. Stick it.

I pull my arms in as I power into my twisting dismount. My bare feet hit the mat, and my arms automatically extend over my head. The crowd's cheers fill the stadium, while that rush of adrenaline surges through me, the one that always comes after I nail a beam routine.

"I wouldn't be at all surprised if that performance brings her gold. She stuck that landing perfectly."

"She's a born winner," the woman says.

I see Coach Chris, off to the side, clapping enthusiastically. As I run toward him, his face breaks into a wide grin. "That's my girl." He pats my back affectionately.

"Solid routine, Charlie," Coach Rachel says, wrapping me in a firm hug. I'm basking in the thunderous buzz of the crowd, the blinding bright lights—

"Charlotte, what is the main role of Congress?"

Mr. Alto's raspy voice snaps me back to reality. I adjust my glasses on the bridge of my nose and see him standing in front of the class, the study guide limp in his fingers.

"Daydreaming again?" he asks, his jaw set. He's clearly not happy with me. It's not the first time.

"Uh, no." Glancing down at the class discussion sheet on my desk, I squirm. I haven't made a single notation. How am I going to prepare for the upcoming test? Why can't I keep this subject matter straight? "I think . . . it's to keep the House of Representatives in check? So they don't make laws that the American people don't like?"

"No." Mr. Alto's tone has a ring of impatience to it. "The House of Representatives is part of Congress. You need to remember the order of government. This *will* be on the test next Tuesday."

I swallow hard. I'm not a bad student. In fact, up until this class I've easily earned straight As. But U.S. government keeps tripping me up. It's only a one-semester course, but for the first nine-week grading period, I barely squeaked by with an A. So far, this grading period has been far less promising.

"Step up your game, Charlotte," Mr. Alto says, pointing a thick finger at me.

"Yes, sir." I cast a sideways glance at my friend Zoe Parker, who sits beside me. She looks back at me pityingly.

"We'll study together," she mouths.

I nod, although I'm not sure where I'll find time for a study session with her. As soon as this class is over, I'm heading out of town for the weekend and won't be back until Tuesday.

As others answer the remainder of the study questions, I make notes on the class discussion sheet. But at the bottom of the page I've been doodling. *Last camp*, I've written with squiggles and hearts around it. *Your time to shine.* Underneath I've drawn something that looks suspiciously like an Olympic gold medal.

Zoe and I walk out of Mr. Alto's room together.

"We need to sync our schedules," she says. "Figure out the best time for studying this weekend."

"I've got a plane to catch. I'm on my way out now."

"Oh, that's right. Going to your aunt's ranch in Texas." Zoe grins at me and wiggles her eyebrows. "Maybe you'll hook up with a cowboy."

I laugh. "Probably not." It's not that kind of ranch, but I can't tell her that, or that no aunt will be there. Guilt pricks me because I'm not being completely honest with her, but too much is at stake. Mostly my sanity.

"I'm going to miss you," she says.

"I'll be back to school on Tuesday."

"We'll need to start examining our prom options when you get back, consider who we can get to take us."

I give a low laugh. "The prom is only for juniors and seniors. We're sophomores."

"Which is why we need to consider which upperclassman we might get to take us." She smiles brightly, her eyes shining with excitement. "Wouldn't it be awesome to have an older boy take us? We'd be special, getting into a dance that most sophomores only dream about."

Going to prom isn't something I've ever dreamed about, although I do have to admit that my dreams revolve around me doing something else that very few people get a chance to do.

"I'm not going to have time for prom," I admit.

She comes to an abrupt halt in the hallway, forcing me to stop as well. "How can you not have time for prom?" she asks.

It's the weekend right before Olympic trials. My focus has to be on trials if I want to have any chance at all of going to the Olympics. "I think my family is doing something that weekend."

"Get out of it. You can stay with me."

I don't have time to come up with a plausible excuse right now, especially when the odds are that no one will invite me to prom anyway. I don't exactly have guys—much less the required junior or senior—tripping over themselves to talk to or hang out with me. Since the school year started more than eight months ago, I've had very little time for anything other than studying and practice. "I've got to skedaddle, but we'll talk when I get back."

"Text me a picture of a cowboy."

Shaking my head and chuckling at her one-track mind, I continue to the office to sign out.

When I first started gymnastics, life was totally ordinary. I did everything—soccer, ballet, T-ball. But when I turned six, gymnastics took over. I was invited onto our gym's TOPs team—short for "Talent Opportunity Program"—which is a way for USA Gymnastics to find rising talent in kids who are between seven and ten years old. After that there was no turning back. I loved it, and my parents sacrificed to make it work. That was when we lived in Indiana.

When I was eight, my coaches wanted me to be home-schooled because a flexible schedule would give me more time to practice gymnastics, so Mom spent three years home-schooling me. But I missed real life. I missed being around girls who weren't associated with gymnastics, and I missed having boys in my class and going to sleepovers and birthday parties.

Then we moved to Columbus, Ohio, where I started at one of the best gyms in the country. I was eleven. My new coach, Coach Chris, thought I could qualify for the USA Gymnastics Junior Elite program by age thirteen. And I wanted it. I wanted it bad. But I also wanted a life outside the gym. My parents and my coaches worked out a schedule so that I could go to public school (and I did still manage to make Junior Elite by thirteen). So for four years now, I've been going to regular school and I love it. It balances out the crazy in the rest of my life.

And life as an elite gymnast can get crazy. When I was younger, just starting gymnastics, I idolized several elite gymnasts, followed their careers, and imagined the day when I would be where they were. A couple of them had overly enthusiastic supporters following them around, bombarding them with social media posts. It seemed a little scary to have perfect strangers following your life so closely. I read in an interview with one gymnast how challenging it was for her to not buckle under the pressure of trying to please a lot of people, and trying to meet others' expectations. I also remember seeing a YouTube video of a gymnast crying because she was being heckled after a poor showing at a meet.

I felt enough pressure competing. I didn't want to heap others' dreams or hopes for my success onto my plate.

So when I returned to public school, I decided to keep my gymnastics life a secret. In order to maintain some semblance of normality in my life, I perform a balancing act. At school I'm Charlotte with glasses and long blond hair that falls into my face; at the gym I'm Charlie in a leotard and a ponytail. On social media I have my gymnastics followers who leave fan mail on my Charlie Ryland Gymnast account pages. I post videos and pictures there sometimes, but only of gymnastics. Charlotte Ryland is the name on my personal Instagram account, where I never, ever post gymnastics stuff.

I think I've done a pretty good job of keeping the two worlds completely separate. It helps that I'm known only a little bit in the gymnastics world. I'm up-and-coming, and it's not at all like I'm famous. No one seems to have put two and two together, thank goodness.

"Out again?" the attendance secretary asks, winking at me from behind the counter-high desk.

"Yep." I take the clipboard she offers me. I know the sign-out routine.

She knows the truth about me. The principal and one of the counselors do too. Mom and Dad had a meeting with them when they enrolled me at Jefferson High, explaining my rigorous schedule and the need for a few exceptions to the rules.

In order to get in my conditioning training, I have no first-period class. Instead I spend that time at the gym. But my not having that first class doesn't raise any red flags, because other students arrive late, those who are part of work programs or attend off-campus classes at the community college. Final bell rings at three, and I'm able to get to the gym by three thirty. It makes for a long day, but it's totally worth it. My parents also made it clear to the school officials that I didn't want my outside-of-school activities made public. The people who are in the loop have been super-respectful and supportive.

"There's some exciting stuff coming up," the secretary says in a voice low enough that the other office staff can't overhear her. I think she likes knowing what the others don't.

I smile. "Yeah."

"I'm excited for you, Charlotte. You're going to do great."

"Thanks." I adjust the straps on my backpack. "I'll see you next Tuesday."

I leave the building with a spring in my step. Heading to Texas always fills me with anticipation. The ranch is one of my favorite places in the world. Which is odd, considering it's also one of the places most likely to destroy me.

Chapter Two

"Let's go, Charlie," Coach Chris says, his voice low but firm.

I don't like that he has to command me. This is our last day of development camp at the Texas ranch where Team USA meets to practice. Olympic trials are only six weeks away. I've won gold at the Junior Olympics as well as at state and regional meets. I won two World Championships on beam. I know what it takes to qualify for Team USA. But his tone means I'm not ready for the big leagues, that I'm stalling and doubting my abilities. I don't stand for stalling, not in myself. Fear is one thing. Everyone's allowed to have fear. But stalling means I'm letting fear win. That's one reason I love gymnastics so much—every single day I get to look my fear of failure in the face and beat it.

I shake out my hands, rotate my ankles, and hop back onto the beam, feeling the grip of the fabric, soft like leather, against my soles.

I take one more calming breath. Arms extend, knees lock—the perfect form I learned as a six-year-old. It all comes together here. Round-off, back handspring, layout full—my body straight and extended. On a beam four inches wide.

As my feet strike the beam, they make a hollow, booming noise. My favorite sound in the whole world, because that means I'm sticking my skills on my favorite apparatus. I'm flying, my blond hair caught up in a ponytail whipping against my neck. Coming up for breath at the other end of the beam, I pull my arms against my ears, chin up, back arched, fingers straight.

"That's it!" Coach Chris claps once, a single, sharp staccato. He has the short stature and firm body of a former Olympic gymnast. Although his hair has turned white, he's still in great shape. I don't think the word "slacker" is in his vocabulary. "Now higher. I want to see more air between you and the beam. I want flight."

I pivot. No stalling this time. Back in the other direction to do it again.

There's no time to look around, no time to evaluate the other gymnasts and their progress. They have nothing to do with me in this moment. In a different section of my brain, I know another gymnast is practicing a complex back pass on floor, but I don't even glance at her. Behind me the bars creak—probably my best friend, Gwen Edwards—but I block her out too. She has the full attention of the head coach of the U.S. national team, Claudia Inverso. Gwen has had it all day, since she nailed the Kovacs—a release move that involves two flips over the high bar. She's been working on it back at our home gym and has stuck it a few times, but this morning she's making it look easy. She's found her rhythm, and it's amazing. Gwen's Kovacs is the most talked-about skill at camp this week. The big question is, will she be ready to compete with it?

This time I wobble on the landing, fighting to keep my body straight, arms raised up, fingers reaching for the ceiling.

"Precision," Coach Chris states in a soft, clipped tone that sends a shiver through me. The quieter he gets, the more frightening he becomes. My performance is disappointing him. He yells only when he's happy.

I've got his attention, and I'm not letting that go. He stood on the Olympic podium where I want to stand one day. He knows how to get there, understands completely what it takes. I nod in his direction, wipe the sweat off my hands.

Round-off, back handspring, layout full. *Boom.*

"I want you still higher," Coach insists. "Prove to me that you deserve to be here. Get into the mind-set—best in the world."

I thought I was in that mind-set. Frustration niggles at me. But I don't let any annoyance show on my face. Coach Chris believes in me, or he wouldn't ride me so hard.

I nod. Close my eyes. Visualize height.

"Faster." Coach Chris approaches the beam. His steely blue gaze bites into me. "You nail this, Charlie. You're going for gold."

I pivot, raise my arms.

Gold—it's what I've always wanted. When I was a kid competing at the Junior Olympic meets, it was what I earned all the time. But now that I'm here, competing on the world's stage against the best gymnasts on the planet, gold is more elusive. Winning takes everything I've got. Every fiber of my being has to be committed to it.

Higher. Bigger. Fly.

"That's it!" Coach Chris's voice rings out. "Now do it again."

"What I wouldn't give right now for one of my dad's pumpkin doughnuts," Gwen says as she sets her cafeteria tray down across from me and takes a seat.

"Your dad makes doughnuts?" I scoop up a forkful of salad. "That's cool."

"Yeah. They are the best." Chalk from the bars dusts Gwen's dark skin. She looks like she's wearing football pads, because her shoulders are bulging with ice packs. She's not injured—those ice packs are to decrease the inevitable soreness after twelve hours locked in the gym. I've got an ice pack bound to my ankle—the ankle I broke when I was eight. The old injury flares up every time I come to camp.

With a weary sigh Gwen digs into her pile of spaghetti.

I understand her lack of energy. She gave everything to pull off those Kovacs today. Just like I gave everything to my routines. The mental and physical exertion is exhausting, which is why we pay attention to what we eat. We need food that gives us energy and repairs and builds muscles. I've already logged my dinner into my fitness app so that I can be sure I'm getting enough fuel and the proper nutrients to keep my body in its best shape. Doughnuts are never on the menu.

"We're almost done," she says. "Although, I wish I were going to my real home tomorrow. I miss more than the doughnuts. I miss my parents." When we're finished here, she'll return to her host family, the Gundersens. A nice family, but still . . . not the same as home. Gwen's family lives in Georgia. She lives with the Gundersens in Columbus so that she can train with Coach Chris, who has a track record for training Olympic champions. She's nearly a year older than I am, which means her competitive clock is ticking. (A female gymnast's career ends when she is relatively young.) We instantly connected the first day she showed up at Gold Star gym.

"Come over when we get back," I tell her. "My mom promised to make no-bake cookies."

Gwen pokes at her food. "Those yummy things with the peanut butter, right?"

"Yep. We'll celebrate wrapping our last camp before trials."

Gwen twirls spaghetti onto her fork. "Sounds like a plan."

She says it with as much enthusiasm as someone saying, *I have a dentist appointment.* I know it's really hard for her to be away from her family. I need to get her mind on something else. Something to remind her that the sacrifice she's making to be trained by one of the best coaches in the country is worth it. "Your Kovacs looked amazing today. You're really nailing it."

Gwen nods. A smile tugs at the corner of her mouth. "Thanks. Yeah, I'm feeling pretty good about it." She pops a cherry tomato from her salad into her mouth, studies me. "Coach was getting after you today."

I was really hoping no one had noticed. "I should have been pushing harder. He knows it. I know it."

"You've won two golds on beam at the World Championships. He should trust you to push when it counts."

"We can't slack off. Not for a second. Besides, *you* got gold in the all-around at the World Championships, and you were rocking it during the last set."

She grins. "We really need to get T-shirts that read, 'Mutual Admiration Society.'"

"I'm glad we can compete and still be friends," I tell her.

"Hey, who else is going to understand the demands and stresses of this life?"

That's too true, and it's part of the reason why I don't tell anyone at school about my aspirations to make the Olympic team.

"How are things at school?" Gwen asks, as though she read my mind. She's always been homeschooled, so Jefferson High is a mystery to her.

"My government class is giving me fits," I admit. "I brought the study sheet—"

"I don't know why you don't homeschool so you can have a more lenient study schedule."

"I don't want my life to be only gymnastics." Which I've already told her a zillion times.

Her brow furrows, and she gives me a serious stare. "But we have such a narrow competitive window, Charlie. If we don't make the Olympic team this time, that could be it for us. We'll be at retirement age before the next Olympics roll around."

I want to laugh at the absurdity of retirement at sixteen or seventeen. Unfortunately, she's not exaggerating by much. During the 2012 Olympics, the girls on the U.S. team ranged in age from fifteen to eighteen. That means that when the next Olympics roll around in four years, we might be too old. It sounds crazy, but it's true.

I don't want to think about everything that is riding on the next few weeks, or all the sacrifices that our families and we have made to get here. I decide to return to an earlier subject. "I wish you hadn't mentioned doughnuts. Now I can't stop thinking about them."

Gwen laughs. "I'll have my dad bring us some when they come to Detroit for trials." Her parents never miss a competition.

"When do you get to go home next?" I ask.

Gwen gives me a hopeful smile. "If everything goes as planned, it'll be a while."

Grinning, I give her a fist bump. "It's going to be a while, then."

Because if everything goes as planned, we'll be heading to the Olympics.

Chapter Three

Rain drives down and runs in mini rivers along the sides of the ranch's dirt roads. The rivulets glisten in the light of the single streetlamp. I'm squatting outside the gym, under a tiny awning, my back pressed against the glass doors. This is the only place I can find at the entire ranch where my phone gets okay reception.

I had five missed calls from Zoe and three texts that read *Call Me!!!!!* I couldn't ignore that many exclamation points.

"You are so hard to get ahold of!" she says when she answers her phone.

"Sporadic reception at the ranch. So, what's up?"

"Michael Hartman."

She says it like he's famous—a movie star or some celebrity—but I'm drawing a blank. "Who?"

I hear her exasperated puff of air. "He's on the wrestling team, and he's a *junior*. Anyway, there was an event at the park today to raise money for the animal shelter. Bubbles and Barks. You could get your dog washed, and the money went to the shelter. People were standing around with little bottles of soap, blowing bubbles. There were food trucks. It was like a carnival. So I took Minnie."

Minnie, her Yorkie, is a precious little thing that always makes me smile.

"I'm standing in line to get a snow cone, and I suddenly hear, 'Cute dog.' I turn around, and it's Michael. Talking. To. Me!"

"She is pretty cute."

"I know, right? Plus I had her decked out in her pink polka-dot bows. Michael says, 'Bet she hates the bows, though.' I assure him that she does not. Then he says, 'My dog would kill me in my sleep if I did that to him.' I look down. He has a bulldog on a leash sitting there. I say, 'Of course he would. He'd want to wear a football jersey.' And he laughed."

"The dog?"

"No! Michael!"

I'm smiling, imagining the exchange, wishing I'd been there. Zoe is so comfortable around people, even those she barely knows or just met. Sometimes I envy the ease with which she can move through social situations. I always worry that I'll give too much away, that people will figure out who I am. A measure of fame comes with being an Olympian, and I'm not quite ready to embrace a total lack of privacy. Coach Rachel was seventeen and at the Olympic trials when someone posted a picture of her at a party, in the pool, topless. Some say it was the resulting publicity of her scandalous behavior that caused her to be so distracted that her routines were judged below par and she missed a chance to go to the Olympics. Not that I would ever go topless. Still, I'm not ready to have every aspect of my life scrutinized.

"So then what happened?" I ask, anxious to get to the juicy tidbit that was worthy of five exclamation points.

"That's pretty much it. The snow cone guy interrupted us by asking for my order, so I gave it to him, and he fixed my snow cone way too fast."

"Oh. I thought maybe there was more."

"Michael did say 'See you around' as I was walking off. That could mean something."

"Do you like him?" I ask.

"I think so. Yeah. I mean, we have study hall together. Not that he's ever really noticed me. Today was the first time he's ever talked to me." She pauses, then asks, "You think it was the Minnie factor? That he was just taken with my dog?"

I hear the disappointment in her voice, like the reality has hit her that maybe the guy was just making conversation to avoid boredom while waiting in line. "No. You have a class together. He knows who you are, and obviously he wanted to talk to you."

"I think I got excited for nothing. I do that, don't I? Read too much into things. He was just being nice."

"Maybe tomorrow you could just say hi to him in class. See how it goes."

She groans. "I wish you'd been there. Then you could have judged the situation. Confirm whether I overreacted."

"If I'd been there, he might not have talked to you."

"There is that. So . . . any hot cowboys? I'm still waiting for my picture."

"It's not a working ranch." Another lie. There is way too much work going on at this ranch, just not the cowboy kind. Gwen and I spent time in an ice-filled tub after our last workout, in order to increase our blood flow and help our muscles recover from the strain we'd put on them during our grueling practice. Plus the cooldown helps trigger a deeper sleep. It's not my favorite treatment, but the benefits are worth it. "No cowboys."

"Bummer."

"Well, listen. I should probably go. We'll figure it all out when I get back."

"There's nothing to figure out. You were right. It was nothing."

"I didn't say it was nothing."

"It's just that it would be so nice to have a boyfriend, especially one who could take me to prom. Don't you want a boyfriend?"

"I don't know," I say. But I do want a boyfriend. It would certainly fall into line with the normal life I want. "We'll talk."

"Okay. See you Tuesday."

I say good-bye but linger for a moment after I hang up,

analyzing the sudden ache in my chest, because Zoe was sharing her weekend with me and I wasn't sharing mine with her. But she doesn't need to know about my gymnastics. Not yet, anyway. At least not until the Olympics are a sure thing. There will be no keeping gymnastics a secret anymore . . . *if* that happens.

I tuck my phone under my arm and sprint toward my cabin, trying to dodge raindrops. But by the time I make it to the doorway of the room I'm sharing with Gwen, I'm drenched.

Gwen is already in her bunk, lying on her back, eyes closed, headphones attached. She left one lamp on for me. I tiptoe across the room, set my phone on the floor next to my open suitcase, and grab a towel. I dry off and slip into a flannel tank and shorts. I've got to pack sometime tonight. Gwen's suitcase stands upright at the door, waiting for her departure tomorrow.

I sort through my clothes, trying to figure out what to wear on the plane. This weekend has been a blur. In the end I choose leggings and an oversize shirt and toss them onto my bunk.

"Charlie?"

Gwen's voice takes me by surprise.

I pivot on my heel. Her eyes are open. She slides off her headphones. "Do you think we'll make it?"

It's the one thing on both our minds, so of course I know what she's talking about. Besides, we haven't trained together for countless hours for the last two years for me to be clueless about how her mind works. "I think so. We've got the best coaches, and we're beating up our bodies every single day. It's going to pay off. Nothing is stopping us. Tight mind, right?"

Gwen's head thumps the pillow. She shields her eyes with her arm. "I'm tightening my mind, but . . ."

"You pulled off Kovacs after Kovacs today," I say, crossing the room in order to kneel next to Gwen's bed. "That's amazing. You're going to be one of the first ever to put that into a routine in competition." I pull out one of the lines Mom always uses on me. "Let yourself enjoy it!"

Her lips tighten, but she nods. "Okay."

The way she says it reminds me of the way she responds to Coach Chris when he's speaking in his nerve-racking, quiet voice. Gwen's "okay" means she's taking what he says and planning to do it ten times better. That's the way she is. A perfectionist to the core. It's no wonder we get along so well.

I take her hand and squeeze it briefly. We're friends, we're teammates, we're competitors. We both want a spot on that Olympic team, when there are only so many spots to go around.

It's one of those moments. When someone is vulnerable with you, it kind of makes you want to be vulnerable with them. I want to assure Gwen that inside I'm just as nervous as she is, that I'm not as strong as I come across a lot of the time. But instead I blurt out, "I wish I had a boyfriend." Okay, so Zoe isn't the only one with guys on her mind.

That gets Gwen's attention. She rolls onto her elbow and stares at me hard, her eyes questioning. "What brought that on?"

I can't help but twist my lips into an ironic smile. "Zoe." I've told her about Zoe, but I've never told Zoe about Gwen. Another thorn of guilt pricks me, because I consider them both my best friends, but I'm not completely honest with one of them. "She wanted to tell me about this guy who gave her some attention today, and I just . . . I'd just like a guy to give *me* some attention for a change. Don't you ever think about having a boyfriend?"

"I'm homeschooled. Where am I going to meet a guy?"

"But if you met someone who was interested in you, wouldn't you want to pursue the possibilities? Not just blow him off?"

"I get that it would be amazing to have a boyfriend, but it's not practical right now. We have to go steady with gymnastics, with practice and competitions, not a guy."

"Don't you get tired of delaying everything?"

"Sure I do. But think about it. Where are you going to find the time for a boyfriend?" she asks, and raises one finger. "You have two hours of conditioning before school." Another finger. "School." Another finger. "Five hours of training after school. And when you get home, you have to eat and study. And sometime you have to sleep. How are you going to work this guy in? Do you think he's going to understand when you're too tired to even text him?"

"He might." If he was the right boyfriend.

"You'd have to tell him about your gymnastics life."

Then how would I know if he likes me for myself and not because I'm an almost-famous gymnast? I want him to fall for the Charlotte version, the one who wears thick-rimmed glasses and is far from being the most popular girl at school.

"You won't even tell *Zoe* you're a gymnast," she reminds me.

"All this"—I flail my arms at the walls of the cabin, but I'm talking about the ranch and what it symbolizes in general—"I mean, would anyone at school get it? I mean, *really get* why I'm doing this? They'd just think I was weird. Or stuck up. Or something."

And the pressure would increase because they might take more of an interest in my success and my failures.

"They'll get it when you make the Olympic team," Gwen says. "Then they'll all be proud to know you."

"But then they'll treat me differently. And they'll ask me about gymnastics at school. And I'd have a lot of friends who aren't real friends." School is my safe place right now, my place to get away from the pressure, to be an average kid. I don't know how it would affect my gymnastics if at least half my life weren't *normal.*

"A boyfriend isn't practical, Charlie," Gwen says kindly. "Not now. Not when so much is on the line. Not if you really want the dream."

"Of course I want the dream! Are you serious?" That's why

I'm keeping up this balancing act, because it's helping me get there. I want the dream more than anything else.

Gwen falls back onto the pillow, smiling. "Good to hear. For a minute there, I thought I'd lost you to *being normal*."

"I'm planning to be anything but normal at the gym, so you'd better watch your back!" I punch her playfully in the arm.

"Oh, I have no doubt." She's laughing. "I believe in you, Charlie. You got this!" She ducks sideways, clutching her sides with laughter, to avoid my second play-punch.

"You got this" is our inside joke. Back when Gwen was in level eight—the first level where a gymnast chooses her own routines—at her Georgia gym, I guess someone from the crowd yelled "You got this, Gwen!" right before she started a run on vault. She was competing with a Yurchenko—round-off with a back handspring onto the vault, with a full flip off the vault— but she over-rotated and landed flat on her back. It was one of those catastrophic moments that brought an edge of superstition to Gwen's competitive career. After that the phrase "You got this!" became a serious taboo. When Gwen moved to Gold Star two years ago, we were all ordered not to say it.

"We're so close to making it," I say, letting out a ragged breath of excitement. There are certain moments when I think about what we're doing and how far we've come, when the Olympics seem not only reachable but right at my fingertips. There's a bubble of excitement that grows in my chest, making me so light that I could float to the ceiling.

"Close," Gwen agrees, seizing my hand again and squeezing. "Just remember that you've got to follow your heart, and right now, as much as I wish the reality were different, it can't go chasing after boys."

My heart. What my heart wants is easy. It wants an Olympic gold medal. It's my brain that confuses things.

In the end, is my wanting to be ordinary going to cost me my dreams?

Chapter Four

"And what did Coach Chris say?" Mom leans forward, a piece of glazed chicken dangling from her fork. Dad picked me up at the airport. Now we're sitting around the dinner table. I've just finished telling Mom about my new series on beam.

"He didn't say much," I say. "You know Coach. But I could tell he was happy."

Dad grins at his plate. He's not one to say much either. "That's great, Charlie. I'm proud of you."

I can't help but smile. "But that wasn't the coolest thing that happened. There was Gwen's Kovacs! She has totally nailed it. I was so excited."

"What's a Kovacs again?" Mom asks. She and Dad are pretty good about keeping up with my gymnastics skills, but they certainly don't obsess about it. Since I've never even attempted a Kovacs, this is new territory for them.

"It's that release move I was telling you about. Here, let me pull up a video." I pick up my phone—second nature.

Dad clears his throat. "Dinner rule."

"Oh yeah." I push my phone back under the edge of my plate. "I'll show you after dinner. It's so amazing!"

"Eh." My brother, Josh, shrugs me off, but his dimples are showing. "You know, flip around a bar a few times. No big deal."

I poke him in the arm, hard. "Whatever."

"Ow! Watch it! These biceps are an endangered species!"

"I know, right? Fading away before our very eyes."

My phone buzzes before it starts ringing. I glance at the screen, cheating on our no-phones-at-the-table rule. But I've got to silence it, right? It's Zoe.

"No phones at the table means no phones at the table," Josh says, deepening his voice to sound more like Dad. We're only eleven months apart, and Josh is a year ahead of me in school. Thankfully. He gives me enough grief as it is. I can't imagine what it would be like if we were in the same classes.

"I didn't answer it!" I cry. "You are such a pest."

Dad scoots back his chair. "Never a dull moment around here. I can tell you two missed each other. But as much fun as I'm having watching this display, I've got to get back to work." Four years ago my dad got laid off from his job. It was the first time I encountered the fear of uncertainty, the possibility of losing my dreams. I didn't handle it very well, worrying that with no money coming in, I'd have to give up gymnastics. But somehow Mom and Dad scraped the money together for my lessons. It was a huge relief two years later when Dad patented an improved spring used in car suspension, which led to a start-up business manufacturing and distributing his invention. He always says his next big innovation is going to be an improved spark plug. Knowing about the sacrifices that my parents made for me, I'm even more determined to stand on the podium at the next Olympics, to bring home the gold.

Dad carries his plate to the dishwasher. "You know where I am, Charlie, if you want to show me that video of the kovanoff thing later."

"Kovacs, Dad. Kovacs!"

"Kovacs," Dad repeats, winking. "You might have to repeat that a few more times before it sticks."

After loading his plate, he disappears down the hallway. Dad seems to be working all the time, locked away in his home office with the QUIET, PLEASE. BRAINS AT WORK sign pegged to the door. At least I know who I inherited my sense of discipline from.

Mom picks up her plate too. "I've got some bookkeeping to get done. Charlie, you're on cleanup duty tonight."

I stifle a groan. The ranch isn't the best place to get homework done, and I've got a killer amount this week, including that stupid U.S. government exam. The last thing I need is dish duty. But everybody's busy around here. Dad with his business. Mom with the freelance accounting she took on when Dad lost his job—not to mention the bookkeeping she now does for Dad's business. Josh with his . . . video games.

Okay, not everybody's busy. But I guess it's only fair that we all pull our own weight around the house.

I shovel the last of my chicken into my mouth. "I'm done too. Sorry to leave you all alone, poor baby," I say to Josh, and carry my plate into the kitchen.

"We need to talk."

I spin around. "What? What's wrong?"

Josh sets his plate in the sink, leans a hip against the counter, and crosses his arms over his chest. "I ran into Zoe at school today, and she wanted to know why I wasn't at my aunt's ranch in Texas." He raises his eyebrows and gives me a pointed stare.

"You never run into Zoe at school." Juniors and seniors have their lockers nowhere near freshmen and sophomores. And they seldom have the same classes.

"Yeah, I know. It was a freak thing."

"So, what did you tell her?" I hold my breath, waiting.

"That it was a girls' weekend thing and I wasn't invited."

My breath whooshes out. "Thanks, Josh."

He shakes his head. "How's this double life working for you, *Charlotte*?"

He's calling me Charlotte to make a point. He knows why I'm leading this double life. He just doesn't agree with it.

"It's working just fine." I retrieve a Tupperware container from the cupboard and grab some tongs. "I'm sorry. I should have told you what I'd told her, just in case you ran into her. It just never occurred to me that you would."

Josh shakes his head. "This is so wrong. She's supposed to be your best friend."

"I know that, but everything will change if I tell her." I point the tongs at him. "Don't you dare say anything to her!"

"I won't," Josh says. "I know it's important to you that people not know who you really are."

I scoop the leftover chicken into the container, snap on the lid. "They know who I am. Just not that I'm in gymnastics." So I'm weird. What's new! I'm also balancing an insane amount of schoolwork and an elite gymnastics career. Boundaries are important. My conversation with Gwen last night reminded me why I'm doing all this. But Josh has never understood.

"It's just that . . ." Josh pauses.

"I already know what you're going to say," I tell him as I put the leftovers into the fridge. "No need to say it."

I grab the washcloth to wipe down the counters. Josh brushes past me. He's got several inches on me, which would make him tall, if I weren't so short.

"Don't be mad at me," I plead softly. "I'm doing my best."

Josh gives me a sympathetic look. "I know. It just seems like there has to be a better way than living a lie."

As I plop down onto my bed, I decide that I'm not going to let Josh make me feel guilty for not telling Zoe the whole story about my life. I hit my favorites contact list on my phone and tap her name. She picks up on the first ring.

"Hey!" she exclaims. "Are you back yet?"

"I am." I can't help but smile at hearing her voice. Her unbridled excitement is refreshing after a couple of days of my sometimes being too tired to move.

"Can you come over?"

I emit a little groan. It's only seven thirty, but . . .

"I can't. You know my parents don't let me go out on a school night."

"They are so rigid."

I can't let them take the full blame, especially when I support the reason behind the restriction. "Even if they said yes, I have way too much homework to catch up on after being at the ranch all weekend."

"You didn't tell me it was a girls' weekend. How was it? What did you do?"

"We got massages."

She sighs. "I'd love to go to a spa."

I did get an athletic massage, but it wasn't really a spa experience. No scented candles and calming music. No long, soothing strokes that make you want to drift off to sleep. It was mostly deep tissue work to keep the muscles loose. Sometimes it hurts a little, although I'm always glad afterward that I went through it.

"So what did I miss at school today?" I ask.

She releases the tiniest of squeals, and I know this is why she called earlier, that she's been sitting on this news, waiting to share. "Michael said hi to me in study hall. Actually he said, 'Hey there.'"

"That's great." I'm going to have to pull out last year's yearbook and look this guy up.

"I know, right? I mean, he didn't sit by me or anything, and he only said the two words, but he gave me a smile that was kind of shy. And so cute."

"What did you say to him?"

She moans. "'Hey.' I couldn't think of anything else. My mind went totally blank."

"You should have asked him how his dog was doing."

"Brilliant! Why didn't I think of that?"

I've been interviewed a few times by gymnastics magazines and shows, and have even had some media training on how to get around questions I don't want to answer, so I have a little experience with thinking fast. "Now that you know he might say hello to you, write down some questions to ask him so you'll be prepared next time. People like when you show an interest by asking them about themselves."

"I'm definitely interested."

"Just don't"—how to say this without being mean or giving the impression that I have no faith in her ability to interest a guy?—"you know . . . get hurt."

"Read too much into a little attention?"

"Yeah. I mean, he'd be the luckiest guy in the world to have you as a girlfriend—"

"But he can have anybody. I get it. You're right."

"No! That's not what I meant." I don't want her to get hurt, but then, there are always risks when you reach for your dream. Gwen and I could fall short of making the Olympic team—and it'll be devastating if we don't make it—but that doesn't mean that we stop working toward our dreams. "If you really like him, do what you can to get his attention. Go for the gold!"

Her laughter tinkles over the phone. "Maybe I will. It's kinda scary, though."

I know that feeling well. "But it'll be worth it. Even if it's only practice for the next guy."

"You're right."

We hang up, and I stare at the ribbons and gold, silver, and bronze medals displayed on the opposite wall. All reflections of my achievements. I really hope my advice to Zoe helps her achieve her goal, because I know how painful it is not to always get the gold.

Or in the case of government, how painful it is not to know the right answers when the teacher calls on me or when I'm taking a test. I drag myself off the bed and sit down at my desk. I pull out the study sheet, pick up a highlighter. Time to get busy. Two questions later my gaze drifts over to my computer.

I could use a break. I bring up my Charlie Ryland Gymnast Facebook page and read some of the comments on the latest video I posted. I have 450,000 followers—people who love gymnastics as much as I do, who keep track of our competitions and offer encouragement and support. I love my Team Charlie supporters, and I enjoy knowing that so many people care about my success. Gwen has more than a million followers. She was featured in *People* magazine last year as the gymnast most likely to make the U.S. team. She became a celebrity overnight. While I think it would have been awesome to be featured, Charlotte Ryland would have been outed as Charlie Ryland. All the inattention I enjoy at school would have faded away. And I might have heard unkind comments directed at me in the hallway, the same sort of comments I'm reading now.

I know I shouldn't take trolls seriously, because there are some people whose main goal in life seems to be to make other people feel bad.

She really needs to do something different with her hair.

Gwen Edwards is still my favorite. Charlie doesn't hold a candle to her.

She looks pudgy. Needs to tighten up.

I miss the good old days of gymnastics, when gymnasts were actually good and they cared about style and weren't trying to do all the tricks!!!!

Of course, there are a lot of nice comments too.

She's amazing!

Go, Charlie!!!

So excited to watch her in the Olympics!!

I actually clicked Like on that one. I hardly ever Like

comments, but sometimes I want to show my gratefulness to the positive people of the world.

Still, the critical ones mess with my brain. When I've finally had enough of doubting myself, I close Facebook and return to the boring domain of U.S. government.

In spite of what Josh and Gwen believe, keeping my two worlds separate is pivotal to my sanity. I don't want to hear ugly comments as I'm walking down the hall. I don't want people saying some of the unkind things to my face that they are willing to post on the Internet.

School is a no-gymnastics zone. I need to keep it that way.

Chapter Five

The school hallway is jam-packed as I thread my way through the crowd. This is one disadvantage to being short. Making my way through a herd of people is like being in a corn maze. I've got to have a pretty good sense of direction to even find my locker.

I'm almost there, having sustained only one bump to the shoulder, when Zoe materializes in front of me. She has a habit of doing that—hopping out from behind some random hallway walker and exclaiming "Hi, Charlotte!" directly into my face.

"Hey, Zoe!"

She wraps me in a huge hug that, taking both our backpacks into consideration, blocks about a fourth of the hallway. Since she's considerably taller, my face is smashed into her chest. People continue to move around us, like we're a boulder in the middle of a stream. "I'm so, so glad you're back," she says, rocking me back and forth. "I missed you."

"I missed you, too," I say, patting her back. "Have you seen you-know-who yet?"

Straightening, Zoe glances up and down the hall, studying faces, as if she's expecting to locate him immediately. "I wish. Our paths never cross until study hall. But I've got my questions ready."

"That's great."

"We'll see."

"Think positively."

She grins. "Will do. So in between your massages, did you get a chance to study for the government test?"

U.S. government is our second class after lunch. I groan. "Not enough."

"I wish your parents weren't so strict. If you could have come over last night, I could have helped you. I'm actually good in this class. I mean, it's almost like we exchange personalities when we walk through the door of that room. Usually I'm the one who needs help, and you're—" She breaks off with an awkward giggle. "Sorry, that sounded mean."

"No, it's not mean. It's true. I don't know what my problem is. Maybe I just don't care enough."

"How can you not care about government?" Zoe asks me with awe. "I mean, like Mr. Alto always says, it's the most important class in school, because it matters. We've all got to vote someday."

"Yeah." It still doesn't sound that interesting. I mean, I love my other subjects. I've always been a voracious reader, so my lit classes are fun. So is history, because I get to learn about other times and people. Then there's math and science, which are fascinating to me. After gymnastics and high school, I totally plan to go into premed and become a doctor. I haven't narrowed down which kind yet. But it's just another reason why I want to go to a real school, and not be homeschooled. I figure it'll be easier to get into a college that has a top-ranked premed program.

But halfway through the government test, I'm really wishing that I had gone over to Zoe's to study. I don't know why I'm struggling with this. Other than the fact that I absolutely do not care about politics at all. Is there anything more boring? I'd rather watch grass grow.

I've only just started on the final essay question when the bell rings.

"That was a snap," Zoe says as she grabs her backpack and stands up.

I promised my parents long ago that my grades wouldn't suffer if they allowed me to compete at an elite level. I have a sinking feeling that my all-As track record is a thing of the past, that after everything they've done for me, I'm going to let them down.

"Are you okay?" Gwen asks during bar workout.

"I'm fine." But I can tell that my reply doesn't fool her.

I take my rep—we're working on dismounts into the foam pit. I'm still thinking about that stupid government test.

Because it contained a series of essay questions as well as multiple choice, I know we won't get the results back until next week. I almost asked Alto to grade mine right then and there, when I handed it to him. But I would have been late to my next class.

"Let's go, Charlie! Kill it!" Gwen's voice rings out, with all the energy she brings to every practice.

I don't quite make the last rotation on my full twisting double. As I come up for air out of the foam, Coach Chris looms above me.

"You with me today?" he asks.

"Yes."

"Are you sure about that?"

"Yes."

"Try it again. I need a tight mind from you, Charlie. Tighten up."

"Got it." I climb out of the pit, ignoring Gwen's worried expression.

"Let's go, Charlie." Coach Chris's voice is deathly quiet. "One more time."

The other girls waiting for the bar shuffle back to give me room. I adjust the hand grips I wear to prevent me from slipping, and take a breath. It's not unusual to have everyone's eyes on me. Besides, these are my friends, my teammates, my most ardent supporters. Why does it feel like they're adding stress today?

Before I can climb back up, Gwen seizes my shoulders and flips me around to look at her. "You are so going to nail this, girl!"

I nod. But even as I climb, I can't feel it.

Focus on this moment, I tell myself. *It's all that matters.* I have to flip this attitude, concentrate. Keep the gym and school separate. Don't let one bleed over into the other.

I release, tighten my body as I flip—once, twice . . . and face-plant into the foam.

If this were any other year, I might come up laughing at myself. But it's not any other year. The summer Olympics will be held this August—that's only three months from now. But I can't jump that far ahead. I have to take it one step at a time. I have to give it my best at the trials and make Team USA. Then I can focus on what I need to do for the Olympics.

"All right," Coach Chris says, jaw tight. "Rachel, take over here. We'll try to at least get her double polished."

"But I need a full twisting double," I protest. "I can do this, Coach!"

"Not today." He doesn't make eye contact with me. "Gwen, get up there and show her how it's done."

I glance at Gwen. She looks apologetic as she climbs for the bar, but she has to do what Coach Chris says. I know he pits us against each other so that we'll push ourselves to get better—but neither of us like it. I'm thankful for a best friend who's humble enough not to let it go to her head when she's the one on top. She casts me one more pleading look before swinging into her kip, the piked swaying motion that gives her the momentum to begin her routine.

"All right, Gwen. Go, girl," I call out, but my voice sounds halfhearted.

Coach Rachel, who's been standing on the sidelines, arms folded across her chest, nods. "Come on, Charlie. Let's see what we can do."

Gold Star consists of two huge warehouse-style buildings. I spend all of my time in the building used by the elite gymnasts and the optional gymnasts who compete using routines of their choice. Rumor has it that the building used to be a Sam's Club. I doubt that's true, but those are the kinds of dimensions we're talking.

I follow Coach Rachel to the set of practice bars away from the foam pit, my stomach queasy. It's not that I dislike her. But this is a demotion. Coach Chris is sending me a message— *Perform. I'm not going to waste my time.* There's no challenge in a double dismount. I had that in my level-nine routine when I was eleven!

"Having an off day?" Coach Rachel asks when we're out of earshot of the group.

"I don't have time for off days."

"We all know you can get the full twist in there," Rachel says. "You've got to get your head back into the game."

I nod. I know how dangerous it is to lose focus. Coach Rachel knows too. I've never talked to her about what happened to her own Olympic dreams when she was a gymnast, but I know she was an elite on the national team twelve years ago. I've also heard the rumors that she didn't have the mental toughness to pull through during crunch time, that she let herself get distracted by the uproar those topless photos created. She's still well-known in gymnastics circles. She went on to have an incredibly successful college gymnastics career, and she's a well-respected coach now. But there's always that hint of shadow when people talk about her, like everyone knows she didn't live up to her full potential. Ever since I started training with Coach Chris and Coach Rachel, I've been determined not to follow in Rachel's footsteps.

"It's not a boy, is it?" she asks.

"I don't have time for boys."

"That's right. You don't. They're a complication you don't need right now."

I guess she would know, but just because her experience was bad, that doesn't mean they all are. It's a moot point, though, since my distraction has nothing to do with the opposite sex. "It's school. I'm struggling with government."

"You have to learn to compartmentalize," she says. "When you walk through the gym door, school and personal issues have to stay on the other side."

"I know." I hate being chastised, especially over something I completely understand.

"Good. Now get up there. Let's see some doubles. Or we

can start with a flyaway if you need to back up a little." I don't like her tone of voice, like I've suddenly become a little kid who doesn't know the drill. But I bite my tongue and hold back all the sarcastic things I'd like to say. She's my coach. I respect her station.

In the locker room after practice, Gwen joins me. She pulls out her scrunchie and finger-combs her tight black curls. "Seriously now, are you okay?"

I sigh. Practice didn't get any better once Coach Rachel took over. She acted snippy and imperial most of the time, and I let my poor performance get into my head. Athletes have to learn not to take a mistake personally, to brush it off. "I don't know." Frustrated, I set my deodorant down a little too hard, and it clangs against the metal in my locker. "I did poorly on an exam today and couldn't shake off my disappointment in myself."

"You have to bring a clear mind to practice. You know that." Gwen reaches over to tap my forehead. "Where's your toughness, girl?"

I shrug her away. "I'm trying."

She smiles. "You're allowed to have a bad day once in a while. As long as it doesn't become a habit."

It's hard hearing Gwen repeating pretty much what Coach Rachel told me. "Yeah." I grab my duffel bag. The walls of the locker room feel like they're closing in on me. I need to get home. "I bet my mom's waiting. . . . See you tomorrow."

As I'm heading for the door, my phone rings. It's Zoe. I

hesitate, because I'm still bogged down with my frustration about my lackluster practice. I don't want her to hear it in my voice. On the other hand, maybe she'll distract me from it. For sure she won't ask me how practice was.

"Hey," I say. "How was study hall?"

"Not bad." Her voice is laced with satisfaction that I wish I could feel. "Michael and I talked about our dogs."

"That's great."

"Yeah, it was. So listen, I was wondering if you might want to catch a movie Saturday. There's a new romantic comedy out, and it seems like it's been forever since we've done anything together."

It has been. Saturday mornings I have training until noon, but I've always kept Saturday afternoons and evenings as a no-gymnastics-no-study zone. I try to do something just for me. "I'll check with Mom, but it shouldn't be a problem."

"Great. I'll have my sister drive us over, pick us up after. We're going to have so much fun."

The excitement in her voice is infectious. And an outing to the movies is just what I need to reset my mind. If I can just get through the week.

Chapter Six

Getting through the week wasn't as difficult as I expected. Alto didn't return our tests, so I didn't have to deal with that reality yet. I regained my equilibrium and focus, which means my practices were no longer frustrating. Challenging, but not frustrating.

Still, I am so ready for time away from it all. As Zoe and I purchase our tickets for the romantic comedy she wants to see, I start to feel a little underdressed. I'm wearing jeans, a red top, and comfortable sneakers, while she's in a short white skirt, a lacy green top, and white sandals. Her hair is curled and perfect, and I'm pretty sure she's wearing the barest hint of blush and eye shadow. I've never known her to wear anything other than mascara.

We walk into the crowded lobby, and she suddenly stops like she can't decide what to do next. We're jostled as people wedge by us to get to the concessions stand or into the hallway that leads to the individual movie theaters.

"Maybe we should head on to our seats," I suggest.

Rising up onto her toes, she glances around. "Yeah. Uh . . ." She drops her heels, looks at me. "Maybe we should get some buttered popcorn."

Popcorn I could do. Butter, no. I don't need calories that really don't do anything for me.

"Are you okay?" I ask. She seems really preoccupied by everything happening around us.

"Yep. I'm just excited about seeing this movie. Let's get in line at the concessions stand."

We find the shortest line and take our place. She's still looking around like she's never been in a movie theater before.

"Zoe, are you sure you're all—"

"Hey, sorry we're late."

At the sound of the guy's voice, Zoe spins around, her face lighting up like it's been hit with a spotlight. "You made it!"

"Yeah, but I had a heck of a time finding you. It's so crowded." The guy has blond hair that's cropped short. Beside him is a grinning guy with dark brown eyes and a mop of curly brown hair.

"Hey. I'm Bobby." He extends a hand toward me.

I look from him to the other guy, to Zoe, and back to him. "I'm confused."

"Hello, Confused. Nice to meet you."

Zoe laughs.

"I told you he was funny," the blond guy says.

I've got a bad feeling about this. "Zoooeee," I say in that

low, frightening tone that Coach Chris uses when he's not happy about something.

"Sorry," she says brightly, obviously totally missing the warning tone I'm emitting. "This is Michael." She points to the blond guy.

I figured that out.

"And his friend Bobby. They're going to sit with us." She turns to the guys. "And this is my bestest friend, Charlotte."

Suddenly my ability to think shuts down. Fast.

"We'll get popcorn and drinks," Michael says. "You wait here, avoid the mash of people."

They move up into our spots in the line, and Zoe grabs my arm to pull me back a little.

"Is this a date?" I ask quietly when we're out of their earshot.

She looks a little guilty. "Not literally. I'm not allowed to date until I'm sixteen."

"But you knew he'd be here."

She nods. "We came up with the idea during study hall."

"And you set me up with his friend?"

She shrugs. "My mom might think something was up if I came alone. And I couldn't invite my sister on a double date. For one thing, she's too old for Bobby. Plus she might tattle."

Her sister is a freshman at the local community college, and she and Zoe don't have a lot in common.

"You didn't think you needed to tell me what you were planning?" I ask.

She pouts. "I didn't think you'd come if I did."

I probably wouldn't have.

"That's *Bobby Singh*," she says in an excited whisper, as though that explains everything.

Still not getting it, I lift my shoulders and shake my head.

She sighs. "He's on the wrestling team with Michael. Bobby is one of the best, actually. Hasn't lost a match yet."

I only stare at her.

"Just go along with it, okay?" she pleads.

"Only because I love you."

She grins brightly. "We're going to have the best time."

I suppose I could do this for her. What is the worst that could happen? Bobby Singh could turn out to be a total jerk?

Although, based on the warmth in his eyes and his smile when they return to us, each carrying a cardboard tray holding two bags of popcorn and two drinks, I think that is probably unlikely. It's at this moment that I realize I've never been anywhere with a guy other than my brother. I'm trying really hard not to feel self-conscious about this arrangement.

"So which movie?" Michael asks.

"The romantic comedy," Zoe says.

"Let's go."

"Wait," Bobby says. "We bought tickets to the action flick."

"So? Tickets all cost the same," Michael reminds him. "It's not like the chick flick is going to sell out, so we're not stealing seats."

Balancing his tray in one hand, he takes Zoe's hand with the other and starts walking toward the ticket taker. Which leaves me to walk beside Bobby. The top of my head doesn't quite reach his shoulder. He's wearing a short-sleeved polo shirt. He has some serious muscles going on in his arms. I'm impressed, because I know the amount of work it took to get them there.

"Man, I think he has it bad for your friend," Bobby murmurs. "Chick flick."

"If you want to go to the action flick, go ahead. You don't have to miss it because of me."

We hand over our tickets, and the ticket taker gives us our theater numbers.

"Nah, that's okay," Bobby says when we're heading down the hallway. He grins at me. He really has a nice smile. It creates a tiny dimple in his left cheek. "You didn't know all this was happening, did you?"

He's figured it out. I shake my head. "No, sorry."

"No problem."

We don't say anything else until we're all seated. Zoe and I sit beside each other, and the guys bookend us.

Bobby hands me a bag of popcorn and a drink. "Hope Coke is okay," he says.

"That's fine." I take a sip, and my mouth puckers at the sweetness of it. I can't remember the last time I had a non-diet drink. I pluck out some popcorn, the butter coating my fingers. I pop it into my mouth. I may have moaned at the deliciousness of it, because Bobby asks if I'm okay.

"I'm doing great." I will not think about the calories. I can work them off tomorrow. Right now I'm just going to enjoy the sensual overload of too much butter and sugar.

He leans toward me, and I go still.

"I come to the movies for the popcorn," he says quietly, like the movie has already started and he doesn't want to bother anyone. "Guilty pleasure."

I look over at him.

He grins again. "I'm on the wrestling team. We have weight classes, which means I have to maintain a certain weight for competition. So I have to log in everything I eat, keep track of calories, make sure everything I eat serves a purpose, provides energy, builds muscle, that kind of thing. But when I come to the movies, I cheat big-time. I figure as long as I limit my cheating, it's okay."

I want to tell him that I totally get what he's saying, that I have to watch my diet too, but then he'll want to know why, and I can't tell him I'm a gymnast. He's in the school part of my life. "That has to be hard, watching what you eat."

"Total pain, but it's worth it. I love wrestling."

I hear the passion in his voice, and I can so relate to that. "I've never been to a wrestling match."

"You should come to a meet next fall. I've got some moves."

I imagine he does. He's lean but solid. I bet his opponents

underestimate him, which gives him an advantage. He probably comes across as totally relaxed and nonthreatening. Like now. He seems completely comfortable with this blind date, but then, I get the impression that he was prepared for it. I wish I had been as well. I would have worn something a little nicer. Internally I shake my head. What am I thinking? I don't need to impress him.

He's just being a good friend—like I am.

The previews start up, and he settles back into his chair. Zoe touches my arm, and when I look at her, she gives me puppy-dog eyes that ask if all is forgiven.

I'm still a little irritated with her for springing this on me. On the other hand, no matter what she calls it, it is a date. My first. And that's exciting. I am actually sitting here at the movies with a guy who bought me popcorn slathered in butter and a sugar-rich drink—things I never buy myself.

I give her a small smile and a nod. *We're still friends.*

Then I lean back to watch the movie. I'm trying really hard not to want more from this moment. Bobby and I are both here so that our friends can be together. We're not here for each other. There's nothing between us. There never will be.

Because Gwen is right. I can't get sidetracked by a boyfriend until after the Olympics.

After the movie ends, Bobby releases a deep sigh. "Guess that wasn't so bad."

I smile at him. "You survived a chick flick."

He pats his chest. "I should get a badge."

"I'll work on it." The words are out before I've really thought about them. Am I flirting?

He grins, and that dimple appears. "I'll hold you to it."

I'm not sure what to say to that.

The theater has cleared out, so we all get up and head into the hallway. Zoe and Michael come to a stop near the exit doors that lead to the parking lot.

"That was fun," she says.

"It was. Can we give you both a ride home?" Michael asks.

I hold my breath, wondering how I'm going to explain to my parents that a guy they don't know brought me home.

Zoe looks a little sad when she shakes her head. "My sister will be out there waiting for us."

"Okay. We'll see you around."

I turn to Bobby. "Thanks for the popcorn."

"Sure." He points a finger at me and winks. "Don't forget the badge."

Then he and Michael walk off, back toward the theater lobby. I have a feeling they're buying another set of tickets to the action flick.

"What badge?" Zoe asks.

I shrug. "It's just a little joke."

"The two of you have an inside joke already? Do you like him?"

"I don't *not* like him."

"I think he likes you."

I don't want to admit that I kind of wish he did. I head for the door. "He was just being a good friend to Michael."

She catches up to me. "But I saw the two of you talking."

"It would have been rude to ignore each other." I shove open the door and step out, and immediately see Zoe's sister sitting in a car at the curb.

"You won't say anything to my sister about Michael, right?"

"Your secret is safe with me."

"Thanks. You're the best friend in the whole world." She leans in, a mischievous glint in her green eyes. "And admit it—it was exciting having a date."

"It was exciting in the way that having a heart attack is exciting. I was totally unprepared."

"Okay. Next time I'll give you some warning."

"There better not be a next time."

Her sister honks.

Laughing, Zoe sings out as she races to the car, "We'll see!"

I rush over to join her, a part of me hoping that there will be a next time.

Chapter Seven

"I can't believe she did that!" Gwen exclaims with a laugh.

"I know. It was totally crazy. But that's Zoe."

I'm sitting with Gwen on a soft leather couch in the near dark in the Gundersens' media room, sipping a kale shake, trying not to remember the soda I had the night before. The room has an awesome sound system, and we use it when we're trying to select the music we want to use for our floor routines. Everyone in levels one through five has the same floor music and the same routine. It's not until the optional levels, six through ten, that gymnasts get a chance to choose their own music. Gwen and I take choosing our music very seriously. But before we started listening to various possibilities, I told Gwen about the unexpected date night.

"She seems like so much fun," Gwen says. "I'd love to meet her sometime."

Doing something with my two best friends would be awesome, but—

"It might get complicated trying to come up with an

explanation for how I know a famous gymnast."

She snorts. "I'm not famous yet."

"But if she did an Internet search on your name . . ."

"What if she does one on yours?" Gwen asks pointedly.

"Searching for 'Charlotte Ryland' brings up pages for only Charlotte Ryland. 'Charlie Ryland' brings up results for Charlie and Charles. No Charlotte. So I don't think people are going to connect thick-framed-glasses Charlotte with ponytail-wielding Charlie."

She laughs in disbelief. "You actually did a search?"

"I started worrying about it."

Gwen releases a scoff that echoes with disapproval. "I don't know why you're not proud of your accomplishments."

We've discussed this ad nauseam. "I am proud of them. I just like having a safe place where I don't have to deal with the pressures of pending fame every minute."

"Search engines will probably connect the two names when you're standing on the podium at the next Olympics," she says.

"I know, but until then I have a little bit of anonymity."

She starts to chuckle.

"What so funny?" I ask.

"I'm imagining someone at the breakfast table, looking at your picture on a cereal box, grabbing a marker, drawing black glasses on your face, and announcing, 'OMG! That's Charlotte Ryland!'"

Laughing, I slap playfully at her arm. If we do well at the Olympics, endorsements will definitely be in our future. "That is not going to happen. Plus, at school I wear my hair so that part of my face is covered."

She laughs, and so do I. We both realize that's a pretty lame attempt at a disguise. "Okay, so then they'll grab a yellow highlighter—" she begins.

I push on her, get up out of my seat, and raise my kale shake. "Stop! Or I'll pour this on you!"

Sobering, she places her hand on my shoulder. "Things are really going to change, Charlie."

I settle back down. "I know. Endorsements, speaking engagements, being invited to huge charity events."

"We're going to be pulled in all directions."

"Does it scare you?"

"Sometimes." Gwen sighs. "All I really want is to do gymnastics."

I grin. "The endorsements pay better."

Nodding, she smiles too. "Yeah, they do."

"I'd like to be a spokesperson for a worthwhile cause," I admit.

"That would be cool."

Sipping on my shake, I imagine it: the lights, the attention, the cameras constantly flashing. It's not the reason I got into gymnastics, but it's where the road I'm traveling leads.

"Everyone at your school will know who you are, Charlie," Gwen says.

"Yep. I won't be the last person picked as a science project partner anymore."

"You're not the last person picked now."

"But I'm not the first. Suddenly I'll be the first."

"And you'll get all these guys asking you on dates—"

"That's why I don't tell them." I twist around to face her. "I don't want a guy to ask me out because I'm on a cereal box or in a sports clothing commercial. I don't want someone to be my friend because they think hanging out with me makes them important."

She nods. "I get it. But you're not going to be able to hold on to the anonymity forever."

"I just want to hold on to it for now."

On Tuesday afternoon I'm getting my books out of my locker when Zoe suddenly appears at my side.

"Hey!" She squeezes my arm, leans down slightly. "Michael sat beside me in study hall yesterday. Then he texted me last night to say good night. So romantic."

I shut my locker door, trying not to wish some guy were texting me. Though, her excitement is contagious. "That's great! I'm happy for you, Zoe."

"And guess what else?"

"He sent you flowers?"

She shakes her head. "*Someone* wants your phone number."

My pulse spikes. But I focus on bringing it back to normal. "Who?"

She rolls her eyes. "Bobby. Who else? So, can I give it to him?"

I shake my head quickly. "No."

She blinks at me, clearly not expecting that answer. "Why not?"

"My parents aren't going to let me date." I'm pretty sure that's true. Either way, I don't have time for a boyfriend.

"But you can talk to guys."

"I just think it would give him the wrong idea."

"That you're interested? Aren't you? I thought you thought he was nice."

"He *is* nice. But I have a lot going on right now with that off-campus program I'm in."

A lot of students are involved in off-campus programs such as internships or classes at the community college, so I use "off-campus program" as a vague reference to explain why I have to be excused every day for tardiness. Of course, I actually spend the time at the gym working out. Fortunately, Zoe has never asked for details ever since I mentioned that the program involves the practical harnessing of physics principles. Which is true, since momentum and aerodynamics have a role in gymnastics, but I didn't have to go into those specifics because

Zoe cringes away from any science-oriented discussions.

"The one that gets you out of first period?" she asks now.

"That's the one. We have to do a lot of stuff after school. My life is just crazy."

She shrugs. "Okay."

I don't quite trust how easily she gave up, but I'm grateful that she's not going to pester me about it. Gwen's right. I can't be distracted by a boy until after the Olympics.

As we head down the hallway, Zoe asks, "So, you heard what happened to Mandy Carrigan yesterday afternoon, right?"

"Mandy?"

"Yeah. She plays soccer."

"Uh . . . maybe?" I have no idea who she's talking about, but that's typical. Zoe follows school gossip like it's a sport, and I'm usually a little more out of the loop. "What about her?"

"Word is going around that her appendix burst. She had to be taken from the nurse's office in an ambulance!"

"How awful!" I say. "Poor thing."

"I know." Zoe pulls her curly red hair back, then releases it. "And for it to happen at school! That has to be the worst! I heard she threw up in the middle of her civics class and was burning up with fever. You know Wilson, right? Wilson James? Football player? He carried her to the nurse, and the whole time was just like, 'I hope she's not contagious.' But she wasn't, of course, because it was an appendix."

"Wow," I say as we reach the classroom. Mr. Alto sits at

his desk, bent over a stack of papers. Looks like he's finally finished grading our exams.

"I'll tell you the rest later," Zoe whispers as she darts to her desk.

"All right, all right." Mr. Alto's voice scrapes like sandpaper. He claps his big hands. "I've got exams to return here. And today we're starting our projects, which are twenty percent of your semester grade."

I slide into my seat and set my folder on the desk. A project that's twenty percent of my grade? I have to take a deep breath, hold it, and exhale slowly to calm my galloping heart.

When I ease open my eyes, Mr. Alto's standing next to my desk, handing me my exam.

I stare at the C- written in red marker at the top of the paper, and groan. My parents aren't going to be happy. They're going to want to meet with my teachers, let them know about my "special circumstances," and ask for considerations like giving me assignments in advance, making exceptions when it comes to taking tests and quizzes. Basically treating me special. Kids are going to start wondering why rules are changed for me, and Charlie Ryland is going to find herself exposed. I need to handle this before my parents feel a need to get involved.

After class I sidle up to my teacher's desk. "Can I talk to you, Mr. Alto?"

"Of course, Charlotte," he says. "Pull up a chair. What's on your mind?"

I settle on the edge of the seat he's patting. "I've been monitoring my grades online, so I know that the score I got on the exam you passed out today is going to hurt my overall average. Is there anything I can do for extra credit?"

Mr. Alto rubs his chin with a blunt-tipped finger. "It might help if you didn't keep daydreaming in class."

"I don't know why I can't stay focused. Government is just so . . ." I don't think it'll help my cause if I confess that I find it boring. "Not my thing."

"Because you don't understand it. Let's look at your grade situation more closely." He opens his laptop, taps a few keys, leans in. "Here we are. You've currently got an 82 average."

"I need to get an A, though." I know it sounds ridiculous, but it's true—at this point any other grade will raise flags at home and potentially get in the way of my college plans. "Can I retake any of the tests?"

Mr. Alto shakes his head. "I don't allow retakes in my class."

"Is there anything else I can do? I want to keep up my GPA."

"Have you got big plans?" he asks.

Besides the Olympics? "Premed . . . hopefully."

"Those are big plans." He pats my forearm. "I think part of the problem is that you need to see government in action."

"Okay," I say slowly. If he's going to make me go on a field trip to Washington, DC, I honestly do not have time for that.

"Student council," he says.

"Excuse me?"

"We have a fine student council at this school, and I happen to be the adviser. I'd like you to get involved, see how it works. Do you know Mandy Carrigan?"

I lift a shoulder. "Does she play soccer by any chance?" This has to be the same girl Zoe was telling me about.

"That's the one. Mandy's our student body secretary. But she's recovering from appendix surgery. There were apparently some complications, so she may be out for a while. We're looking for someone to fill in for her for a couple of weeks. I'm offering you the chance to earn some extra credit, and an opportunity to learn about government in a hands-on way. Tomorrow at lunch you'll attend the meeting and begin serving as temporary secretary until Mandy returns. If you take this on and get good grades on future tests and projects, it could be enough to bump your overall grade up to an A. But no guarantees."

There's no guarantee that I'll make the Olympic team either, but that hasn't stopped me from working my butt off.

"I'm in," I tell him. I hope I won't live to regret it.

Chapter Eight

"Charlie!" Mom cries as soon as I walk into the kitchen the next morning. She grips a piece of toast in one hand and her phone in the other. Her large purse, already slung over her shoulder, overflows with papers. "Charlie, Coach Chris just called. *Gymnastics NOW!* magazine has a reporter and photographer at the gym. They're interviewing Gwen and want to interview you, too. It'll be great exposure for you and the gym."

Gymnastics NOW! Wow! That they want to feature me is a big deal. A really big deal. It means I'm on their radar as a true Olympic contender. They think I have a chance. My stomach is flipping, my heart pounding. It's practically a gymnastics meet inside my torso.

The last time I was in a photo shoot, Gwen and I had just found out we'd been chosen to compete at the World Championships, and we had to pose for a series of photos that would become our official publicity shots for events. Nobody could've wiped the smiles off our faces that day if they'd tried.

Now those pictures hang, larger than life, high up on the walls of Gold Star's optional/elite gym.

But . . . "This morning?"

"Yes. As soon as you finish your workout. The shoot shouldn't take more than a couple of hours. Do you have any tests this morning?"

"No. But I need to be at school during lunch."

Mom slips her phone into her purse. "We'll stop to grab a quick bite when I'm taking you to school after the interview. I'll talk with the principal, make sure you're excused from your morning classes. This is kind of a big deal, sweetie."

"I know, but, Mom . . ." I did not want my parents to find out about this. "I have to *do* something during lunch."

Mom leans back against the counter and studies me. "During lunch? During lunch you eat."

"I have to go to a student council meeting today."

She looks thoroughly confused, and I can't blame her. "Why?" she asks.

I release a deep sigh. "It's for extra credit. For government."

"Why do you need extra credit? Is your teacher not allowing you to make up work when you're out of town? Do I need to have the principal speak with him?"

"No, Mr. Alto is good at taking my work late. And I've been there for all my tests. It's just that I'm not doing so well on those tests. I'm afraid I'm going to get a C in this class if I do poorly on one more exam. So I spoke with him. I'm going to serve on the student council for a couple of weeks. The meetings are at lunch, so I have to be there for lunch."

"Why didn't you tell me about this?"

"I didn't want you worrying. My grades are my responsibility. I can get my grade up."

"I'm going to worry anyway. You take on so much."

I shrug. "That's why I didn't say anything."

"Do you want to do the interview?" she asks.

"I do. If I can get to school before lunch."

"We'll make it happen. Now go grab your favorite leotard and makeup bag. I'll run you over there."

I would have preferred to skip my morning workout, but Coach Chris never lets us miss a practice. So when I'm finished, I take a quick shower, scrape my hair up into a severe ponytail, and add a deep-purple scrunchie that matches my favorite deep-purple leo. I rush to apply eye makeup that also matches my leo. Then I head to the area of the gym where the journalist is waiting and the photographer has set up a white backdrop, with lights illuminating it. Gwen is standing there. She smiles at me, gives me a little wave.

"I'm Marcia," the journalist says, shaking my hand. "This is Todd."

The photographer looks up from whatever adjustments he's making on his camera to give me a smile and a nod.

"We're glad you could make room in your schedule,"

Marcia says. "I understand you go to public school. That's a bit unusual, isn't it? Aren't most gymnasts homeschooled so that they have more time for practice?"

I don't think this is part of the interview. She's just trying to put me at ease. "Many do," I confirm. "But I enjoy the public school experience. My parents and the school administration are very supportive when it comes to working out a schedule that allows me to do both."

"Lucky girl. Before we get to the interview, we'd like to get a couple of photos with you and Gwen—best buds and all that. I know she needs to get to practice."

"No problem, but just so you know, I only have about an hour before I have to leave for school."

"We'll make it work."

I prance over to Gwen, give her a quick hug. Then Todd has us face each other, raise one arm, put the other hand on our hip, bend one leg—

Click, click, click.

He poses us side by side, back to back, and when he's finished taking those, he tells us to just do what we want. We go for sexy, presenting our backs, looking over our shoulders. Then for some reason we just start giggling. All the while, Todd is clicking away.

Finally they send Gwen to her practice, and Marcia approaches me, holding up her phone. "Mind if I record the interview?"

"Not at all." I prefer it, actually. There's less chance of being misquoted.

"Great. Why don't we get comfy over here? It shouldn't take too long. Then Todd can get some shots of just you."

I'm not sure if she's being sarcastic about the comfy part, because we end up sitting on the floor. There are very few chairs in the gym. But she seems okay with it as she opens a small spiral-bound notebook and studies what looks like a list of questions.

"When's this story coming out?" I hazard to ask while she's reading her notes.

"Next month. In time for Olympic trials."

"Cool. Did your interview with Gwen go well?"

"Yeah, she has quite the story, doesn't she? Moving all the way out here from Georgia. She mentioned that you two are best friends. I tried to work it out for you to have your interview and shoot together, but your coach said that wouldn't work because of your schedule, but we got the photos of you together, and that's probably just as good. How is it competing against one of your best friends?"

"Fantastic, actually. We push each other to do our best. I don't think I'd be where I am in gymnastics without Gwen."

Marcia laughs. "That's pretty much what she said about you, too. So how long have you been doing gymnastics?"

I start the story I've told during at least half a dozen interviews for blogs and magazines like this one that appeal mostly to gymnasts and those interested in the gymnastics world. I've never been too concerned about anyone at school reading the interview and figuring out that Charlie Ryland is Charlotte Ryland. The gymnastics world is just so insular—people outside it don't tend to pay attention. Still, it's a weird sensation, feeling so excited for something, like being featured in a magazine—practically famous!—but with this underlying hope that no one I know actually sees it.

When I'm finished, she asks, "What's your favorite part of gymnastics?"

I smile. "That's easy. The travel. I've been to places that I might not have gone to otherwise—Belgium, London, Paris, Canada, Australia. Plus all the various cities in the States. I love meeting people from all around the world. Even at competition, when I meet gymnasts from other teams, I feel an instant connection because I know how hard they worked to get there."

"Sounds like you have a lot of respect for your competitors."

"I do. Coach Chris tells us that the only one we're really competing against is ourselves. Our performance determines whether we stand on the podium."

"Being an elite athlete is pretty much a full-time job," she says. "Plus you're going to school. How do you keep the pressure from getting to you?"

"Family and friends are essential to keeping things real. I spend time hanging out with Gwen or Zoe—"

"Who is Zoe?" she asks, her brow furrowing.

I wasn't thinking. I didn't want to bring my school life into the interview, but now it's already there. What I told her earlier might be off the record, but I'm pretty sure she's going to mention that I go to public school. "My best friend from school."

She smiles broadly. "How does she feel about hanging out with an Olympic hopeful?"

I can't answer truthfully, can't say Zoe doesn't know that my dream is to make Team USA. Because that would lead to a whole other set of questions and would start us down a path I don't want made public. I remember my media training and how I learned to respond to a question without actually answering it. "Zoe keeps me sane, makes sure I have something to think about other than gymnastics."

"She sounds special."

"She is."

She moves on to the typical questions: What is my favorite skill? What am I working on? What are the judges going to see from me at the Olympic trials that they haven't seen before?

"More confidence," I assure her on the last one. "A better command of each apparatus and the floor routine. I've been working hard. This is my year."

She grins, her eyes reflecting warmth. "Based on what I'm hearing, I believe it is, Charlie. Good luck. Now let's get some more photos."

Todd has me stand in front of the white backdrop. I strike

a pose, arms up, one leg extended like I'm about to run across the mat for my floor routine.

"All right, beautiful! Let's see those dimples." Todd hops sideways and then darts forward to move a piece of stray hair out of my face. "Perfect. Relax. Keep that smile. There you go."

The camera shutter chatters.

I bring my arms down, extend them out, make them parallel with the floor. I toss my head back. I've posed for enough photos to know my good side.

"Love your shining eyes! You're made to be in front of a camera, you know that? You sparkle."

He's a total cheeseball, but I *do* feel pretty sparkly.

"Let's get some on the beam," Marcia says. "That's her strong suit. You don't have to actually do a routine. Simply balance yourself on the beam."

"But where's the fun in that?" I ask saucily.

So I do a couple of forward flips, backflips, and a few other maneuvers. Todd's laughing, telling me he's getting some great shots. I'm having so much fun hamming it up that I forget about the time. It's only when my mom-radar picks up her face peering anxiously at me through the glass of the parent viewing area that I remember there's a time limit.

"Oh gosh," I say. "I've got to get to school. Did you get enough shots?"

Todd lowers the camera and steps back, flipping through the images on his camera. "What do you think?" he asks

Marcia, who moves in to better see the photos. They talk among themselves for a minute as he flips through the shots.

"You did great," he finally says. "Sure, if you've got school, you've got school."

Mom waves me over. "How was it?"

"Fantastic!"

"You're glowing." Mom touches the tips of my hair. "You look beautiful, honey. I'm sure it will be a gorgeous spread with you and Gwen."

I nod. "I can't wait."

As I hurry to the locker room to change from Charlie back into Charlotte, I can't curb the tingles that reach to the ends of my fingertips. If I make the Olympics, I'll be doing this sort of thing all the time—but it won't be limited to media coverage that only gymnasts know about. It'll be broader outlets that appeal to a wider audience. I'll be public, out in the open. My life will never be the same. . . .

I'm not sure if I'm excited or terrified.

Chapter Nine

I arrive at school in time to hear the bell signaling the beginning of lunch. Before making a mad dash for Mr. Alto's classroom, I have to check in and get an absent slip for the two classes I missed. Because I didn't have a lot of time, at the gym I changed out of my leo into a long T-shirt, leggings, and sandals. In the car I swapped my contacts for my glasses and brushed out my hair so that it now flows past my shoulders.

I'm out of breath and a little nervous when I finally make it to Mr. Alto's classroom. Not too tardy, but I'm apparently the last to arrive. I have no time to settle in and get comfortable with this situation.

Most of the desks have been pushed back, leaving room for a dozen to be arranged in a circle. Seven girls and four boys are occupying the seats, and the students all look at me, those with their backs to the door turning around. I stare in disbelief. Bobby Singh is glancing over his shoulder at me. His mouth spreads into a wide grin.

Mr. Alto is sitting on the edge of his desk. "Come on in, Charlotte," he says. "Take your seat."

Which must be the empty one, the one directly across from Bobby. Trying to hide the fact that I'm flustered by his presence, I drop into place. I let my hair fall into my face as I slowly unfold the top of my paper lunch bag and draw out my mostly squished turkey sandwich and my hulking bag of fresh veggies.

Mr. Alto clears his throat. "Everyone, say hello to Charlotte. She's agreed to fill in while our secretary's out of commission."

There are a few murmurs, but the only voice I really hear is Bobby's saying, "Hey." I don't know why I'm so tuned in to the sound of his voice, except that it's deep and rich and shivers through me.

"Charlotte, you probably know who everyone is, but if not, you'll learn their names when you call roll." He hands me a sheet of paper with a list of names on it.

"Is this within the rules of our student government?" a girl sitting beside Bobby asks, giving me a small smile of acknowledgment. I know who she is. Everybody does. Kristine Altman is student body president and captain of the girls' varsity soccer team. "I mean, can someone just come in here and fill in for someone without being elected?"

Kristine's words aren't mean-sounding, but they are pointed, as though she's truly challenging the legalities of my substituting for the secretary. I wouldn't have even thought to care if it was okay for someone to replace someone else without an election.

"I'm your adviser," Mr. Alto says, his big voice filling the classroom. "The bylaws state that yours truly has to approve a fill-in, and since I'm appointing the fill-in person, I'm pretty sure it's okay."

"But shouldn't we get to choose?" another girl asks. I have no idea who she is, but she and the girl next to her have their hair arranged in matching topknots. They're also wearing matching yellow-and-black Jefferson High Yellow Jacket hoodies with a soccer emblem on the shoulder, signaling that they're also on the soccer team. Their desks are so close to each other, their shoulders touch. "I mean, I can think of tons of people who would love to fill in. What about them? This doesn't seem fair."

I take an awkward bite of sandwich. I so wish I weren't sitting in this room right now. Maybe Mr. Alto should have warned them about me before I actually showed up.

Bobby is shaking his head, tightening his mouth as though to stop himself from speaking. He seems impatient with the questioning of my right to be here. I wish I'd paid more attention to the student council. If I'd known he'd be here . . . Well, I still wouldn't have said no to the opportunity to bring up my grade, but I wouldn't be sitting here wondering what he thought when Zoe wouldn't give him my number. Since he smiled at me, he couldn't have been too upset.

"I'm the adviser," Mr. Alto repeats, more firmly this time,

bringing my attention back to him. "It's only a couple of weeks. I'm excited for Charlotte to see what student government's all about. She's a girl with a good head on her shoulders, a hard worker, and I can tell she's a great leader. A diamond in the rough, just waiting to find her place of leadership in our school. I'd like to encourage that. So, again, I'm appointing her temporarily. When Mandy gets back, Charlotte will have to step aside and wait till next year, when she can run for an office." He winks at me. Embarrassment causes heat to rise in my cheeks. I mean, don't get me wrong. I'm glad Mr. Alto thinks so highly of me, but did he have to say all that in front of the entire student council? In front of Bobby? He's going to think I'm the teacher's pet. No one likes a teacher's pet. Although, why do I care if he likes me?

The boy to the left of me is tapping his pen against the desk, obviously bored.

"Thanks, Mr. Alto," I say belatedly, because everybody seems to be waiting for me to say something.

"All right." He slaps his hands together. "Let's get this meeting under way, shall we? Kristine?" He wanders over to a seat in the corner and settles in, crossing his arms over his chest, grinning contentedly.

Kristine shuffles some papers. "Okay. I hereby call this meeting to order."

I take another quick bite and fold the front cover of my notebook back, click my pen so that it's ready.

"Do you have the agenda?" Kristine asks, eyeing me.

I swallow my bite of sandwich too early and have to take a gulp of water to get it down. My eyes are watering by the time I can answer. "Uh, sorry. I didn't know I had to do that."

She flicks her blond hair over her shoulder. "I provide the talking points, but Mandy always puts the agenda together because she is amazingly organized. So I'll just work from my talking points. Go ahead and take the roll."

"What's the point?" Bobby asks. "We all know everyone is here."

"Mandy's not," Kristine says.

"That's obvious," Bobby tells her. "I just don't think we have to be so formal."

"Then you should have run for president. I want the roll called."

I appreciate Bobby trying to make things easier for me, but I just want to get this done with as little trouble as possible. I rattle the paper Mr. Alto handed me. "I've got it. No problem."

I call the roll, grateful for the opportunity to put a name with every face.

"All right," Kristine says when I'm finished. "The first item to discuss is prom."

There's a collective groan from the four boys in the room. I kind of get their lack of enthusiasm. I know Zoe really wants to go, but I haven't given it much thought. It's not like I have a guy in my life who would be willing to shell out the money it takes to go to prom. Then there is the fact that he has to be a junior or a senior. And with the trials coming up, I've been pretty much ignoring everything else. Which might be one reason why I'm here.

"I know, I know," Kristine says, waving her hand. "It's not something that student council usually involves itself in, but some of us are very, very concerned that this year will suck if we don't step in. The prom committee"—she sniffs—"hasn't even selected a location yet, and prom is only three weeks away, which is why I made an executive decision and told Deidre that we were taking over. I mean, we owe it to the juniors, and especially to the seniors, since it'll be their last prom. So the first order of business is to come up with a theme."

Tasha Nguyen raises her hand. She's one of the topknot girls. She has black hair, while the other topknot girl—Jane Stables, I learned during roll call—has blond hair.

"Yes, Tasha?" Kristine says.

"How about *Frozen*? We could have ice sculptures and—"

"What are we? Twelve?" Kristine asks.

Tasha's cheeks burn a bright red. I feel sorry for her. I thought her idea had potential.

One guy's hand shoots up.

"Brandon?" Kristine calls on him.

"How about a *Star Wars* theme? We could call it Prom Wars."

"Yeah!" the other guys shout. The ones sitting near Brandon knock their knuckles against his in a show of solidarity.

Kristine rolls her eyes. "No."

"This isn't a dictatorship," Brandon says. "You have to put it to a vote. Isn't that right, Mr. Alto?"

Mr. Alto looks up from his phone. "That's right."

I have to admit that I'm finding it a little interesting that everyone is taking the workings of the student council so seriously. It's remarkable that they not only know all these rules but care about them. It matters to them that things are handled correctly.

Kristine sighs. "All right, then. Do I have a motion?"

Brandon raises his hand again. "I move that the prom theme is Prom Wars."

"I second," a guy named Alex says.

"It has been moved and seconded," Kristine says. "All in favor raise your hand."

Four hands shoot up. All belonging to the guys. Bobby catches my eye, gives his head a little jerk like he has the power to mentally raise my hand. But I have visions of a sci-fi convention atmosphere. If Zoe's wish comes true and Michael asks her to prom, she would kill me if lightsabers were being wielded.

"Ah, come on," Brandon whines. "Don't y'all want the guys to want to go to prom?"

"It'll become a costume ball. They'll all dress up like Han Solo," Tasha says.

"What's wrong with that?" Brandon asks.

"Everything," Tasha says.

With a huff of air Brandon slouches down in his chair. "You guys are no fun."

"The motion does not carry." Kristine looks pointedly at me. "Did you get all that for the minutes?"

I give her a thumbs-up. "Got it."

"Okay, so any other theme suggestions?"

I glance around. The girls' brows are furrowed in concentration, although I suspect that most just don't want to have their ideas shot down by Kristine. The guys have all crossed their arms over their chests in defiance. I guess they've given up.

I'm trying to think of something that could be fun and different. Last year I competed in a world competition in Paris. Gwen brought home the gold with her bar routine, while I brought home a gold on beam. We didn't get to do a lot of sightseeing, but still I fell in love with the City of Light. Tentatively I raise my hand.

"Charlotte," Kristine says.

"I'm not sure if I'm allowed to contribute—"

"You've been appointed to replace Mandy," Kristine cuts in. "You have full student council member status."

She has such confidence, has obviously devoted some time to learning the rules. I have to admire that.

"Okay, then. What if our theme is A Night in Paris? Paris is the city of love. We could put twinkling white holiday lights all over the ceiling and—"

"Boring," Kristine says.

"I like it," Bobby says.

Kristine glares at him. "Really?"

The three other guys are looking at Bobby like he's lost his mind.

"Prom is in three weeks," Bobby says. "We're short on time, so it's not like we want anything elaborate. Maybe we could create a little river, make it romantic. You want romance, right? I just think it has potential."

"Okay." Kristine smiles at him sweetly, like he's special. I can't blame her. He has definitely won her over with the romance aspect. He has won me over as well. It's too bad I won't be going to prom to see his vision of my theme. Even if by some miracle I were invited, it's too close to Olympic trials. I have to cocoon my thoughts that close to competition. I can't allow any distractions. Prom would be a major distraction, with shopping and appointments for hair, nails—

"Vote!" Brandon yells, and I realize that just thinking about prom is distracting. I almost forgot I am supposed to be taking notes.

The vote is nine to three in favor—Bobby is the only guy to vote in favor. It gives me an awesome sense of satisfaction to make a notation that I brought forth a motion that carried. Maybe I misjudged how much fun government could be.

Of course, I also have to acknowledge that if Bobby hadn't supported my idea, it might have gone nowhere.

"Okay, next order of business is a venue-scouting expedition. Unfortunately, at this late date we have only one possible alternative to the gym, so we'll check it out Saturday night," Kristine says. "Everyone meet at the Roll-R-Rama at eight to evaluate its potential. Then we'll discuss and vote at the next meeting."

"Cool, a roller rink," Brandon says. "I could get into Rollerblading at prom."

Kristine rolls her eyes. "We won't be skating at prom. We just need to visualize the venue's suitability."

My hand shoots up, and Kristine calls on me, obviously impatient. But she's not the one my question is for. "Mr. Alto, I don't have to go Saturday, right?"

"Of course you do," Kristine says impatiently before he can answer. "You're the appointed secretary."

I'm still looking at Mr. Alto, who's studying his phone as though it's the most important part of his world. "But you said I would have to participate only during lunch."

He finally lifts his gaze to me. "Government is not always predictable. You made a commitment. You have to see it through when something unexpected comes up."

I know all about dealing with unexpected issues—like when my dad got laid off from his job. I don't need this class to teach me that. Nor do I need it to teach me about seeing things through. Even when I've known that my performance in the first two events of an all-around competition wasn't good enough to receive a medal, I still gave the last two events my all. I didn't stop giving it my best. I want to continue to argue that he's reneging on our arrangement, but not with eleven other students as witnesses to a battle I'm probably going to lose. Okay, to be honest I don't want to lose in front of Bobby Singh. So I clamp my mouth shut and decide to just be glad that it's Saturday evening, when I don't have practice.

"Can we move on now?" Kristine asks me with a pointed look.

I nod. "Sure."

"All right, then. Our last bit of business is to divide up into committees," Kristine says. "I have them mapped out here. Bobby and I will handle the music, find us a good DJ. Who wants to be on the decorating committee?"

By the end of that discussion, I'm on the refreshments committee with the guys—minus Bobby—with Brandon serving as chair. The remaining council members are on the decorating committee, and Jane is their chair.

The bell rings.

Grateful that I survived, I slap my notebook closed and push to my feet, very much aware of Bobby standing and waiting, his gaze on me. I give him a shy smile as I reach him.

"I didn't know you'd be here," he says.

I shrug. "It just came up yesterday."

"I was wondering how my I SURVIVED A CHICK FLICK badge was coming."

"Sorry. I haven't had time."

"Yeah, Zoe said you were really busy. I had fun Saturday."

"Me too."

"But you don't want me to have your number." Statement, not question. I feel bad that I told Zoe not to give it to him; plus now it's awkward.

"Life is a little crazy right now."

"I have no problem with crazy."

I don't know what to say to that.

"Bobby!" Kristine calls out. "Got a minute? I need to talk with you about something."

Bobby gives me an apologetic smile. "Later."

"Yeah." I'm disappointed and partly relieved, because, even knowing it might be a bad idea, I was about to apologize and give him my phone number. Nothing can happen between us this close to trials. Too much is at stake for me to risk a distraction. So it's good that Kristine needed to talk with him before I made that mistake. Although, I suspect she wants to do more than just talk with him. It seems like she might have a little crush of her own on Bobby. Not that it should matter to me.

I head for the door. Just before I step into the hallway, I glance back. Kristine has her hand on Bobby's arm, stroking those fine biceps of his. Yep, she definitely wants more than conversation.

When I walk out, I see Zoe leaning against a locker, her eyes big and bright. She hurries over and falls into step beside me.

"So how was student council?" she asks.

I glance over at her. I told her yesterday why I wouldn't be able to join her for lunch. "Did you know Bobby Singh was on the student council?"

"Of course I did."

"You didn't think to mention it?"

She grins. "I was afraid you'd get nervous, chicken out of going." Her eyes widen, and she grabs my arm and staggers to a stop. "Wait a minute."

She peers into my face, our noses almost touching. "You're wearing makeup. You do like him! I knew it. I knew I should have given him your number, that you were just playing hard to get."

"Zoe, I didn't even know he was on the student council."

"Yeah, right."

"I didn't."

"Then why are you wearing makeup?"

The bigger question is why didn't I go to the trouble of washing it off? Because I knew I was going to be late, minutes seemed to matter, and I didn't think anyone would notice.

"I had some extra time this morning and was just messing around."

"It looks really good. If I get invited to prom, will you help me with my makeup?"

I want so much for her to get invited to prom. "Absolutely."

"Thanks." She starts walking again. "So you and Bobby. How did that go?"

"It was a little awkward," I tell her. "You know, since I didn't let you give him my number."

"I could still give it to him."

"Don't. I have even less time now that I'm on the prom committee."

"How did that happen?"

"Part of being on the student council."

"That is way cool. If you need any help, I'm free."

I smile at her enthusiasm, her willingness to help me out. "I'll definitely keep that in mind."

"To have a role in creating the prom will make it extra special when we go."

We reach our lockers. "Family commitment, remember?"

She wiggles her eyebrows. "Bobby Singh, remember?"

Before I can comment, she dashes over to her locker. Chuckling at her one-track mind about going to prom, I begin to spin the dial on my combination lock. Zoe can't honestly believe that Bobby Singh would ask me. We've talked a couple of times because our paths have crossed, but our conversations have hardly been prom worthy. And if he did ask—

I shake my head to rid it of that thought. No way would he ask. No way am I going to prom. I'm on the committee. But that's it. I don't have time for anything else.

Right?

Chapter Ten

As I'm rushing to my locker before last period, I wish I were tall with long legs so I could cover a greater distance faster. It's tiring trying to get from one building to the other in the allotted time. As I near my locker, though, my pace slows while my heart accelerates.

Bobby Singh is leaning against the metal. When he sees me, he straightens, grins. "Hey."

"Hey." I'd ask how he knew which locker was mine, except I'm pretty sure Zoe told him.

"So student council," he says. "Are you stalking me?"

I roll my eyes. "No. And you showed up at *my* locker. I didn't show up at yours."

"Good point. So, what did you do to get on Alto's bad side?"

I release a deep sigh, a little embarrassed to reveal the truth. "I did really bad on a test and need to bring up my grade, so he's letting me sub for extra credit. I didn't know you were on the student council."

"Most people don't pay attention to the governing student body."

I scrunch up my face. "Do you really govern?"

His laughter echoes around the lockers. "This school would fall apart if we didn't give our full attention to prom."

"You really wanted the Prom Wars theme," I say.

"I really did."

"Thanks for backing up my Night in Paris idea."

"I thought it was a nice compromise. I promised Brandon that we'd hang some X-wing fighters from the ceiling."

I shake my head. "I wish I could see that. Kristine will have a fit."

"Probably. You don't have a date to prom?"

Without answering, I duck my head, slip past him, and start working the combination on my lock.

He moves in beside me, leans a shoulder against someone else's locker. "So about prom . . ."

I hold my breath. He's not going to ask me, is he? I barely know him. Anyway, I'd have to say no. It's the weekend before trials in Detroit. I have to stay totally focused. But this is Bobby with the milk-chocolate eyes. A guy who actually made me glad that I had to spend some time in a student council meeting.

"Or, more specifically, the prom venue. I was wondering if I could give you a ride to the rink Saturday."

Okay, he's not asking to take me to prom. That's for the best. It really is. Still, I can't deny the disappointment that spreads through me. After working to make my expression neutral, I twist my head around to look at him. He appears very serious, also a little nervous.

"Like Zoe, I'm not allowed to date until I'm sixteen." Not that it's ever come up in conversation with my parents, but knowing that I have the trials looming, I can pretty much guarantee what their answer will be. A resounding no. And it's easier to say that I can't date than to try to come up with a reason why I can't go with him—the reason being that he would be a total distraction that I can't afford right now. Gwen is right about that, because whenever he is near, I am thinking only about him.

"It's not a date. It's just a ride for the student council scouting expedition. A non-date. I can pick you up at seven thirty."

"I need to check with my parents."

"Okay. Let me give you my number, and you can text me when you know."

I put him into my contacts.

"I'd better scoot to gym," he says with an adorable grin. "I have to run extra laps if I'm late."

I watch him dash down the hallway. I consider the non-date with Bobby Singh. Saturday night could turn out to be a lot more fun than I expected.

While my family sits around the table that night wolfing down eggplant Parmesan, I try to gauge the perfect moment to ask my parents about Saturday night. I keep running through different ways to approach the subject. With each one that I reject, my stomach knots up a little tighter. I feel like I'm at a competition or something. Best to just do it.

"Mom, Dad, I was wondering if it would be okay if I go out Saturday night to check out a possible venue for prom."

Mom looks at me, her brow furrowed. "That seems an odd request."

In retrospect I probably should have started at the beginning. "It's a student council thing."

"You're not on the student council," Josh says.

I glare at him. "I'm filling in for extra U.S. government credit."

"Since when?" Dad asks.

"Since today. I told Mom about it." Belatedly, but still, I did tell her.

"She did," Mom confirms. "But do you really have time for this? Your grades are important, but I'm worried that you're taking on too much. With the trials approaching—"

"The student council meetings are at lunch, so they're no big deal. This thing Saturday night is a onetime thing, only for a couple of hours, and you wouldn't have to do anything. Bobby Singh offered to give me a ride."

"Bobby Singh!" Josh exclaims. "You're going out with Bobby Singh?"

"I'm not '*going out*' with him." I make quote marks in the air. "We'll just be in the same car."

"Who's Bobby Singh?" Dad asks.

"Only the best wrestler at school," Josh says. "Half the trophies in the wrestling trophy case have Bobby's name engraved on them."

"Do you know him personally?" Dad asks.

"Yeah. We have math together," Josh answers. "He's a nice guy. Popular. I can't believe he's taking you out." He gives me a pointed look.

"He's not 'taking me out.'" Air quotes again. "We have to look at a possible venue for the prom, and he said he'd give me a ride." I dart a quick glance at Mom, then Dad. "So is it okay?"

"I don't know," Dad says. "You're a little young to be dating."

"It's not a date," I insist. "The entire student council will be there."

Mom laughs. "If you were thirty, your dad would think you were too young to be dating. But I do have to wonder if you really need to go at all. Saturday evening is usually when you get a chance to relax."

"This will help improve my government grade, and it definitely won't be stressful." I'm not sure that last part is true, but after talking with Bobby today, I really want to spend some time with him. "He'll pick me up at around seven thirty."

"That does sound like a date," Dad says, his eyes suspicious.

"It's not," I assure him.

"I suppose if it's just a couple of hours, it'll be okay," Mom says.

"But this Bobby Singh has to come into the house," Dad adds. "I want to meet him."

I refrain from rolling my eyes. "Okay. I'll let him know."

As soon as I can after dinner, I escape to my room so that I can text Bobby to let him know I can go. I've just picked up my phone when there's a rap on my door and it opens.

I glower at Josh. "Why do you knock when you don't wait for me to answer?"

"To warn you that I'm coming in." He closes the door and leans against it. "Bobby Singh? Really?"

I shrug. "His friend Michael likes Zoe, and that's how I met Bobby."

"And you didn't know he's sort of a big deal?"

"Well, I do now. But we're only hanging out because of student council."

He grins. "If you're looking for normal, hanging out with Bobby Singh definitely isn't it. Everyone knows who he is."

"I didn't."

He shakes his head. "You need to get your head out of the gymnastics clouds every now and then."

"Hence Saturday night."

"You might not think it's a date, but I'm betting that Bobby does."

"He said it wasn't."

He opens the door, steps out, and then peers back in. "Of course he did."

He closes the door, and my heart does this little double somersault in my chest. Bobby said it wasn't, but did he say that just to get me to say yes? I wouldn't be totally disappointed if Bobby wanted it to be a date, but then I hear Coach Rachel and Gwen in my head, telling me to avoid boys and stay focused. Bobby is definitely hot enough to be a distraction.

I text him.

Saturday night is a go, but you have to come in to meet my dad even tho it's not a date. Sorry.

No problem.

See you then.

If not before.

I don't know what to say to that, so I just set my phone aside. I've never really developed any flirtation skills, since there has been an absence of boys interested in me. I think about searching for tips on the Internet but cast that notion aside. I don't have time for that. I have to focus on my history homework.

But before I can get through the assigned chapter, another text lights up my screen. This time it's Zoe.

You & Bobby on Saturday!!!

How did you know?

Michael. How did you get your parents to say yes to a date? Need tips.

I wonder exactly what Bobby told Michael. *Not a date. Has to do w/student council.*

She texts a sad face, then a happy one. *Michael asked me to go to prom. Mom ok'd it. Can you believe it?!?*

Can't believe you didn't lead w/that! Great news! I'm happy for you! And going to prom is a date.

Not a date. An exception. According to Mom. Will you help me find a dress?

Absolutely!

She texts a string of happy faces.

I set my phone aside and return to history. Another text lights up my screen. Bobby.

Pressure is on to make prom a success. Michael's taking Zoe.

I heard. Don't think Kristine will allow prom not to be the best.

True.

I almost ask him if he's going, but I don't really want to know. I told him I was too busy. No way he'll ask me.

What are you doing right now? he asks.

Studying for history. Gotta get back to it. Sorry!

No prob. See you Saturday.

Saturday. I hit send and silence my phone, then stuff it into a drawer where I can't see it. Out of sight, out of mind, right? There's just one problem. . . .

Phone or no phone, I can't seem to stop thinking about Bobby Singh.

• • •

I'm tying up my hair in the locker room at Gold Star when my phone pings. I check the clock on the wall. I officially have ten minutes before practice starts, and Gwen isn't in the locker room yet. Sometimes she stays between practices to do school at the gym, but she must have gone back to the Gundersens' today.

I hazard a glance at my phone, and my heart gives a little lurch, not a thoroughly unpleasant sensation. It's Bobby.

Hey, I wondered if you wanted to grab a burger Saturday before we go to the rink.

I would, but I'm afraid I'd be stepping onto a slippery slope, moving close to date territory. My parents might rethink letting me get a ride with Bobby.

Thanks, but my family already has dinner plans.

Not a lie, exactly. We do have plans. We plan to eat dinner.

Okay, it was just a thought.

A good thought. I glance at the clock on my phone. Almost time for practice. Where's Gwen? *Sorry I can't do it.*

No problem. What are you doing now?

I stare at the screen. I don't want to tell him what I'm doing, but I do need to end this conversation. I settle for: *Hanging out with some friends. I need to go.*

Later.

I silence my phone and toss it into my locker, but I'm smiling as I jog out onto the gym floor. To my surprise Gwen's already out there, working on beam with Coach Chris.

"Am I late to the party?" I call to them from the floor.

Gwen stands on the beam with her hands on her hips. "No, I just had a personal with Coach Chris today. Needed some help with a couple of things. You're good."

"Warm up, Charlie, and get over here with us," Coach says. "All right, Gwen. Let's see that series again."

After a few fast laps around the gym floor, I join them at the beam.

"Why don't you start with vault today?" Coach says. "I want to see how you're doing with your Amanar."

To get an Olympic placement I desperately need the level of difficulty that the round-off onto the board followed by a back handspring onto and over the vault into a two-and-a-half twisting layout will give me. I've been working on this one for a while. The challenge is that I have to get enough height so that I have time for all the twisting before I land on the mat.

Another challenge is that vault is my least favorite apparatus. I figure that's probably because an awkward landing following a vault routine caused me to break my ankle when I was eight. Sometimes memories of that experience will mess with my head when I'm flying in the air, and make me doubt my ability to land solidly.

But not today. Today I shove all those doubts away as I race up the runway. I hit the springboard, sail up, land perfectly on the vault, push myself off, and go high enough that I can get all my twists in before I land with a thud, my feet positioned perfectly, with no wobbling or sidestepping. I end with my presentation—arms straight up, back slightly arched, every part of my body in perfect alignment.

Then I make a fist and jab it through the air. "Yes!"

I start to leave the mat, and come up short at the sight of Coach standing there with his arms crossed. "Not bad," he says. "Let's see you do it again."

"How was practice?" Mom asks as soon as I slide into the passenger seat. It's her usual greeting.

"Fantastic! Best practice ever! I not only nailed my Amanar, but I also managed a decent full twisting double dismount from the bars. I was on fire. Before we get to trials, Coach Chris thinks I can pull off a full twisting double back. You know, where I'm rotating backward instead of forward."

"That's fantastic."

"I know, right? It will up my difficulty . . . and I need all the points I can get. I mean, Gwen's Kovacs is putting her through the roof. I feel like if I can at least meet or exceed the bar she has set, then I increase my chances of making the team. I mean, there are only five positions on the team. Every point is going to count." I know Gwen isn't the only competition I have to face, but she is recognized as one of the best in the world. I use her as my mark.

Mom eases the car out of its parking spot. "Wow."

"What?"

Mom shakes her head, but she's smiling, too. "I'm glad you and Gwen have each other. You really push each other to be your best."

We do push each other, but it's a friendly competition. I want Gwen to make the Olympic team almost as much as I want to make it myself. I know how hard she works and want her to have every success. After today's practice I'm in a very positive frame of mind. I think we'll both make the team. There's nothing to stop us.

Chapter Eleven

By Saturday evening I'm a nervous wreck. More nervous than I am before a competition. Maybe because I've prepared for competition. I know my strengths and how to adjust for my weaknesses.

But I have no idea whatsoever regarding how I should prepare for a night with Bobby.

"You should put your hair up," Zoe says from my desk, where her face is visible on my laptop screen. She wanted to come over and help me get ready, but I wasn't certain how I would explain all the photos on the walls that trace the history of my gymnastics career. Or the trophies and medals arranged on a bookshelf that is outside her range of vision now. All she can really see is my bed.

So I lied about having to do something with my family that wouldn't allow time for her to come over. But I didn't have the heart to ignore her text asking if we could video chat.

I slide the brush through my long blond hair, moving my hair so that it partially covers one side of my face. "I'd feel exposed," I tell Zoe. Although, I did consider putting in my contacts and going without my thick black-rimmed glasses. But this is a Charlotte night, not a Charlie one. It's such a Charlotte night that I didn't even tell Gwen about it, and I'm feeling a little guilty about that because I've never kept anything from her before. But I didn't want to hear her words of caution regarding the dangers of hanging around with a guy.

I spin around to face Zoe, hold out my arms. "What do you think?"

I'm wearing skinny jeans and a green top.

She smiles. "Green is your color. He's going to love it."

"This isn't a date, Zoe," I remind her.

Her grin gets mischievous. "Could be."

"It's not. It's because of student council."

"Getting to go out with Bobby Singh makes that C- so worth it."

With a sigh I slip into some ballerina flats. "Not really. I still have to type up the minutes from the meeting."

"Don't you have some heels?" she asks.

I do. But I'm not willing to risk turning my weak ankle and causing a sprain. It probably wouldn't happen, but one misstep could ruin my chances of making the Olympic team. "That's too dressy. We're just going to the roller rink to check out space for prom. We'll probably be doing a lot of walking."

"I just don't see the harm in putting in some extra effort."

I can't do anything to turn this night into more than it is. I hear the rumble of a car. I look out the window, and my heart speeds up like a locomotive. I quickly move back to stand in front of the monitor. "He's here. I have to go."

"Have fun!"

"Bye, Zoe." I disconnect our video chat, close my laptop, take a deep breath, and head out of my room.

By the time I get downstairs, Bobby is standing in the foyer talking to Mom, Dad, and Josh. Bobby seems completely at ease. Probably because for him this isn't a date; it's simply a ride. He's just being nice.

Bobby says something, and Josh laughs a little too long, a little too loudly, like he's trying to be cool, trying to impress the wrestling champ. My brother, who always seems so comfortable around people, is acting like a lunatic. And I know it's because he sees Bobby as someone popular, someone he'd like to hang out with.

If people at school knew I was an elite athlete with Olympic aspirations, they'd be acting the same way around me. They wouldn't show me their real selves. The sad thing is that I think Bobby would probably like Josh if he weren't working so hard to be likeable.

Josh is saying something about someone in their math class asking the stupidest question of all time. Bobby is nodding like he cares, but his gaze shifts past Josh and lands on me. He grins. The dimple forms.

I'm wishing I'd gone with the contacts, my hair up, and heels.

"Hey," Bobby says.

"Hi." Do I have to sound so breathless?

Josh is still talking. Dad's large hand lands on Josh's shoulder. Josh goes quiet, looks at me. I can tell he's not happy that I've arrived.

"I didn't realize I know your brother," Bobby says, tipping his head toward Josh.

"Small world," I say, wondering if I could sound any more lame. "I guess we should go." Before my brother embarrasses himself any further.

"Ten o'clock," Dad barks. Mom looks like she's trying really hard not to laugh.

"It's not a school night," I point out.

"You're fifteen," Dad reminds me.

"Maybe ten thirty," Mom says, and Dad glowers at her like she's a traitor.

"Ten thirty," Bobby says with a grin, as though he was in on the negotiations and wants to lock it down before Dad says, *Ten fifteen.* "Nice to meet you all."

"We know each other," Josh reminds him, clearly unhappy to be included in the just-met category.

"Sorry. I just meant it was nice to meet your parents," Bobby concedes, reaching over and opening the door for me.

We walk out, but he can't shut the door, because my parents have followed us and are now filling the doorway. As we continue on, I pretty much want to die.

"Sorry about all that," I mutter once we move beyond earshot.

He gives a low chuckle. "Not a problem."

"So do you really know my brother?" I ask.

"Not *know* know. I know who he is."

"He's not usually quite so exuberant. I think he was trying to make an impression."

"I get that from time to time." We reach the car, and he opens the passenger door for me. *Not a date*, I repeat to myself. *He's just being polite.*

"Doesn't that bother you?" I ask.

"Sometimes. But I like that you didn't know who I was when we met."

"How do you know I didn't know?"

"Because you said it was okay if I went to the other movie. And you weren't clinging to my arm like you'd forgotten how to walk."

As I slip into the car, I wonder if he often has to deal with girls like that. "I'm not much of a clinger," I tell him.

He grins. "I like that about you. And you're with me now. By choice."

"But it's not a date."

He winks. "Definitely not."

With that, he slams the door closed. Warning bells are going off, because Josh might have been right. Bobby might be thinking that this is a date.

Worst of all — I'm kind of hoping he is.

• • •

As the car moves smoothly through the traffic, though, I decide that Bobby isn't considering this a date. His black jeans and dark-gray T-shirt don't exactly scream, *I went to a lot of trouble to impress this chick.* Although, the soft cotton does nothing to hide the fact that he is in great shape.

"Do you like wrestling?" I ask.

"I love it. Love all sports, actually, but I'm too short for basketball, too small for football, and too slow for track. But wrestling works for me because I compete against guys my size. I'm only five-seven." He darts a quick glance at me before returning his attention to the street. "Is my size a problem for you?"

I laugh. "Are you kidding? You're still a foot taller than me."

"Good to know."

I feel my cheeks grow warm. "I mean, it's a total non-issue, since you're only giving me a ride."

"That's true," he concedes. "You mentioned that you can't date until you're sixteen. When will that be?"

I stole that excuse from Zoe. I have no idea when my parents might let me date. "Mid-June."

"That's not so far off," he says.

I look out the window. It's not far off. I need to change the topic. "Do you like being on the student council?"

"It keeps me out of trouble."

I chuckle. "Yeah, I bet you're a real troublemaker."

He gives me that grin again. "I have my moments."

The roller rink comes into view. He pulls into the parking lot, parks, and turns to face me. "Be warned. Kristine is going to make this excursion into a big deal—like securing-world-peace big deal."

"She likes being president."

"She loves being president."

We're both smiling as we get out of the car and head toward the building. I spot Kristine standing near the entrance with a few of the other student council members near her. Her eyes narrow as we approach, and she taps her cell phone. "You're late."

"So?" Bobby asks. "We still beat half the members."

"That's not the point." She flicks her hair over her shoulder. "We can go in and start checking things out. I have free passes for all the council members." She hands one to everyone else standing around her, then gives the remainder to me. "Since you're secretary, please wait out here for the late members. Everyone else, inside."

Bobby looks at me. I'm not sure if he expects me to protest at being given this chore, or expects me to be upset that we have to separate.

"Go on," I tell him. "I'll be fine."

Kristine touches his arm. "I need you with me so that we can figure out if there's a good place for a DJ to set up."

"I brought Charlotte. I'm not leaving her out here alone."

"Brandon?" she calls out. "Will you stay with Charlotte, please?"

He shrugs. "Sure."

Bobby gives me an apologetic look.

"It's fine," I assure him. "Everyone will be here soon."

"Okay. Find me when you get inside."

Kristine loops her arm around his and starts to lead him away. I'm not sure why I'm so bothered by her possessiveness. Her hip keeps tapping against his. I'm surprised either of them can walk, with her snuggled so close to him.

"Man, she wants them to get back together so badly," Brandon says. "It's pathetic."

I jerk my attention to him. He's leaning against the wall. "What?"

He curls up one corner of his mouth. "You didn't know they used to be an item?"

I shake my head.

"For about three years. They broke up right after winter break."

Well, that explains some of the hostile vibes she sends out whenever I'm talking with Bobby.

"How could you not know that?" Brandon asks.

"I must have missed that edition of the *Jefferson High Yellow Jacket Enquirer*."

He laughs. "You're funny. You should consider running

for student council next year. Better yet, run for president."

I almost throw out my usual line about no time, but I realize that I don't have to explain myself or my decisions to him. Plus he's just making conversation, so I settle for a noncommittal, "We'll see."

It's another twenty minutes before everyone arrives. Apparently not all the members are as committed as Kristine. Once all the passes are gone, Brandon and I head inside. We walk through the short hallway where tickets are sold and skates are rented. At the doorway into the main area, we show our passes. As soon as we stroll into the dimly lit area, Brandon sees someone he knows and veers off. I wander to the railing that circles the wooden-floored area where people are skating. I can't remember the last time I came to a roller rink.

Mirrored balls hanging from the ceiling send light dancing around the skaters. The skating floor is pretty packed. There's an area circling the rink, where those not skating have congregated to talk. I can see an occasional bench. On a few of them, couples are kissing. That would definitely work for prom. I try to imagine twinkling stars across the ceiling.

"What do you think?"

I jump at Bobby's unexpected voice breaking into my thoughts. He's standing beside me at an angle so that my shoulder is almost pressed against the center of his chest.

"I think what matters is what Kristine thinks," I answer honestly. I try to picture him with her, and the image just doesn't compute. She's beautiful and popular but a little on the harsh side.

He shrugs. "She likes it. We figure we can set the DJ up over there." He points to the opposite end of the rink.

"That would work. I assume the rink itself will be the dance area."

"That's what some of the committee members were saying before you came in."

"We could set up little tables in the area around the rink, like sidewalk bistros in Paris. Have little refreshment stations."

"That could be fun. Have you been to Paris?"

I nod. "I went last year. It's a beautiful city." I glance around. "Are we supposed to be meeting up with the other student council members somewhere?"

"We're actually finished. Well, except for the decorating committee. Kristine is talking things over with them, but everyone else is free to leave."

I furrow my brow. "We went to all this trouble to come here just so we could take a peek and then leave?"

He grins. "Apparently so." Leaning forward, he places his forearms on the railing. "Do you skate?"

"Not in a while."

He glances back over his shoulder. "Do you want to? We have free passes. We might as well use them."

An image of us skating around the rink, holding hands, flashes through my mind. I want to accept his invitation, but then other images bombard me. Losing my balance, landing hard on my wrist or shoulder. Someone tripping me. Me twisting my ankle. This close to trials, I can't take the risk. "I'm way out of practice. I'd probably do a face-plant."

He turns, presses his back to the railing. "I wouldn't let you fall."

So he's planning to stay close enough to grab me. The temptation to say yes is so strong. What would it hurt? Just for a few minutes—

A series of shrieks echoes around us. I jerk my attention to the skaters and see three sprawled on the floor, legs and arms entangled. People are dodging around them as they slowly sit up. I could end up in a pile just like that. A scrape wouldn't be a big deal, but a broken bone or torn muscle could ruin everything.

"Thanks, but there are just way too many people out there," I tell him, hoping he can hear the genuine disappointment in my voice.

"All right, then." He looks up at the ceiling. "You mentioned putting twinkling lights on the ceiling. I wonder if there's something we can do so that we could have some shooting stars."

"That would be cool." And definitely romantic. "I've never seen a shooting star."

He jerks his gaze back to me. "Never?"

He sounds so mystified that I'm a little embarrassed I

brought it up. "Well, I've seen them on TV and in movies, of course." I think. Surely I have.

"Since we're part of the group responsible for making sure the prom experience is all that it can be, we need to do some further research."

He grabs my hand and starts leading me away from the rink. I notice how his large hand envelops my small one, how warm his skin is against mine. "Where are we going?"

"Someplace special."

We are in the middle of nowhere. Or it feels like the middle of nowhere.

Bobby drove out of town, then down a two-lane country road, and finally pulled off the road and into a field. I can see a few other cars parked out here. Apparently we're not the only ones into stargazing.

We're reclining on the hood of his car. It's so dark out here. No lights to brighten anything up.

"It's better when there's a meteor shower," he says, "but we ought to see something tonight."

"Before I turn back into a pumpkin," I say, subtly reminding him that I have a curfew.

"If you're Cinderella, it's only your clothes that will change. It's my car that will become a pumpkin. Unless you're thinking I'm Prince Charming. . . ."

He is charming. I can't believe he went to this much

trouble to show me a shooting star. I also wonder if he knows about this place because he brought Kristine here. I clear my throat. "So . . . Brandon mentioned that you and Kristine . . ." I let me voice trail off, although I roll my head to the side and study him through half-lowered lashes. With the darkness surrounding him, I can't tell if he's blushing, but he does turn toward me, and I feel his gaze land on me.

"You didn't know about us?"

Slowly I shake my head. I wanted to attend public school so that I could have normal teen experiences. But I'm beginning to think I'm walking around with my head in the clouds—or my thoughts constantly on the gymnastics mat.

"I guess that makes me unusual," I admit self-consciously.

"I like that you're unusual. I like that you don't care about all the gossip that goes around the school."

"Well, I wouldn't go that far—to say that I don't care about gossip."

"What kind of gossip do you like?" He turns his attention back toward the stars. I do the same.

"I don't like any gossip, but I do *care* if there is gossip going around about me." It's one of the reasons why I keep my elite gymnast status a secret, of course. I don't want people speculating about my triumphs and failures.

"I haven't heard any gossip about you," he says.

I grin. "And I like it that way."

"Is there some I should know about?"

He sounds genuinely interested, as though he's trying to make a decision—about us. Only, there can be no us. Not right now.

"Nope. I'm pretty boring."

"You're not boring, Charlie."

I nearly choke. I swallow hard. "Why did you call me that?"

"You just don't look like a Charlotte to me."

Sitting up and crossing my legs beneath me, I push my glasses up the bridge of my nose, let my hair fall forward, suddenly very self-conscious. "I like 'Charlotte.'" And he might randomly search the Internet for a Charlie Ryland. I don't want that name in his head. Or for it to catch on at school.

He pushes himself up as well. "How about 'Shar,' then?" he asks.

"What's wrong with 'Charlotte'?"

"There's nothing wrong with it. It's just long, formal. Does it bother you that I want to call you something else?"

"It just seems . . ." Strangely intimate for him to have a unique name for me. "I don't know. But a princess is named after me, so there will probably be a whole slew of Charlottes in a few years." And if I win gold at the Olympics, some über-fans might name their kids after me too. "And don't think I didn't notice how you changed the subject."

He slips a single finger beneath the curtain of my hair and moves it aside, back over my shoulder. A pleasant shiver courses through me.

"What do you want to know?" he asks quietly.

"Why did you break up?"

He looks off into the distance. "We started dating freshman year. We were both athletes. It seemed a good fit. She was different then. Not so . . . interested in the spotlight. We'd just started high school. No one knew who we were."

I can see that. Three middle schools meld into Jefferson High. It means there are a lot of new people to meet.

He lies back down, his gaze on the stars. "She's good at soccer. Really good. I have a talent for wrestling. Soon people knew who we were, and everything became a big deal. She wanted to be popular, talked about. Being with me became more about my trophies than about me. Don't get me wrong. I'm happy for her success—soccer captain, student council president. But we just weren't in sync anymore. She wouldn't come out here with me to look at the stars, because it's too dark for anyone to see that she's out here with me looking at the stars."

He shifts his gaze over to me. "I don't know if that makes any sense."

It does. It makes so much sense. It's one of the reasons why I don't tell people I'm an elite gymnast. "She seems to want you to get back together."

"It's not me specifically. If the quarterback broke up with his girlfriend, Kristine would be after him. Football is way more popular than wrestling."

I'm not sure if it's true that Kristine would throw Bobby over for a football player. Bobby—wrestler or not—is nice, fun to be with. I unfold my legs and stretch back out over the hood of the car, resting my back against the windshield.

"I'm glad you broke up if you weren't happy," I say.

"I wasn't miserable, but we weren't right for each other anymore. Have you ever had a boyfriend?"

I laugh. "The no dating, remember? Makes it hard." And the focus on training for the Olympics.

"That doesn't mean there wasn't someone you liked."

"No one." I stop just short of confessing that I like him. Flirting is one thing. Giving him hope where there is none— What am I thinking? I'm probably reading way too much into his asking for my number and giving me a ride.

"There!" he suddenly says, pointing off to the right. "Did you see it?"

"No." I can't hide my disappointment. "I was looking in the opposite direction."

"Okay, don't focus on any one part of the sky. Just relax and look at all of it."

"It's so amazingly big."

"Immense. I always feel so small when I'm out here."

"Do you do this often?"

"When there's something special like a meteor shower or an eclipse. Hold on." He pulls out his phone.

"Is it time to go?" I ask.

"Not yet. I've set an alarm, but I'm checking an app that will tell me . . . Yes!" He turns off his phone, shifts closer to me. I can feel the warmth generated by his body. "Keep your eyes on that portion of the sky. You're going to see a bright light moving fast. Not a shooting star but—right there. Follow the line of my finger. Do you see it?"

"I do. Is it a plane?"

"It's the space station." I hear the awe in his voice.

"Wow! That's awesome."

"Yep. Circles the earth every ninety minutes. It isn't always visible to us. We got lucky tonight. Right place, right time."

"It's almost better than a shooting star," I say.

"Nothing's better than a shooting star."

The space station disappears over the horizon. Just as it does, I see a streak of light arcing across the sky.

"Oh, there's a shooting star!" I cry.

"Make a wish," he orders.

So many things to wish for. Making the Olympic team. Gold in Montreal. Gwen making the team, her bringing home gold. Raising my government grade. Zoe getting to actually date Michael.

I turn to look at Bobby. He's watching me. Our faces are so close, so close. I want more light so that I can see what he's thinking, see if he's looking at me as intensely as I'm looking at him.

"I wish I didn't have to be home by ten thirty," I say.

His grin flashes in the pale moonlight. "You shouldn't have said it out loud. A wish doesn't come true if you say it out loud."

It doesn't always come true if you only think it either. Because before the star burned out, before I told him what I'd wished, I actually silently wished that he would kiss me.

Chapter Twelve

Sunday afternoon I pick up the phone when it rings even though I know I shouldn't. There are student council notes to type and tests to study for. But as interesting as cellular respiration is, I've got to steal a break.

"Hey, Gwennie," I say, massaging my temple with my free hand. My studying would be going better if I didn't keep thinking about Bobby. He had me home with two minutes to spare last night. More than a dozen times I've thought about texting him just to thank him again for the ride, secretly hoping it would lead to his texting me back or, better yet, calling me. Pathetic.

"You're not going to believe it!" Gwen's voice is practically thrumming with excitement.

"You somehow made the Olympic team without having to go to trials?"

"No!" She laughs. "Are you going to guess for real, or should I just tell you?"

"Um . . . you won a million dollars?"

"No. But I feel about as happy as I would if I'd won a bunch of money."

"Seriously? Okay, then I know it has something to do with either gymnastics or your family."

"Very intuitive," Gwen says. "It's something about my family."

"They're moving to Columbus!"

"No. If that were true, I'd be pounding on your front door and doing back handsprings in your yard."

"Okay. So, tell me!"

"My dad paid me a surprise visit this weekend, and . . . are you ready for this? He bought me a car!"

"Seriously?" I cry. "That's great!"

"I know! No more having Mrs. Gundersen driving me to practice. I'm free, Charlie!"

"I'm really happy for you, Gwen." I won't have time to take driver's ed until after the Olympics. With homeschooling, Gwen was able to work it in, plus she was old enough to take the classes before our schedules got crazy busy. "What color is it?"

"Look out your window."

"What!" I rush over to my window, pull back the curtain, and gaze out. Wearing jeans and a red top, Gwen is leaning against a red Mustang. "I'm coming down."

I slip on flip-flops and race down the stairs, shouting that Gwen is here. Before anyone can respond, I'm out the door. When I reach her, I give her a big hug. "It's beautiful."

"I know. Want to take a spin in it?"

I think of the stack of books sitting on my desk. "Definitely. Let me okay it with Mom."

A few minutes later I'm sliding onto the leather seat, inhaling the new-car smell. "I have to be back in half an hour."

Gwen looks crestfallen. "Why? We can't go anywhere in half an hour."

"There's a park nearby. We can go there."

She starts the car and carefully pulls into the street. "I thought Sunday was your relaxation time."

"I'm behind on my studies. And I went out last night."

"Oh?"

"Student council thing. I told you I was serving as secretary for extra credit in government."

"Honestly, Charlie. . . ."

"I know, I know—but if it weren't for school, I wouldn't be meeting some cool new people." As if on cue, my phone dings, and Gwen raises an eyebrow at me. I glance at the text, and my heart speeds up. It's Bobby.

Had fun last night.

I hesitate, knowing I should ignore it. Now is my time with Gwen.

"Who is it?" she asks. "You're blushing."

"Bobby."

"That guy from the movie?"

"Yes."

"Why is he texting you?"

I quickly explain about last night, then say, "It's no big deal," even as I text him back.

Me too.

Want to grab a bite somewhere?

I smile. *Can't. With a friend right now.*

Later.

I slip my phone back into my shorts pocket.

"You like him," Gwen says.

"Yeah, I do." I can feel the disapproval shimmering off her. "Take a right up here. There's a little park."

A few minutes later Gwen and I are sitting on swings, our feet planted, just rocking back and forth.

"Did you notice I have a navigation system?" Gwen asks, and I'm glad we're turning the conversation back to her car, which was the whole point of our outing.

"No, I didn't. That's cool. You'll never get lost."

"The map is on the console, but you didn't notice it because you were distracted. I know you like him, but what if he causes you to be inattentive or all dreamy-like at competition? What are you not going to notice?"

Groaning, with my foot I flick a pebble toward the grass. "I won't be distracted, Gwennie. And at competition I won't have my cell phone on me."

"But won't you be wondering if there's a text waiting for you? I would. If I had a guy interested in me, I'd be thinking about him all the time. My focus would be fractured, and I'd have this little nagging piece wondering what he was doing."

I shoot out of the swing, twist around, and face her. "Bobby is not going to distract me. We're not dating. He hasn't asked me out. He just gave me a ride." Although the text he just sent was sort of asking me out. "And he doesn't keep texting me when he knows I'm busy." He's respectful that way, never intruding.

"So you're going to tell him you're busy preparing for the Olympic trials?"

I dig my toe into the dirt. "No."

"We've worked so hard for this, Charlie. You know how any alteration in our routine can throw us off. And guys are unpredictable. You don't want to end up like Coach Rachel."

She's right, and yet . . .

"He wouldn't do anything to ruin my Olympic chances, Gwen."

"Do you know that for sure?" she asks. "What if you have a fight right before trials or—"

"We're not dating!" I exclaim, frustrated because I'd begun to think maybe we could. "I don't even know if we're friends."

"You don't text people who aren't your friends."

"If you met him—"

"You won't even let me meet Zoe."

With a growl I drop back down onto the swing. "He broke up with his girlfriend because she wanted so much attention. He doesn't like a lot of attention."

"You're going to have a lot of attention after the trials."

"If I make the team."

"He's making you doubt."

"No, he's not. I want it all. The regular life and the spotlight. I know I have to make sacrifices right now for the spotlight."

"We all do. My dad told me to go easy on school for a while. With trials so close, my parents want me to focus on gym."

I swallow as I think of my stack of books at home. "That's probably good advice."

"If I can't finish junior year now, it won't be the end of the world. I can always come back to my studies in the summer . . . like, after the Olympics in August."

"Right." For Gwen, setting assignments and tests aside is not a big deal. For me, on the other hand . . .

I heave a sigh. At least if I can pull off the rest of this semester, I won't have school hanging over my head when the Olympics start. I will be free and clear, totally focused. "Since ignoring school isn't an option for me, I need to get home to study."

"That's an additional reason why you don't need a boyfriend pulling you in another direction right now," she emphasizes.

"No boyfriend." Not that Bobby has said he wants that role in my life. Still, as we walk back to the car, I keep hoping to feel a buzz in my pocket, to get a text from Bobby.

• • •

When I walk into Alto's classroom on Wednesday for the student council meeting, I notice two things straightaway. Bobby isn't sitting by Kristine, and his arm is draped over the back of the seat of the empty desk beside him, as though he's been saving it. He grins at me, straightens, and his arm falls away, an invitation for me to sit there. Two other seats are open. I have to choose.

Ignoring Gwen's warnings that are going off in my head, I take the seat beside Bobby. His grin grows; his dimple winks at me. I don't even bother taking my lunch out of its sack, because my stomach is knotting up so tightly that I know I won't be able to eat.

The last two council members rush in and noisily take their chairs. Kristine calls the meeting to order, but she certainly doesn't sound happy to do it.

I call roll, pass out the minutes that I typed up—feel a sense of pride when they get a satisfactory nod from Alto and are approved by the council. I glance over at Bobby. He winks at me, and I refrain from adding that to the notes I'm taking for the next set of minutes.

Kristine clears her throat harshly, and I give a little jump. When I look at her, she narrows her eyes back at me. "First order of business," she says curtly, "is the venue for prom."

The motion to use the skating rink passes unanimously.

"With that out of the way, I'm going to adjourn the meeting," Kristine says.

I breathe a sigh of relief as I close up my notebook. Typing up these minutes will be a snap. The short meeting gives me time to meet up with Zoe in the lunchroom so that I can quickly eat my sandwich and veggies.

"We'll use the time to break up into our individual committees to discuss plans. Food committee, back corner by the window. Decorating committee, opposite corner. Bobby, we'll just meet here."

"We figured everything out Saturday night," Bobby says. "I thought I could help out the food committee."

"We have a few things to discuss," Kristine says.

Bobby leans toward me, and his breath tickles my cheek as he says, "I have an idea for the food caterer. I'll text you later."

I'm glad someone has an idea regarding food, because when I join my group, the guys on my committee are just exchanging video game strategies.

"Uh, excuse me." My interruption causes them to stare at me like I've sprouted three heads. "Shouldn't we discuss food?"

"Hot dogs," Brandon says.

"Really?"

"We don't care." Alex's words confirm my suspicions. "Just do whatever you want."

"But we're supposed to decide together."

"We decided that whatever you want is what we want." Brandon looks to the other two guys for confirmation. They nod.

"But I might not even be on the student council by the time prom gets here," I remind them. "I'm only temporary."

"I went to see Mandy yesterday," Alex says. "I don't think she's coming back this year."

What? Wait! This was supposed to be for only a couple of weeks.

When the bell rings, I stop to have a word with Mr. Alto. "So how is Mandy doing?" I ask. "Any idea when she'll be back?"

"I don't know if she will be back before school's out—but if she does return, her mom wants her to take it easy. She's resigned from the student council."

"So what does that mean? For me, specifically?"

He smiles as though he's about to tell me that I aced an exam. "It means you get to finish out her term." He holds up the minutes. "These were excellent, by the way. I'm impressed, Charlotte."

"Impressed enough to give me an A in the class?"

He chuckles. "Impressed enough to not give you a C."

I'm still reeling when I walk out into the hallway. Zoe is waiting for me.

"Are you okay?" she asks as we head for our lockers. "You look like you're trying to process bad news."

"I'm not getting off student council anytime soon."

"Bummer."

"No, that's just it. I'm not upset about it. That's what I'm trying to process. It's a little more fun than I thought it would be." I've never had time to be this involved in any school club or organization. It's giving me the sort of high school experience that I envisioned when I decided to return to public school in the first place.

"Are you going to run for student council next year?" Zoe asks.

Am I? If I make the Olympic team this year, everyone will know who I am by then. I'd probably win—but it would be Charlie winning, not Charlotte. People would vote for me because of my gymnastics record, not my school record. On the other hand, that will be a part of my life that I can't escape. "I don't know."

"If you run, I'll run."

Smiling, I look at her. "Really?"

"Sure. We could take over."

"It's not a dictatorship." Which I would have never said before I attended a meeting.

"I know. I was just . . . Oh, looks like we'll have to discuss this later." She's wearing a big smile. "Have fun."

I don't know what she's talking about, until I near my locker and see Bobby standing there. "Hey," I say to him.

"Hey. What did your committee decide about the food?"

"We didn't." Then I remember what he said before we broke into our committees. "You said you had an idea?"

"My aunt has a catering business. She'll have some ideas.

We could go talk with her, see what she suggests. I can't do it during the week because I have wrestling practice after school until seven, then there's homework, et cetera. So I was thinking Saturday evening."

"We?" I ask.

"She'll give you a better deal if she thinks you're a friend of mine."

I want to ask him if I am a friend of his. I have to be, if he's going to this much trouble for me. I'm a little surprised by how happy the thought makes me. "I hate to take up your time with this. You're not on the food committee."

"I don't mind. I don't have any plans for Saturday."

"Okay, then. That would be great."

"I'll pick you up around four."

"Would it be all right if I ask Zoe to go with us?" I need someone else's opinion about the food for prom, because it's too easy for me to say yes to things when Bobby grins at me.

"Sure. Michael can come too. The more the merrier."

He says good-bye. I'm smiling as I open my locker and grab my lit book. I slam the door closed and nearly jump out of my skin because Zoe is right there, almost in my face.

"Did he ask you to prom?" she asks excitedly.

"No." I'm not even going to go there, because as tempting as it is, it would be a bad idea on so many levels. "But we're going to check out some refreshment possibilities for prom. Would you and Michael want to come?"

She shakes her head. "Mom won't agree to a date."

"It's not a date," I remind her, grinning. "It's a food-scouting-for-prom expedition."

A smile lights up her face, and her eyes glow. "Brilliant! She has to say yes to that." She gives me a hug. "Thanks, Charlotte. You're the bestest friend ever!"

Watching her skip down the hallway, I can't help but think that the bestest friend ever wouldn't keep secrets from her.

Chapter Thirteen

My parents don't object to my going on a food scouting expedition with Bobby. They aren't hovering in the entryway when he arrives either. Although, Josh is there.

"Hey, man!" he says, going through some sort of strange ritual with Bobby that includes sliding palms and tapping knuckles.

"How's it going?" Bobby asks.

"Good. I finally asked Morgan Whitcomb to prom, and she said yes."

"You're going to prom?" I ask, a bit dazed. I had no idea he was interested or that he even liked anyone.

"Yeah."

"Do Mom and Dad know?"

"Of course they know. I need a tux. Don't look so shocked."

"Sorry. I just didn't realize you were interested in prom."

"I'm not. But I'm interested in Morgan."

I've never met her, and he's never mentioned her before, but then, we don't typically share that sort of information.

Josh looks at Bobby. "Are you going to prom? I figured we could double."

I shove on Josh's shoulder. "You can't just invite yourself along," I point out. He and Bobby don't hang out together, and it makes me uncomfortable that Josh is using this opportunity to barge into Bobby's life.

"It doesn't hurt to ask," Josh says.

I want to tell him that it makes him look desperate. He's acting toward Bobby just like I expect people to act toward me when my truth comes out.

Bobby's cheeks turn red, and he avoids looking at me. "I haven't decided," he says quietly.

"But you're doing all this stuff to make prom happen," Josh says.

"That's because we're on student council. And we need to get to it."

We walk outside.

"Just let me know!" Josh calls out before closing the door.

"I can't believe my brother just invited himself to go to prom with you," I say as we head for Bobby's car.

"We've been talking more before and after class," Bobby says.

"Best-friends more?"

He laughs. "No, not that much. But I noticed that whenever he mentions you, he calls you Charlie."

Inwardly, I cringe. I probably shouldn't have made such

a big deal of it when Bobby called me Charlie. I should have just let it go. "Typical older brother stuff. He does it because he knows it irritates me, and now he's just in the habit of it."

"I get that," he says. "Siblings can be the worst sometimes."

"Yes, they can. I hope he's not being a nuisance to you. Where you are concerned, I think he has some serious hero worship going on. He considers you 'the incredible Bobby Singh.'"

Bobby winks and opens the door for me. "I am pretty incredible."

He is, but I'm not going to say that. When he gets into the car, I ask, "Are you picking up Michael and Zoe?"

"No, they're meeting us at Tasty Bites. That's my aunt's place. I thought that would be easier." As he pulls out into the street, he darts a quick glance at me. "You suggested that they help us because you figured this was a way for them to have a date without it being a date."

"Yeah. Zoe's mother is pretty set against her dating until she's sixteen too. And that won't happen until July."

"That was nice of you."

I shrug. "She really likes Michael."

"He likes her, too. Obviously."

We're quiet for a while, but it's not a thick, uncomfortable silence. Maybe because the stereo is on, and the theme to *Rocky* is playing low.

"You like movie sound tracks?" I ask.

"I like the ones that pump me up. I have a playlist that I listen to before I get out on the mat. Kind of like a pep talk. Do you want me to turn it off?"

"No, I like it." Although, I wonder why he needed a pep talk before arriving at my door. I wonder if this is more than something we're doing because of student council. I understand how helpful music can be to get you into the right mind-set, though. I listen to my favorite songs before competition because I find it calming. "I wouldn't recommend listening to the sound track from *Titanic* before a meet."

He grins. "Trust me, you won't find that one on my playlist. I go for sound tracks to movies that end victoriously." He gives me another sideways glance. "Just so you know, there was room on that plank for Jack."

"But then we wouldn't have cried."

"You cried?"

"Not as much as Zoe. We saw it in the theater last summer. It was part of a classics series being shown. I'm surprised you've seen it. You know, since it's a little bit of a chick flick."

"It wasn't my choice," he says simply, and I hear what he's not saying. He watched it with Kristine.

He pulls into a strip mall and parks near a building with an elegant sign that says TASTY BITES. Zoe and Michael are standing outside, holding hands, talking. She is smiling so brightly. I'm happy for her, but I have to admit that I want that someday—to find so much joy in being with a person.

"Hey!" she cries out as we approach. "We were beginning to wonder if you'd set us up for a date and weren't going to show."

"We got waylaid by Josh," I admit. "He had some questions for Bobby."

"Is he thinking of joining the wrestling team?"

I give a short laugh. "No way. He hasn't got a competitive bone in his body." I seem to be the one who inherited all those. "Okay, not true. He is competitive when it comes to video games. But I don't think he has any interest in athletics. He just thinks it would be cool to hang out with an athlete." A known athlete. Not one who doesn't tell anyone she's an athlete.

"Bobby gets that a lot," Michael confirms.

"Josh is harmless," Bobby says. "Let's see what my aunt has to show us."

The shop is quaint, with only a few cloth-covered tables. The long length of the display case makes me think that most people must take their orders to go. And everything looks delicious.

"Bobby!" An older woman with salt-and-pepper hair comes out from behind the display case and gives him a hug.

"Hello, Aunt Sasha. These are the friends I told you about." He introduces us. "Aunt Sasha is married to my dad's older brother."

"It's nice to meet you, Mrs. Singh," I say.

"Oh, please, call me Sasha. Bobby tells me you need some

refreshments for your prom. Make yourselves comfortable at a table. I have some samples to bring to you."

"I'll get them for you," Bobby says to his aunt, and he follows her into the kitchen as the rest of us settle at a table.

"He's introducing you to family," Zoe whispers to me. "That's a big deal."

I roll my eyes, shake my head. "We're here because of prom, and that's it."

The tray Bobby carries out and sets on the table has the cutest little items on it: various pastries, tiny sandwiches, and little egg rolls.

"You want something that people can just pick up and pop into their mouths," Sasha says. "Nothing messy."

The cucumber-and-cream-cheese sandwiches are delicious. And the avocado egg rolls are to die for. I'm not sure what's in the teeny tiny flaky turnover, but it's sweet and melts in my mouth.

"We should have all of these," Zoe says with excitement.

On the one hand I agree. On the other . . .

"They look like a lot of trouble to make," I say. "How many people are going to be at prom?"

"Four hundred or so," Bobby says.

I look at Sasha. "That's an awful lot of work."

She waves a hand dismissively. "It's my passion. What's the point of doing something if it's not your passion?"

Gymnastics is my passion. I consider all the hours I devote

to it. I can't disagree with her about the hard work being worth it when you love something.

"Besides, I'll give the school a big discount. They'll acknowledge my business. It's good publicity. I'll work up some figures and e-mail them to you."

I give her my e-mail address and thank her profusely. I can't believe how excited I am about the opportunity to present this as a possibility at the next student council meeting.

When we're all standing outside, I turn to Bobby. "Thank you. That was so easy."

"Aunt Sasha loves doing it. Now let's go grab some real food."

I bite into my double-meat cheeseburger. I want to laugh out loud as my taste buds nearly explode with sensations. Warm juice dribbles down my chin. I quickly wipe it up with my napkin. I'll pay for this meal later when it makes me sluggish.

"I thought you were bad only at the movies," I say to Bobby.

We're sitting across from each other in a booth at the back of the restaurant. Zoe is beside me, Michael across from her.

Bobby takes a sip of his chocolate shake. Guiltily I spoon out some of my strawberry malt. I decide to focus on the calcium I'm getting.

"What I usually eat is not something you offer a girl on a date," Bobby says with a grin.

My heart rate spikes. "This is a non-date," I remind him.

"Right. Still not something you offer a girl."

"Charlotte probably would like it," Zoe says. "She brings the most boring lunches."

"I noticed," Bobby says.

"There's nothing wrong with vegetables. They get a bad rap for no reason." Although, I'm not sure I'd eat them if I didn't have to.

"I'll take a burger any day," Michael says.

We move on and talk about movies. Bobby's favorites involve the Avengers. We talk about TV shows. His favorites involve Marvel superheroes.

"I'm sensing a trend here," I say. "Do you have a secret ambition to be a crime fighter?"

"No, I'm more interested in getting into sports medicine."

"Really? I'm interested in that too."

His head jerks back a little, and his brow furrows. "You didn't strike me as being into sports . . . at all."

I don't want to lie, but I don't want to confess everything either. I drag a fry through the ketchup, stalling, trying to figure out how much isn't too much. And also wondering why I want to share more of myself with him. "I was into gymnastics when I was younger."

Leaning back, he grins. "I can see that. You have the size and build for it. Why'd you give it up?"

"When I was eight, I broke my ankle." True. "It's been giving me trouble ever since." True.

So I haven't exactly lied. I just omitted the complete truth.

"Gymnastics is hard," Zoe says. "I did it for a couple of years. Until I got too tall."

I stare at her. "I didn't know that."

"I wasn't very good. Mostly I got participation ribbons. Although, I suspect those came from my mom and not the actual meet. She's always worrying about my ego."

"Athletics isn't for everyone," Michael says. "Someone needs to sit in the stands and cheer us on."

"I'm definitely up for that," Zoe says, smiling brightly.

"Bobby's got a big meet coming up," Michael says.

I look at Bobby, not bothering to hide my confusion. "I thought wrestling season was in the fall."

"High school wrestling season is. But I go to meets outside of school. I'm training for the Juniors in Fargo."

"What's 'Juniors'?" I ask.

"Junior Nationals. I'm trying to qualify for Junior Worlds."

"You qualified last year," Michael says. "This year should be a snap."

Bobby's smile is a slow burn. "No guarantees, man. You know that."

"This guy's a beast," Michael says.

"Wow, that sounds serious," I say.

"Nah, Junior Worlds is just another competition."

"This guy is too modest," Michael says. "Only the best in the United States go. Kind of like the Olympics of high-school-age wrestling."

"Is it like Junior Elite in gymnastics?" I ask, without thinking.

"I have no idea what that is," Bobby says. "But it sounds about right."

"Some Junior Elites go to international competitions and represent the United States," I mumble. I've been to three. Twice I've taken gold on the beam. I've taken a couple of silver and bronze. "It's not quite the Olympics, but they have the opportunity to go to the Olympics later, when they're older."

"Yeah, that's probably similar," Bobby says. "If I can make the team, I'll go to an international competition in Brazil."

"So, you're really good at wrestling," I say, eager to get the subject back on track. "I mean, this isn't just a hobby or a school sport?"

"No, I train all year-round," Bobby says, picking up a fry. "It's club wrestling. We're serious."

My heart pitter-patters. "That's exciting." And it also means we have a whole lot in common. Maybe I'm not so abnormal after all, for taking a sport so seriously.

"Do you go too?" I ask Michael.

"No, I'm strictly into high school competition only. I enjoy burgers too much."

"Speaking of," Bobby begins. He sags back against the bench, pats his stomach. "That was a mistake. I'm just glad I don't have a competition this week. A pound over or under my weight class, and I'd be in trouble."

I smile at him. "I think you could take anyone on."

He shakes his head. "No, I'm used to facing guys who weigh a certain amount. I'm pretty good at judging weight distribution, knowing how to unbalance them in my weight class. But outside of that, I'd get clobbered."

I can't see him getting clobbered, but I like that he's so modest.

"Although, Michael's right. Eating healthy is no fun. I didn't think my spouting off about which foods are good for energy and which are best for repairing or building muscle would interest you. But I spend a lot of time studying what I should eat to remain a lean, mean wrestling machine."

I give him a big smile. "I'm definitely going to come watch you in competition sometime."

He grows serious. "I hope you will."

I imagine what it would feel like to dismount from the balance beam, look up into the stands, and see him sitting there, cheering me on. I'm tempted to confess that I'm an athlete too, that I compete and watch what I eat. That I'm a lean, mean gymnastics machine. He might get it. More than anyone else I've met outside of gymnastics, he might get it.

But things between us would shift. He would look at me differently. And I don't know if I'm ready for that.

Chapter Fourteen

On Monday, Zoe catches up with me as I head to my locker right before lunch.

"I had so much fun Saturday night," she says. "Thanks for arranging it."

"I had fun too."

"I don't understand why my mom is so strict about me dating. I'm almost sixteen."

As I'm opening my locker, I give her a sympathetic glance. "I don't get it either, but my parents are the same way."

"What. Is. That?" Zoe cries, her gaze zeroing in on something inside my locker.

Following her gaze, I see a scrap of folded paper lying face-down in front of my books.

She snatches it up before I can reach for it. "It's clearly from a boy," she says.

"How do you know that?" I pinch the note from her fingers, laughing.

"Sorry," she squeaks. "I got excited. You read it first. Of course you should read it first."

"How do you know it's from a boy?" I narrow my eyes at her and hold the note in my fist so that I won't give in to the temptation to look at it. "Did you plant this here? Is this a joke?"

"No!" she squeals. "I swear! I'm trained to recognize a note from a boy. See, it's their handwriting, the way they fold stuff. That's definitely a note from a boy."

"Okay. I'm going to read it now. Can you handle that?"

"Yes, absolutely. Just tell me who it's from and what it says."

I keep my face expressionless, even as my pulse quickens while I silently read it.

> *Charlotte—*
> *I know you can't date yet, but I'm hoping your*
> *parents will make another exception and let*
> *me take you to prom. As a friend. Not a date*
> *but another non-date. That is, if you want to*
> *go with me.*
> *—Bobby*

"It's from Bobby. He's asking me to prom."

"I knew it! I knew he was going to ask you. All the signs were there Saturday night."

I can't help it. I laugh. "What signs?"

"The way he talked to you like Michael and I weren't even there. The way he looked at you."

"How did he look at me?" I ask as I slam my locker door closed and start walking toward the cafeteria.

Zoe patters along beside me. "Like you're the most amazing girl he's ever met."

I know she's exaggerating. Still, I can't help but hope there's a little truth in what she's saying.

"You're going, right?" she asks. "We can double. I'll help you find a dress."

Before this moment I hadn't seriously considered going to prom. I convinced myself it would be a distraction. So I'm a little astonished by how much I want to go. Although, I know it's not so much about going to prom as it is about going with Bobby. I really like him. And we would just be going as friends, so how could it be a distraction?

"I have to check with my mom." I hope she says yes. She'll probably say no because the trials are so important, but like Josh said, it doesn't hurt to ask.

"Tell her what I told my mom. It's not a date. It's just a special event. A high school moment. A memory."

But it's not something I've been working toward for most of my life. The trials are. I have a feeling that I'm going to need a stronger argument for going, because there are two more possible proms in my life—but maybe only one Olympics.

"Oh my gosh, aren't you excited?" Zoe asks. "I mean, what

are you, a zombie or something? You look like a zombie! What is wrong with you?"

I'm running a thousand scenarios through my head, a thousand ways to ask, but none of them end with my mom saying yes. "I don't know that she's going to let me go, Zoe."

"But you're on the committee. You should be there. It's not fair if you can't be there."

Unfortunately, gymnastics has taught me that life isn't always fair.

Mom holds up a finger when I open the car door and slide into the seat after school. She's on the phone. After she hangs up, she pulls away from the curb and offers an inattentive, "How was school?"

"Interesting."

She lets out a sigh and flips her bangs out of her eyes. "I've got a client upset with me because the numbers aren't adding up like she wants. I'm an accountant, not a magician. If she spends the money, that's what's going to show up on paper."

"I'm sorry you have to deal with that."

She waves a hand. "It is what it is. It'll all work out." She blinks, puckers her mouth as though she's in thought. "So what was interesting that happened at school?"

I take a deep breath, release it slowly. "Bobby asked me to prom."

Mom nods slowly, seems to be focusing really hard on the

road, but I have the feeling she's focusing more on my words. "What did you tell him?"

"Nothing yet. I needed to check with you. To see if it was okay."

She shakes her head. "I don't think it's a good idea, Charlie. Not this close to trials."

"It's just one night."

"Not really. You're going to be thinking about it every day until it happens, and then depending how it goes—good or bad—you're going to be thinking about it for days afterward. Days when you have to be seriously focused on competition. It's bad timing, sweetie. You're going to have to say no."

Even knowing that was probably going to be her answer, I'm surprised by how much it hurts. "You're letting Josh go."

"Josh is not competing a week after prom for something that he has worked for—and made sacrifices for—most of his life," she says. "You can't have everything, Charlie. We discussed this. You wanted to go to public school, and we made arrangements for that. Now your grades are suffering—"

"One class."

"And you've had to take on the extra responsibility of student council and having to help with planning prom. Coach Chris called me to let me know that you've been struggling with some of your dismounts. He's concerned that something is going on at school—"

"Nothing is going on at school."

"Then it's things going on outside of school, and that leaves Bobby."

I shake my head. "It's not him."

"Then what is it?"

"I've just had some off days."

Mom sighs. "Maybe I'm wrong. We can ask Coach Chris if he thinks it's a good idea for you to go to prom."

But we both know Coach Chris will say no. I let my gaze wander out the window, watch the neighborhoods flash by with their play structures in backyards, their carefully manicured lawns, their trimmed bushes.

"I'm sorry, Charlie, but the trials are too important. You've worked too hard for them."

There's an elementary school up ahead, so Mom slows the car. I watch the kids walking from school. Some have their hands shoved into their pockets; others run, with their backpacks jouncing.

Then I see one little girl with her hair brushed back into a tight bun. Her pink sweats have LOVE GYMNASTICS blazoned down the leg. She must be singing, because her lips are moving, and she smiles privately as she walks, as if she's keeping a wonderful secret. Just as we're pulling past her, she takes off in a little run. She leaps, lands, and spins, then keeps walking, as if leaping and spinning down the street is a completely normal thing to do.

My mouth curls up into a soft smile. I was once that little girl. I wanted to be on Team USA more than I wanted anything else in the world. I wanted to balance on beams and hit the vault and go flying.

Mom's right. I worked hard for this opportunity. Making the Olympics is too important. I can't throw it away over a cute guy. I want to go, but prom will be a distraction. I'll be preoccupied thinking about what kind of gown I want to wear, how to fix my hair, how to do my makeup. I'll wonder if Bobby thinks that we're more than friends. I'll wonder if he might kiss me. And if he doesn't, I'll wonder why not.

This stinks. I just wish I knew how to break the news to Bobby. I really don't want to hurt him. Because the truth is, I like him a lot.

Later that night, after practice and dinner, I'm lying on my bed, staring at my phone, trying to figure out how to respond to Bobby's note. Texting is probably better, will be less embarrassing for him. It has to be hard on a guy when a girl turns him down.

Sorry, I can't. I wasn't planning to go to prom and I . . .

Delete. Delete. Delete.

How do I say this?

I got your note. Thank you for the invite, but I'm busy that night.

Ugh. That is so much worse.

Suddenly there's a thudding on my bedroom door, like someone's kicking it. "Come in."

"Open the door, please!" says Mom.

When I swing it open, she's standing outside, holding a bucket of water and ice in one hand and a homemade smoothie in the other, complete with a rainbow straw and miniature paper umbrella. A heating bag filled with rice is pitched over her shoulder. She shuts the door with her foot while handing me the smoothie. "I thought you could use some comforting. Grab a towel."

I keep a towel in my closet for just this purpose. I spread it on the floor, and Mom sets the bucket on top of it. I sit on the edge of the bed and dunk my feet into the ice water. "Thanks, Mom."

She arranges the heating bag around the back of my neck and wraps a fluffy blanket around my shoulders. The goose bumps are already standing out on my legs from the ice water. "I know you're disappointed about prom. I talked with your dad, and he agrees with me. Now just isn't the time to add something else to your schedule."

"I get it, Mom. I do." I don't like it, but I get it.

Mom kicks off her slippers, climbs onto the bed, and settles behind me. "Drink your smoothie and soak your feet. Relax."

The frigid water around my feet doesn't exactly feel relaxing, but over years of needing to ice my ankle, I've gotten used to it. The smoothie is delicious, although the paper umbrella that would normally make me smile doesn't tonight.

Mom starts rubbing my sore shoulders. It's not the

working-the-knots-out-of-my-muscles massaging that I get at the gym, but a gentle stroking that could easily lull me to sleep. My eyes close.

"I remember that day so well, when the switch happened."

"The switch?" I ask.

"The day when you decided that you wanted gymnastics for yourself. Before that I think you did it because it was fun, because you knew you were good at it, because you knew that Dad and I enjoyed watching you. But you were about twelve, I think, when the switch happened, and suddenly you *owned* gymnastics. It was at that moment that I knew there would be no stopping you."

Opening my eyes, I take a slow sip of the smoothie. I don't remember that as clearly as Mom does. Being twelve seems like a lifetime ago.

"You have such a narrow window, sweetie, to realize your dreams. If you don't make this Olympics, you might make the next one, but after that . . ."

She doesn't have to say it. After that I will most likely hit my expiration date.

"You just don't need any additional drama in your life right now," she continues. "I never should have let you go out with Bobby to begin with."

"It was for school," I remind her.

"I shouldn't have gone along with the extra work you're doing. I should have spoken to your teacher, taken care of it—"

"I took care of it," I insist. "If I can do well on the final, I'll get an A."

"Still, all the work."

"It's fine, Mom. I actually enjoyed it." I twist around, and she moves to the side just enough so that I can see her clearly. "I understand what you're saying. I really do. I'm not mad. I'm just disappointed. I love gymnastics. I want to make Team USA. I want to go to the Olympics. That's my number one priority."

"Good. Because we've all made so many sacrifices for you."

"I know. And I appreciate every one. It's just that sometimes I wonder if life is ever going to slow down for me. If I'll ever be *normal*."

"Charlie," Mom says with a short laugh. "I'm sorry to break it to you, but I think you might find normal . . . boring."

"So, what are you saying?"

Mom smiles. "I'm saying you should . . . embrace your crazy."

"Embrace my crazy," I repeat. "I like that."

I return her smile as I hand her my empty glass. Then I pull my feet out of the ice water and dry them off.

She takes the rice bag, which has cooled down, and the bucket. "Just remember we love and support you. We want you to have the opportunity not only to reach for your dreams but to hold them."

"I love you, Mom."

She kisses the top of my head. "Good night, sweetheart."

After she leaves the room, I lie back on my bed.

Embrace my crazy, Mom says. I think back to when I told Bobby that I didn't give him my phone number because my life was crazy right then. He responded that he had no problem with crazy. Of course, he doesn't know exactly how crazy things around me are about to get. So what would it hurt to add just a little bit more insanity to this wild ride that I'm on?

I pick up my phone, type out a text to him.

I got your note about prom. I have to work around some family things. But I definitely want to go with you.

Chapter Fifteen

"You've got that look," Gwen says as we push through the gym doors and out into the twilight Tuesday evening.

"What look?"

"I don't know," Gwen says, laughing. "It's the look like you're up to no good."

My heart does a little patter. Ever since she got her car, she's been giving me a lift home after practice. I told her that tonight I'd treat her to frozen yogurt as a way to say thanks. But the truth is that I want to ask her for a huge favor. Does Gwen know me so well that she's figured out my ploy? I shrug off her suspicions and say, "We're going for froyo. We *are* up to no good."

"You think Coach Chris would be mad at us?" Gwen asks, glancing back at the gym and his Toyota 4Runner still in the parking lot. I wonder if we look like fugitives, making our escape through the darkness.

I force myself to giggle, but my mind is on other things. "What Coach Chris doesn't know won't hurt him."

"I'm getting the sugar-free peach, sprinkled with organic cocoa," she says. "He can't be too mad about that!"

"But he'd be mad about my chocolate-and-pomegranate combo with Heath bar and gummy bear toppings." I tug her along faster.

The frozen yogurt shop is located in a strip mall a few blocks from the gym. I got permission ahead of time to stay out a little later than normal. Gwen will have me home by nine. That should be enough time for me to persuade her to help me out.

But all dreams of sugar rush out of my head the moment Gwen swings open the shop's doors and my gaze sweeps over a sea of yellow and black.

I can't walk through the door of FroYoLicious. I'm rooted to the concrete.

"Go in!" Gwen cries, prodding me.

Yellow-and-black warm-ups. The frozen yogurt store is full of them. "Uhh . . . maybe this isn't such a good idea."

"You are not backing out now!" Gwen cries.

A quick glance at her face tells me she has no idea why I'm stalling. For all she knows, I'm doubting our decision to pig out on froyo this close to trials. I check over my shoulder. Sure enough, there's a big yellow school bus parked at the back of the lot.

I size up the situation inside the shop. There's a mixture of boys and girls, it seems, all in yellow and black. What I don't get is why they're here. Gwen and I have been to FroYoLicious a dozen times, and I've never in all those times seen another person from Jefferson. In fact, mostly, at this time of night, we have the place to ourselves, which is why I thought it would be perfect for a clandestine meeting.

There have to be at least thirty Jefferson kids here tonight, crammed into the small shop, all at different stages of dispensing and eating their frozen yogurt. I scan the crowd for someone I might know. Mostly they're strangers, but I do spot a kid who sits a couple of rows behind me in Spanish. And a girl I recognize from U.S. government. Is that Alison from AP Lit? Or her twin? I can never tell them apart.

I slip through the doorway, dipping my head and trying not to make eye contact. My hair is firmly back in a messy bun, and my face is glasses-free. Even if there are kids here from my classes, they're not used to seeing me with my hair up, dressed in my warm-ups, so maybe they won't recognize me.

"Wow, it's crowded," Gwen says. Her voice is loud over the jumble of conversations. We grip each other's sleeves as we weave our way through the crowd. "What are all these kids doing here, do you think?"

"They must've had some sort of competition," I say.

"What school are they?" Gwen asks.

I cough and speak at the same time. "Jefferson."

"Jefferson? Your school?"

We've reached the yogurt machines and wait in line behind a couple of girls. I'm not sure I want to answer her when we're standing so close to other people. "Yes," I whisper, "but don't make a big deal about it. I don't really know any of these people. Not well, anyway."

Gwen bounces on her toes. Her eyes skim the crowd. She seems super-excited to be around this many other high school kids. Maybe it's all the boys. Our gym doesn't have a boys' program, so her opportunities are limited.

"Why are they all over here? This isn't exactly near Jefferson," Gwen says.

The girl in front of us turns and gives Gwen a once-over. "We had a meet at Rosa Parks."

"Oh, cool. What kind of meet?" Gwen asks.

I pretend to be reading the flavors on the yogurt machine. I don't think this girl recognizes me from school. I don't recognize her. Thank goodness.

"Track-and-field," the girl says, inching forward in the line.

"That's so cool!" Gwen says. "How'd it go?"

"A lot of us won our events," the girl says, finally offering Gwen a smile. "Where do you go?"

"Oh, I do online school," Gwen says, sending me a nervous side glance. I grit my teeth in a smile, hoping the girl doesn't ask me the same question, but she starts talking to the friend in front of her and seems to forget all about us.

We fill our cups and add toppings, but after we've paid, there's nowhere to sit.

Gwen and I lean against the wall, angling away from a

cluster of girls who are sharing the same wall. "Note to self," Gwen says. "Don't come to FroYoLicious when there's a track-and-field meet in town."

"No kidding," I say.

Gwen licks yogurt off her spoon. "I guess if someone found out you did gymnastics, it wouldn't be the end of the world. They wouldn't know what level you were. It wouldn't change anything."

I shrug. Maybe she's right, but they *might* figure out I'm actually pretty good, and that makes me nervous, because I would have to deal with explaining my double life to people before I'm ready. Talk about a distraction before trials. I need to take things one step at a time: trials, Olympics, loss of ano-nymity at school.

"Oh my gosh! Mom, look!" exclaims a small voice.

A mom and double-daughter combo are approaching us. I know they're talking about us, because they have that look on their faces—the shining-eyed, excited look.

"It's Charlie Ryland and Gwen Edwards!" The mom is practically yelling. "Hi, girls!" She reaches a hand out to pump mine. "My girls go to your gym. We've seen your pictures and followed all your meets!"

I glance around to see if anyone's taking notice of us. A Jefferson girl near us makes eye contact with me and gives me an odd look, but then goes back to her froyo.

The woman's daughters are only slightly shorter than

Gwen and me, but they're probably only ten years old, max. Though, sometimes it's hard to tell with gymnasts. We do, generally, tend to be on the shorter side. They flutter their fingers at us sheepishly.

"Hey, girls. Great to meet you!" Gwen says, flashing her sunny smile. She pumps hands with the mom and then each of the girls. I, on the other hand, glance around the shop, trying to assess if anyone is paying attention to what's going on over here or if we can be heard. But it doesn't seem as though anyone is aware of us, which makes me feel a little silly and paranoid.

"We're such big fans," says the mom. "Do you think they could get something signed by you? I'm not sure we'll ever see you at the gym when you're free."

"Sure!" Gwen cries. Of the two of us, she's definitely the PR person at the moment, while I'm working to keep a low profile.

"We don't have pens or anything," I finally contribute. "I'll check with the cashier. Maybe she has one we can borrow."

"Don't go to that trouble. I'll see what I can find in my purse," the mom says, beginning to rummage. "Thank you so much!"

I nod, smiling, wishing I hadn't let the presence of students from Jefferson unsettle me. As a result I haven't been paying attention to these two young girls, who are obviously starstruck. I would have died at their age if I'd had a chance to speak with an elite gymnast.

"What levels are you in?" I ask, positioning myself so that

I'm giving them my full attention and not worrying about the Jefferson students any longer.

The girls nudge each other. "You answer," one says.

"No, you!"

"They just started at Gold Star," the mom answers for them. "We were at a different gym before. Both did level four last season."

"Are you twins?" Gwen asks.

"No, no," the mom says. "Fifteen months apart. But they started gymnastics at the same time."

"How cool to do gymnastics with your sister," I say. "That must be awesome. I wish I had a sister to do gymnastics with. But I only have a brother, and he just likes to play video games."

"Do you play with him?" one of the girls asks.

"Nope. Can't sit still for that long. I'd rather do cartwheels."

"Me too!" the other girl says. "I love cartwheels."

The mom holds up a pen. "I found one! Here . . . let's use a napkin."

"What about my hand?" chirps one of the girls. "They could sign my hand!"

"Oh, but that would rub off, honey," the mom says, bustling away to find a napkin.

"What is your favorite event?" one of the girls asks, barely daring to look at Gwen.

"Mine is definitely bars," Gwen says. "How about you, Charlie?"

"Beam."

"My favorite is beam too!" says the girl. I give her a high five.

"Mine is bars!" says the other girl.

The mom returns. "Thank you so much!" she exclaims. "You two are such an inspiration to my daughters. I can't tell you how much it means to us to run into you."

"It's fun to meet younger gymnasts," I say, trying to make up for my distraction earlier. "Did you have a good season in level four, girls?"

They nod in unison.

"What level are you doing next year?" I ask.

"Level five," says one girl, who looks like she might be the older one. "Tamara's still working on her flyaway, though."

"I still need a spot," says Tamara sheepishly, referring to the fact that she needs someone to be there to catch her if she falls, and to help her get back into the routine.

"There's nothing wrong with a spot," I tell them. "We all need a little help sometimes. Flyaways are hard when you first try them."

The girls grin at us.

"You're both awesome," I say, signing my name with a flourish. "Keep up the good work and never give up, okay?"

The girls each give us a thumbs-up as they walk off with their mother. Watching them leave, I realize that the place has pretty much cleared out and all the Jefferson High students are gone.

"Whew! So much for a relaxing bit of frozen yogurt after practice," Gwen says. She takes a bite of yogurt, studies me. "So why are we really here?"

Busted. She knows something's up. "Let's sit down."

We settle in at a small round iron table with two iron seats. Not the most comfortable. Gwen turns her unblinking eyes on me and licks her spoon. She's waiting. Patiently. Now that the moment is here, I'm not quite sure how to explain.

"You know more about me than anyone else," I say. "I tell you everything. You're my best friend. I need a favor a week from Saturday. I need you to drive me somewhere, and I don't want my parents to know."

Her brow crinkles. "That sounds ominous. What's going on?"

"Bobby invited me to prom, and I want to go really badly, but Mom said no."

She shakes her head like what I've said makes no sense. "You want to go to prom a week before trials?"

I sigh with frustration. "I don't know why we always have to choose gymnastics over everything else. I think I can do both. Life as we know it is going to get crazier if we make the team. How can I handle the stress of the Olympics if something as simple as going to prom throws me off-kilter? Mom told me to embrace my crazy, and this is part of it. Not sacrificing everything, but doing as much as I can to enjoy this wild ride I'm on."

She studies me, and I see the concern in her eyes. "I get what you're saying. I really do. It's just one night, but what if something goes wrong? I know I'm a broken record, but I can't stop thinking about what happened to Coach Rachel."

"Gwen, nothing bad is going to happen," I hastily assure her. "You'd know that if you met Bobby. He's really nice. And it's my only chance to go to prom before I hopefully make the Olympics, which means I'll be stepping onto the world stage and everyone will know who I am whether I like it or not. Plus I'll get to see the results of all the hard work the student council did to create one romantic starry night in Paris."

"Paris?"

"That's our theme. Paris is such a romantic city, known for people falling in love. It was my idea."

She sets aside her cup of melting yogurt. "Coach Chris will have a fit if he discovers you're not a hundred percent focused on trials."

"That's what I'm trying to explain. I'm going to think about it whether or not I go, so I might as well go. Besides, he's not going to find out."

"If he learns that I was an accessory—"

"It's not a crime," I point out, holding back the need to laugh at her legal terminology. "But again, he's not going to find out."

Leaning back, she crosses her arms over her chest and stares off into the distance. "Prom," she grumbles.

"I know you don't approve."

Shaking her head, she shifts her attention to me. "To be honest, I'm a little jealous. I wish I were going to prom. When we walked in here tonight and there were all those guys . . . Did you see how buff some of them were?"

I smile. "I saw a couple of them looking you over."

"You were too worried about them figuring out who you were to notice them looking at me."

"Not true. Trust me, a couple of them were interested."

She blushes with obvious pleasure. I've never seen Gwen blush.

"So this escape to prom that you're planning, how would it work?" she asks.

"I'd tell my mom that I'm spending the night with you so that we can begin psyching each other up for trials. I'd go ahead and have my dress and everything at your house so I could change there. Then I'll just tell Bobby that I have to meet him at prom. You drive me there. I'll have him drive me to your house when it's over."

"We'll have to figure out a way for Mrs. Gundersen not to get suspicious. I'll think of something."

I can't believe what I'm hearing. "So . . . you'll do it?"

"I've got your back, Charlie."

I almost whoop with joy. I can't believe that I'm going to be able to pull this off and go to prom. "Thanks, Gwennie. You're the best friend ever."

Chapter Sixteen

When I arrive at Mr. Alto's classroom for the student council meeting, I slide into the empty seat next to Bobby. My heart does a little somersault because he looks so glad to see me.

"Did you get things with the family situation worked out?" he asks.

"Almost. But I'll need to meet you at prom."

"I thought we'd do dinner first."

"I can meet you at the restaurant."

"You don't want me to pick you up?"

He looks confused, a little suspicious.

"It's a long story, but I'll be—"

"I'm calling the meeting to order," Kristine says harshly. "Secretary, call the roll."

I do. Then we approve the minutes. Each committee is called on to report. When we get to the food committee, I share the information from Tasty Bites. It gets a resounding approval—even from my committee members, who I figure are just glad they don't have to discuss it anymore—and Mr.

Alto is asked to present it to the administration for a final approval.

Things don't go quite as smoothly for the decorating committee.

"We still have so much to do," Tasha says. "We're trying to build an Eiffel Tower, and we want people to stand beneath an Arc de Triomphe for their prom photos. We just don't know if we'll have everything ready in time."

"All right," Kristine says. "We have to jump on this. The athletes"—she gives Bobby a knowing smile—"have practice, so they are excused, but everyone else will need to meet every day after school and three hours this Saturday to get the decorations done. Then, of course, we'll all be expected to meet the Saturday morning of prom to get the decorations put up."

I can't do any of that. I start to raise my hand, but stop. I'm not going to argue with her about it. I'll just tell Mr. Alto.

Kristine goes on about some other things. Finally she adjourns the meeting. I close my notebook and start to get up to talk with Mr. Alto, when Bobby's hand comes to rest on my arm.

"You were saying?" he asks.

And I remember what we were talking about when Kristine called the meeting to order. Everything suddenly seems so complicated, and I have so much that I need to do. I take a deep breath, calm my racing heart. I can handle all this. It's what I do.

"I'm going to be staying with a friend," I tell Bobby.

"Would it be okay if I pick you up there?"

I don't want to ruin this night for him. I don't want to be a selfish or demanding date. "Let me check. I'll get back to you. Oh, and don't say anything about our going to prom together to my brother." With four hundred people in the building at prom, there's a chance I won't even cross paths with Josh, but if I do, I'll deal with it then.

"Charlotte, what are you not telling me?"

So much, and I hate it, but I don't want him to have doubts about our going, and I don't want him to change his mind. I squeeze his hand. "Nothing. I really want to go with you."

"Okay. I have to scoot to class."

He walks out, and I approach Mr. Alto. He looks up from his phone and smiles. "Charlotte."

"Mr. Alto, I have other commitments that I've made for after school and on Saturday. I absolutely cannot blow them off, so I'm not going to be able to help the decorating committee. If that means that I need to resign from the student council—"

"No." He waves a hand. "I'm really impressed with the minutes you write up, and you've done an excellent job with the food committee. You weren't expecting to have to help with the decorating. I'll excuse you."

I grin. "Thank you."

When I get to my locker, Zoe is waiting for me.

"Okay," she says. "I promised I wasn't going to bug you about this, but I'm dying to know what you told Bobby about prom."

I've actually been totally surprised that she's gone this long without insisting that I tell her. I've waited because I needed to know if Gwen was on board. If she wasn't, then I would have had to back out of what I told Bobby. I can't help the broad smile stretching across my face. "I'm going."

"Yes! Michael and I will double with you. This is going to be the best night of our lives! We're going to have so much fun!"

I hope so. I hope it's going to be as wonderful as we both think it will be, so wonderful that it makes what I'm doing worth the risk.

"The thing is, Zoe," I whisper, "my mom said no, and I don't want Bobby to know, so we need to keep this on the down-low."

Her eyes widen. "Why did she say no?"

I shake my head. "She just thinks it's too much too soon. I'm too young. A bunch of reasons. But I'm going to go. I just need to make sure my family doesn't find out. I'm working on that."

"Okay. Whatever I can do . . ."

"Go shopping for a dress Sunday?"

She smiles. "Absolutely. I still need to get mine."

"Which will be my excuse for going with you. Can your sister give us a ride?"

"Probably. I'll check."

She studies me a minute. "Charlotte. You're, like, being a rebel. I didn't know you had it in you."

I didn't know I had it in me either, but then, I've spent years doing whatever I've had to do to reach for my dreams. Maybe I've been a rebel all along and just didn't know it.

Zoe and I walk across the shiny tiled floor of the mall, the tinkling elevator music filling our ears. I'd say we were walking shoulder to shoulder, except, since I'm a whole head shorter than Zoe, my shoulder hits somewhere above her elbow. As soon as we entered the mall, her sister told us to meet her at that entrance in two hours and took off. Apparently she has no interest in hanging with two high schoolers. That makes everything better for us, since we're here on a mission.

Zoe steers me into a store. "This is the place I wanted you to see. I totally think we'll find something in here."

The shop assistant approaches us. Her name tag reads MINDY. "Can I help you find something?"

"Prom dresses," Zoe says, smiling brightly. "One for each of us because we're both going to prom with the cutest guys."

Mindy smiles, her gaze going from Zoe to me. "First time?"

"Yep," Zoe replies. "For both of us."

"Okay," Mindy says. "Do you have anything in mind?"

"I want long!" Zoe cries. "Glamorous."

"Something short," I say. "Long dresses make me look smaller than I already am."

"You know, that's actually a myth," Mindy says. "The right long length can make you look taller."

"Seriously?" I ask. I love the idea of long dresses—I just never thought I could pull them off.

"Pick out something short that you like. I'll find something for you in long. Then you can decide."

I emerge from the dressing room fifteen minutes later in a hot-pink dress with a swishy skirt that ends around my midthigh.

"This might be too short," I say, tugging on it. "Plus, this pink is too—"

"Bright? Obnoxious? Hideous?" Zoe finishes for me.

I was thinking too Olympics. During the last Olympics the Americans all wore pink leos exactly this shade. "No, I like pink. It's just . . . not looking like I thought it would."

I gaze into the mirror one more time. It is a nice dress, but I have nothing to fill out the bust. And it makes my shoulders look wider than they are.

"All right," Mindy says, holding up a long, lacy navy-blue dress. "Try this."

When I step out of the dressing room, I'm stunned. The lining of the dress is a stretchy material that hugs my body across my chest and just under my arms, and stops midthigh. Lace covers it, rising to the neck and creating sleeves that stop just below my elbows. The lace flows down my body, pooling on the floor, with a slit that ends just above my knee. I do look taller. I look—

"Oh my gosh," Zoe says. "Charlotte, it's gorgeous."

"The key," Mindy says, "is straight lines and solid colors. You'll need to wear heels, of course."

"Of course," I murmur in breathless disbelief.

"What can you do for me?" Zoe asks.

"Tall is easy," Mindy says. "We need to find something that emphasizes your gorgeous red hair. I have a green that I think will work."

"I'll look like Christmas."

Mindy gives her a slow smile. "Let's see it on you first before you make a judgment."

It's a deep-emerald-green, satiny halter gown that shimmers whenever Zoe moves—which she is doing a lot, swinging her hips, twirling around.

"It's stunning!" I exclaim.

"You think so?" Zoe asks.

"Absolutely."

"You should both wear your hair in some kind of chignon," Mindy says, gathering my hair in her hands. "And get your makeup done."

"Charlie's a whiz at makeup," Zoe says. "She's going to do mine." Then she looks at me. "Right?"

"Right."

We both change into our street clothes. I'm a little surprised by how regular I suddenly feel. The gown made me feel so elegant.

At the cash register I take out the credit card that my parents gave me to use whenever I travel with the team.

From there Zoe and I head to a shoe store and purchase shoes—with three-inch heels—to match our gowns.

"We still have a little time left," Zoe says. "Let's go to the food court."

I'm not at all surprised to see Bobby and Michael sitting at a table and sipping smoothies.

"You know," I say to Zoe as she steers us toward them, "you don't have to keep arranging these little trysts without telling me."

"But this way is so much more fun."

"Hey," Michael says as he and Bobby stand. "What a surprise. We just came to the mall to order our tuxes."

"And you had no idea we'd be here?" I ask in disbelief.

"A little birdie might have said something," says Michael. "What can we get you to drink?"

Zoe gets a latte. I go with an iced skinny chai.

"So . . . ," Bobby says, resting his crossed arms on the table. "We thought we should make sure we're all on the same page about Saturday. We've rented a limo."

Zoe gives a little squeal. "I've always wanted to ride in one."

"We'll have it pick us up at Zoe's at six," Michael says.

"Bobby will pick you up, bring you over," he says to me. "We'll grab dinner somewhere and be at prom by eight."

This is happening. This is really happening.

I look at Bobby. "Because of the family thing, it'll work better if I just meet you at Zoe's."

"Are you sure? Because I don't mind picking you up."

"I appreciate that, but everything will be crazy on Saturday. It's just less complicated to meet you there rather than have to figure out all the timing."

He nods. "Okay."

"That works better," Zoe says, "because Charlotte is going to help me with my makeup." She grins broadly. "We're going to have a blast!"

Unless I get caught.

Chapter Seventeen

Coach Chris pulls me and Gwen out from the rest of the development team—the girls he's preparing to take to trials. He wants to work with us individually on bars. On Saturday, Gwen ran into a slight block with her Kovacs that worried Coach Chris, but nothing ever stops her for long. I have my new dismount to work on—a full twisting double back. I've mastered it into the foam pit. Now it's time to put it to the test. Coach Chris is quiet and nervous, chewing gum rapidly as he paces beside the mat. He likes us to be doing full routines this close to competing, especially with the high stakes of this particular competition. It's crucial that we all give our best these last two weeks before trials.

Gwen toe-shoots up to the high bar and begins her series of giants—starting with a handstand and then rotating her body 360 degrees, circling the bar—building up to her Kovacs. I dip my hands into the chalk bin. "Come on, Gwen! Go, girl!"

Gwen comes up high, releases, flips twice, and grabs the bar again. It all happens in a smooth, fluid whoosh. She doesn't even lose momentum, whips right up into a perfect handstand on the high bar and rotates in a pirouette.

"Yeah!" I cry out.

I check to see if Coach Chris is reacting, but his face is expressionless, and if he notices me looking at him, he ignores me. His eyes are trained on Gwen. She whips through her dismount and nails her landing.

"All right, Charlie," Coach Chris says. "Let's go."

I dust more chalk onto my hands. I slide the springboard into place and take my position on the far side of the high bar. Closing my eyes for a moment helps to block out any distraction. After a deep breath I spring into my routine. While I'm flying, everything around me is a beautiful blur.

But when I come to the dismount, my body doesn't cooperate. I hit the floor standing, wobble, stumble, lose my balance and land on my backside.

"Tight mind, Charlie," Coach says. "Tight body. Let's get this done. You want to head back to the pit?" he says, referring to the foam pit.

"No, I got it," I say.

"One more time," Coach says. "Just the dismount."

I hear impatience in his tone, and I don't blame him. I need this dismount if I'm going to stand a chance at trials. I take the bar again.

"Higher!" Coach's voice rings out when I swing around fast in my final 360-degree rotation. I need height to get all those twists in. But when I come down, my feet slide out from under me and I slam onto my back instead of sticking my landing. The jarring pain knocks the breath out of me and makes my eyes water. I struggle for a few seconds to get air back into my lungs.

Coach claps in one, short staccato. "Back to the pit!" he orders.

I shove myself to my feet, my heart beating in my temples. Before I can take a step, Coach is there, both hands on my shoulders. He gives me a steady look. "Usually I'd tell you not to get frustrated, to take your time, it'll come. But we don't have time for that, and you know it."

"I know."

"So, work that dismount over there. You've got the ability. Get back over here as soon as you can and give me something I can work with."

"Yes, Coach."

"He knows about Saturday," Gwen whispers to me later when we're in the locker room.

"He doesn't know," I assure her as I take my bag out of my locker. Inside it I have my gown, shoes, and makeup bag to pass off to Gwen when we get to her car. She's giving me a ride home tonight.

"But he was watching us so closely."

"Because we have to perfect our routines."

"You were struggling tonight," she says. "Were you thinking about prom? Because I can't stop thinking about it and about what will happen if we get caught."

I'm not really worried about getting caught, but I can't deny that prom is on my mind.

"Everything is going to be okay, Gwen."

She glances around before leaning in toward me. "I've never done anything that I'm not supposed to do. It's exciting and scary, but what if my helping you means you don't make the Olympic team?"

"Gwen, it's only one night."

"Coach Rachel thought it was only one dip in the pool topless."

"It's not the same thing. You can't bail on me now. We've made all these plans."

"I keep questioning what we're doing, but I'm not going to bail. And I have some good news. The Gundersens are going to a fund-raiser that night, so they won't be home."

"Perfect! So I could actually have Bobby pick me up at your place."

"And I get to meet him. See what all the fuss is about."

I nod. "We can discuss the rest in the car."

After gathering all our things, we head out of the locker room and toward the doors.

"Charlie, Gwen!" Coach Chris jogs toward us. "Glad I caught you before you left. Talk to your parents"—he nods at Gwen—"or host parents, as the case may be, and let them know I'd like for you to pick up some extra hours of practice on Saturday. Say, two until six."

My stomach drops. Saturday? This Saturday? Of course he's talking about this Saturday. It's the last Saturday before we leave for trials.

"I have tickets to a concert Saturday." I don't know how I got so brazen, lying to a coach's face. I just hope he doesn't ask me for the name of the band or the venue. I'll also have to make other arrangements, because Gwen will be stuck here.

Coach's gaze zeroes in on me. "You're going to a concert?"

I push through. "I thought it would be a good idea to relax, get my mind off gymnastics for a night."

"There is no relaxing a week before we leave for trials." His voice is eerily quiet. "There is no giving your mind a night off. You have to stay a hundred percent focused on the competition."

"You're right," I say, releasing a breath. I offer him a brave smile, while inside I'm fighting the bitter disappointment. Why did I think I could get away with this? "I don't know what I was thinking. I'll give my ticket to my brother. He can take a friend." Why do I keep talking, spinning this lie when it no longer matters?

Coach studies my face. "I know you probably think I'm being obsessive about this, but you need the extra practice. We've got to get that dismount polished before trials."

"I know. I'm a hundred percent committed."

"Good," he says, nodding crisply. "We'll see you tomorrow at regular practice."

As soon as we're out the gym doors, Gwen says, "Wow, I can't believe you lied like that—on the spot without breaking a sweat. I would have been impressed if I hadn't been so worried that he was going to figure it out. I would not make a good secret agent or undercover cop. I don't think I took a breath during the whole exchange."

"I decided I had nothing to lose by giving it a shot. If he figured it out, the worst that would happen was that he'd chew me out."

"He might have decided not to take you to trials."

"I know there is no guarantee that we'll make the Olympic team, but you and I have brought home enough medals from world and regional competitions that he knows we're good. That's why he pushes us so hard, to make sure we reach our potential."

"I hate to admit it, but I'm kind of bummed about having practice Saturday. I was looking forward to helping you get to prom. What are you going to do now?"

"I'll just have to skip dinner and the ride in the limo, tell them to enjoy that part of the evening without me and that I'll meet them at the dance." I look over at her. "That is, if you're willing to drive me over to the skating rink. And if not, I totally understand, Gwen. I shouldn't have put you in this position of doing something we shouldn't be doing."

She gives me a smile as we reach her car. "You'd do the same for me."

"I would," I say. "I totally would. If I could drive."

She laughs. "That would help."

"I just really want to do this, Gwen. And I've never given up on something I wanted. I can't give up on prom, on Bobby. I'll figure it out."

I am strong. I keep fighting. I don't give up.

Chapter Eighteen

The next day I'm able to catch up with Bobby at his locker.

"Hey," he says when he sees me. "I didn't know you knew where my locker was."

"Zoe knew, since it's close to Michael's. I wanted to give you this."

He laughs as he examines the small star-shaped cardboard. On it is written, *I Survived a Chick Flick*. I glued a safety pin to the back of it. I made it as a peace offering and as a way to break the ice regarding what I need to talk with him about.

"I never claimed to have any artistic skills," I admit.

"I like it," he says, smiling. "Probably never wear it, but I like it. Thanks."

He opens his locker.

"So there's something else," I say.

He stops, looks at me intently, gives me his full attention.

I swallow hard. "I mentioned this family situation on Saturday. I can't get out of it, and it's going to go longer than I thought. I can't make dinner at six, so I thought you all could

THE FLIP SIDE · 179

go ahead and eat and I'll meet you at the dance instead of at Zoe's."

"We could move dinner to seven."

"I probably won't even be ready until seven."

"Then we'll eat at eight."

"That'll make everyone late to prom. I don't want to do that to you, not to mention to Michael and Zoe."

"So what if we're not there at eight?" he asks. "We miss a couple of dances and the long line for photos. Prom goes until midnight. We'll have lots of time to enjoy it."

"It just doesn't seem fair to everyone else to make them late because of my schedule."

"Okay, then. I'll check with Michael and Zoe. If they don't want to wait on us, they can go ahead. We'll catch up."

"That's a lot of trouble for you."

"Charlotte, I don't care about prom. I care about going with you."

My heart does a little flip, even as I feel myself falling seriously in like with Bobby Singh. "I thought we were going as friends."

"You're a friend I really, really like."

"I like you, too," I whisper.

"Okay, then, we'll figure this out."

I nod and back up a step. "I'll talk with you later."

"Count on it."

I spin around, slam into Josh. He puts his hands on my

shoulders, steadies me. "What are you doing in this hallway?"

"I didn't realize it was a no-Charlotte zone."

He grins. "I didn't mean that. It's just that you're never in this hallway." His gaze shifts from me to where Bobby is. I glance over my shoulder. Was. He's already left. "Is everything okay?"

"Everything is fine. I have to get to class."

I rush off, breathing a sigh of relief. I do not need Josh getting suspicious. And I need to figure out how to avoid running into him at prom. I have the advantage that he won't be looking for me, but I'll be looking for him.

I fully realize that I'm taking a risk—grasping for the best of both worlds. I hope it's worth it.

Later, when I'm in Mr. Alto's class, Zoe slides into the desk next to mine.

"Did you really think we'd go to prom without you?" she asks, looking at me as though I'm a total disappointment.

"I know how much this night means to you," I tell her. "I feel like I'm ruining it."

"You'll only ruin it if you're not there at all." She reaches across, grabs my hand, and squeezes. "Charlotte, we're best friends. We share everything. We're going to share prom night."

A fissure of guilt hits me. We don't exactly share everything. For the first time I'm beginning to regret that.

Mom motions excitedly to me as I jog toward the car after school. I open the passenger door.

"Look!" she cries, holding out a magazine. "Look at this!"

It's a copy of *Gymnastics NOW!* and my face is on the cover. My gigantic face. The whole cover is me. I'm leaning forward on the beam, looking strong and confident.

"Oh my gosh!"

"I know!" Mom squeals. "Isn't it fantastic? Oh my goodness, Charlie, they did the most amazing job. You look absolutely gorgeous."

I stare at the cover. Is this really me? My hair is a shining gold; my smile is warm and genuine. My eyes are sparkling. I look happy, in my element. Beautiful.

"Why'd they put me on the cover and not Gwen?" I ask. Gwen has won more gold medals at world and national competitions than I have.

"I don't know," Mom says. "I guess your picture worked for the cover. It is an amazing shot. I mean, I— You are breathtaking. But of course I'm biased."

"Thanks, Mom." I can't work myself up to be as excited as she is. I'm worried that Gwen might be disappointed that they didn't put her on the cover. She gets most of the media coverage because she's brought home the world all-around title two years in a row.

"My baby girl!" Mom exclaims, pulling me into a hug. "The article is nice too. And you and Gwen are all over the inside, along with a few of the other girls from the national team."

I can't help but smile every time I flip a page and see the face of one of the girls I've trained with. There are some wonderful photos of Gwen. I laugh at the one of us clowning around for the photographer, trying to look sexy. I can't believe they used it. This is really happening. "Olympic Hopefuls" is the title of the article. "Bringing It On for 2016."

"You're going to get so many more opportunities like this, to be written about, to be featured," Mom says.

"But the success will come with a price." I set aside the magazine and pull down the sun visor so that I can use the mirror to put in my contacts.

"Everything worthwhile comes with a price," Mom reminds me. It's not the first time she's told me that. "As always, focus on the positive."

"I've got less than two weeks left to embrace the crazy that is my life right now. After trials—if I make it—I won't be able to keep my secret any longer. Things are likely to get a lot crazier."

Mom pinches my cheek lightly. "Charlie, enjoy this ride. It's like being on bars. Remember when you were learning your first release move? What was it, a bail?"

"Yeah."

"You've got to let go of one bar to grab the other, right? Otherwise you'll just keep swinging in the same spot and not go anywhere." She reaches over to smooth my hair. "You've always been brave at gymnastics. I know you're going to be brave at life, too."

"Thanks, Mom."

Speaking of being brave—

"So you know we have this extra practice on Saturday," I say.

"Yes."

"Gwen invited me to spend the night with her. We thought we could use the time to start mentally preparing. Get ourselves psyched."

"I think staying so focused on gymnastics this weekend is an excellent idea. You're coming into the homestretch."

"So I can tell her yes, just go right to the Gundersens' after practice?"

"It works for me."

I try not to reveal how relieved I am. Another hurdle out of the way. Prom night is going to happen. As if on cue, I get a text from Bobby. With only one contact in, I have to squint at the screen to read it.

Changed our reservations for the restaurant to eight.

I text back, *Great. I'll meet you there. Where are we going?*

It's a surprise. Can I pick you up?

I glance over at Mom. She's focused on the road. Bobby is going to so much trouble for prom night. I don't want to be a stick in the mud or ruin his plans.

I'll be at a friend's house.

I just need an address.

I type in Gwen's address and lean back. My heart is

thundering. There's no way that Mom knows exactly what we were texting, but I still feel extremely guilty about it.

"Who was that?" Mom asks.

"Zoe." I'm a little surprised that the lie comes so easily.

"I don't suppose you told her about the magazine coverage."

Now I have to continue with the lie. I fight not to squirm, because lying makes me uncomfortable. "No. I'd have to explain things, and I'm not ready to do that yet."

"She's one of your best friends. It seems to me that you could trust her to keep your secret."

"I don't want to burden her with it." Even though I'm burdening Gwen with a big secret. But it's a harmless secret. No one is going to get hurt. Still, I try not to feel guilty. "Besides, in a few more weeks she'll know everything." If I make the team. I'll tell her then, before the Olympics. Or maybe after prom. I have so many balls to juggle to make prom work that I don't want to take a chance of ruining any of it by revealing my other life.

Mom pulls into a parking spot at Gold Star and shuts off the engine. "I don't think things between you and Zoe will change. I know you worry about that."

"You're probably right." I hope she is. I can't imagine not having Zoe in my life.

"Ready for a great practice?" she asks with a huge, encouraging smile.

I take a deep breath, easing my mind into positive mode as I slide my second contact into place. "Everything's going to be great," I say, letting my breath out.

It has to be great. I've got less than two weeks of holding on to my secret identity. I'm going to make it count.

Chapter Nineteen

Practice Saturday afternoon is a test of mental toughness. I shove aside every outside distraction: prom, Bobby, the possibility of getting caught. I concentrate totally on my twists, my flips, my dismounts. If it were possible to give more than a hundred percent, it's what I would be giving.

When Gwen and I walk out at six, I'm practically skipping because I feel almost invincible.

"I think that's the best practice you've ever had," Gwen says. "You were in the zone, sticking your landings."

I jump in front of her, face her, and start walking backward. "Life is only a distraction if we let it be."

She glances around quickly. She's been doing that a lot lately. That and looking guilty. She was so relieved when I told her that Bobby was going to pick me up. As though it lessened her culpability.

"I kept worrying that I was wearing a sign saying, CONSPIRATOR," she says now.

I squeeze her shoulder in reassurance and then fall

back into step beside her. "Helping me go to prom is not a conspiracy."

"Helping you do something you probably shouldn't—"

"You admitted that I just had my best practice. So how can this be a negative?"

When we reach the car, Gwen pops open the trunk and we sling our gym bags in. She slams the lid closed. "It just feels like we're going to get caught."

"We're not. Everything has fallen into place."

We get into the car, and Gwen starts it up. "So tell me what it's like to have a boyfriend."

"He's not really a boyfriend. He's a friend."

She darts me a sideways glance.

"Okay," I admit. "He's a little more than that. I can't wait for you to meet him."

When we get to the Gundersens', it's a little eerie how quiet the house is.

"I can't believe they went out tonight," Gwen says as she leads the way to her room.

"More proof that fate is on our side and I'm destined to go to prom."

Gwen and I are accustomed to helping each other get ready when time is short. After I take a quick shower, Gwen works my hair into a French twist while I apply my makeup. Then I slip into my gown and put on my shoes.

"Wow! Charlie. Just, wow."

Gingerly, taking care walking in the heels, I peer into her full-length mirror. My smile is so wide that if I hold it for too long, my jaws will probably start to ache. "I look tall."

"'Tall' is an overstatement," Gwen says. "'Not so short,' maybe."

The doorbell ringing makes us both jump.

"He's here," I say, suddenly incredibly nervous.

"He's going to love how you look."

"Thanks, Gwen. Thanks for tonight."

"I was wrong, Charlie. I was wrong to think this would be a distraction. You look so happy. You're going to carry that through to the Olympics."

"I'm at least going to carry it through to prom. Come on."

I grab my clutch before walking cautiously down the stairs, gripping the railing, since I'm wearing the tallest heels I could safely toddle around in. Gwen rushes ahead, then waits.

"I guess I should let you open the door," she says. "But hurry. I can't wait for him to see you."

I reach the door, open it, gasp a little. Bobby looks so cute. He's wearing a black tux that fits him perfectly, and a navy bow tie. His hair is wild and curly, his eyes sparkling. I have to concentrate on swallowing so that the drool doesn't leak out the side of my mouth. Because that would definitely not be attractive.

He's smiling, a full-on, enthusiastic smile. "You look amazing."

"Thank you. Come in for a quick sec. I want you to meet someone." When he steps forward, I am surprised to see the limo instead of Bobby's car. "You brought the limo here?"

"Yeah. We thought it would save time to bring it to you instead of having you come to it."

"We?"

"Michael and Zoe are waiting inside."

Tears prick my eyes. I can't believe how much trouble everyone went to so I could have this night. I blink back the tears and turn. "This is Gwen, one of my best friends. She helped me get ready."

"Hey, Gwen," Bobby says.

"It's nice to meet you, Bobby."

"Do you go to Jefferson?"

"I do online school."

"That must be cool. No schedule and rushing from class to class."

"It has some advantages . . . some disadvantages. No prom."

"Speaking of," I say. "We need to go."

Bobby touches my arm. The pleasure of it ripples in tingles down to my fingertips. "I have something for you."

He holds out a small box. Inside is a wrist corsage of white orchids. "It's gorgeous," I tell him, a little breathless. Even knowing that guys usually give girls a corsage for prom, I wasn't thinking about it or really expecting one. It's the first time a guy has given me flowers.

"Do you like it?" he asks, somewhat hesitantly.

"I love it!" I hold out my arm, and he places it around my wrist. "Thank you."

Bobby slips his hand into mine. "Ready?"

His hand is warm, so strong. I can feel every callus on his fingertips. I swallow. "Yeah."

But as we walk out the door, I twist back around. "Gwen, come with us. I want to introduce you."

When we get to the limo, the driver opens the door. I peer inside, see Zoe and Michael sitting together on the seat facing the rear window. "Can you come out for a minute? I want to introduce you to someone."

When they are standing on the sidewalk, I say, "This is Gwen. One of my dearest-friends."

Zoe's eyes round, and her lips part slightly. I can tell she's confused, but I also know she'll be too polite to mention that I've never told her about Gwen. Still, I plow on. "Gwen, this is Zoe."

"It's nice to meet you, Zoe," Gwen says. "I've heard a lot about you."

Zoe's brow furrows, and I'm beginning to realize that I probably should have prepared Zoe for meeting Gwen—or maybe I shouldn't have introduced Gwen, but it didn't seem fair to just leave her.

Zoe seems to recover from her surprise. She offers Gwen a teasing grin. "Charlotte is going to tell me a lot about you later. And this is my boyfriend, Michael."

"It's great to meet all of you," Gwen says.

"I wish you were going to prom with us," I say.

"Maybe next year. You better scoot."

Stepping forward, I give Gwen a big hug. "Thanks for everything."

"Have a great time, Charlie," she whispers, hugging me back. Bobby has moved to stand over by the limo, so I know he didn't hear her refer to me by the nickname I asked him not to use.

I release my hold on Gwen and climb into the limo. Zoe and Michael are already inside. Bobby settles down next to me.

"How do you know Gwen?" Zoe asks.

"I met her through gymnastics."

She looks like I punched her. "Wow. You've been friends a long time."

Not really. Zoe thinks I'm talking about back when I broke my ankle, which is when she thinks I stopped doing gymnastics. I want to veer us away from Gwen before I have to reveal all. That conversation is for another day. I should probably tell Zoe—and maybe even Bobby—everything before I leave for trials. "Really, guys, I'm very sorry that I had to delay your night."

"For the thousandth time," Zoe says, "waiting for you is going to be totally worth it. We're going to have so much fun!"

We pull up next to Constantini's Restaurant a short while

later, a place I've only ever heard about. "You got us reservations here?" I cry. This place has the reputation of being the best Italian food in Columbus. "I was expecting Olive Garden."

"The guys are treating us special," Zoe says as we climb out of the limo.

I've never eaten in a restaurant this fancy before. Bobby talks to the hostess and then returns to us. "It'll just be a couple of minutes," he says.

"That works. I need to go to the restroom." I look at Zoe. "Will you come with?"

"Sure."

"Why do girls have to go in pairs?" Michael asks.

"We just do," I say.

When we get into the restroom, I'm grateful to see a bench. "Sit down," I order Zoe.

"Why? What's wrong?"

I open my clutch and pull out a smaller bag. "I promised to do your makeup."

"I already put it on."

"You can always use a little bit more. I bought some sparkling shadow to match your gown, and some eyeliner."

"Oh!" She plops onto the bench, folds her hands in her lap, and barely breathes.

Placing my finger beneath her chin, I lift her face a little more toward the light. "You can breathe, Zoe."

"Why didn't you ever mention Gwen before?"

I can tell that she's still bothered by the fact that she didn't know anything about Gwen. Very carefully I start to apply the eye shadow. "She doesn't go to Jefferson. She's a year older than us. I didn't think your paths would ever cross. But maybe sometime all three of us could do something together."

"She seems really nice."

"She is. You'll like hanging out with her."

"She looked a little familiar."

I pause, consider, try to remember if I've ever seen Zoe with an issue of *People*. "She just has one of those faces. Now be really still, because I'm about to apply the eyeliner."

She doesn't move a muscle. When I'm finished, I apply a little more mascara, a tiny bit of rouge. "There. See what you think."

She hops up, goes to the mirror, and leans in. "Oh my gosh! My eyes! They're so big. Striking." She spins around. "Oh, Charlotte, thank you!"

"I promised to do your makeup. I keep my promises."

"And I promise this is going to be the best night ever." She loops her arm around mine. "Let's get back to our guys."

As we step into the hallway, I say, "So you referred to Michael as your boyfriend."

She squeezes my arm. "Yep. He says he is, even though I can't officially date yet."

"That is so neat."

"Maybe you and Bobby . . ."

"I don't know that we're ready to go there yet."

"Don't you like him?"

"I like him a lot, but it's a little scary thinking about having a boyfriend." Would he be willing to embrace the craziness in my life—especially the craziness that might be unleashed in another week?

"Well, I'm going to keep my fingers crossed for you. It would be so cool if we both had boyfriends. Anything and everything could happen tonight."

When we enter the lobby, the guys approach us. Michael staggers to a stop. "Wow. What did you do?"

"Charlotte added a few makeup touches."

"You look great." He blushes. "Not that you didn't look great before, but your eyes . . ."

She grins. "I know. Pretty amazing what someone who knows what they're doing can do."

"I don't mean to interrupt, but they're ready for us," Bobby says.

A man with a white napkin over his arm escorts us to our table. The restaurant is quiet, dimly lit, with candles on the table. So romantic. As we take our seats, Michael says, "I don't want to hear about empty calories tonight."

Bobby chuckles. "I promise to keep my healthy eating tips to myself." He leans toward me, grins. "Especially since I plan to be bad tonight and snack on my aunt's goodies."

"Me too." I pat my stomach. "If I have room." His brown eyes are twinkling, and I don't want to look away. Ever.

"Sparkling cider?" asks the maître d', bowing slightly. There's a silver bucket of ice by our table, with sparkling cider already chilling.

I look over the menu. So many choices.

"Bread?" The waiter has appeared by our table again. He sets down a basket filled with assorted rolls and bread slices. "Freshly baked from our kitchen."

We place our orders. Shortly after, our salads arrive. A gorgeous bed of spinach, with olives, orange baby tomatoes, and an artistically situated pile of grated purple carrot. This is all stuff I can feel guilt-free about filling up on. Bobby may not be worrying about calories tonight, but I do have to keep trials in mind. But it doesn't matter—the food is delicious.

An hour later, after our main course and a dessert, I'm stuffed. When the waiter sets down our check, I reach for my clutch.

"No way," Bobby says, putting his hand over mine. "Michael and I have this."

I think about arguing, pointing out how expensive all this must be, but one of the things my mom taught me was to always simply graciously thank people who do nice things for you. "Thank you. It was all wonderful."

"And just think. The best part of the night is yet to come."

Chapter Twenty

The lights outside the rink glimmer through the darkness. A light rain fell while we were in the restaurant, and the parking lot shimmers. The pulse of bass vibrates through the cool evening air. I'm so happy to be here. Every moment of plotting and planning was worth it.

We enter through a propped-open front door. We walk toward a woman sitting behind a table at the door leading into the rink area, collecting tickets. Bobby digs into his pants pocket and hands her ours. "Have a good evening," she says, smiling.

The warm air of the rink smells like sweat and perfume, but it's glimmering in here, with twinkly white lights threaded through trellises. At one end of the rink is a model of the Eiffel Tower. A banner reading A NIGHT IN PARIS hangs from the ceiling, where Christmas lights are twinkling, and glowing paper lanterns are suspended. Then I spot the X-wing fighter in the corner, and laugh.

"You did it!" I say to Bobby. "You got your Prom Wars theme."

"I'm not sure claiming one corner counts as a theme, but Brandon was happy."

"This is incredible," Zoe says. "Before we get separated, I want to get a photo of us."

She pulls out her phone. We all pose in front of the Eiffel Tower. She holds up her phone. "Ack! My arms aren't long enough to get us all in."

Michael takes it from her. His arms are a little longer.

"Say '*Oui! Oui!*'" Zoe shouts.

We all do, and Michael snaps the picture.

"Perfect," Zoe says. "Now let's get the real photo done."

As we stand in line, I glance around. I see Mr. Alto and a few of the other teachers serving as chaperones. One is actually holding a ruler and separating couples, making them stand a certain distance apart. In the area that circles the rink, small round tables have been set up so that the space resembles a sidewalk in Paris. The food and punch bowls are nearby. "I can't believe how the committee transformed everything. I wish I'd been able to help more."

"Hey, you got us the theme and the great refreshments," Bobby says.

"Which, unfortunately, I'm too full to enjoy."

"Me too."

"Seriously, Bobby. Dinner was wonderful."

"I wanted tonight to be special. Our first date."

He's looking at me so seriously, so intently, so hopeful. I

know I should remind him that this is another non-date, tell him that I can't be more than friends, but I don't want to, because I want tonight—and us—to be something more.

Suddenly it's our turn to have our photo taken by the professional photographer. We move into place beneath the Arc de Triomphe. The photographer positions us with my back to Bobby's chest. Bobby's hands come to rest at my waist. Even this small touch sends electricity rippling through me.

"All right, smile!" the photographer shouts.

Snap. Snap. Snap.

"All done. Little lady, you're a natural. Give my assistant your e-mail address, and she'll send you a link to the proofs when they're ready."

Bobby and I both give her our information. Then we move into the crowded space surrounding the skating area, where people are now dancing.

Bobby takes my hand. "We'll get lost in here if we don't hang on to each other." He has to yell to make his voice heard above the pumping bass of the music.

I lean closer. I can't resist. My eyes are combing the crowd, looking for Josh. I can't help but feel a flutter of nerves. And excitement. Because I'm here with Bobby, the best-looking guy in this whole place. I'm here in my beautiful dress, with my hair up in a twist, without my glasses, and with the beautiful corsage from Bobby on my wrist. Confidence surges through me.

Bobby tugs my arm. "Let's dance."

I let him pull me to the dance floor, though I wish I could lose my shoes. There's no way I can dance in these things. I glance around to see if I can spot Zoe and Michael. It's hard to identify anyone specific in the crush of people. Josh will never find me.

Bobby lets go of my arm and starts flapping his like chicken wings.

I laugh. "Is that your version of dancing?"

"It's a warm-up," he says. "Just wait till I get my groove on."

The music abruptly changes tempo, and Bobby's arms change tempo too.

"Oh my goodness," I say, slapping my forehead. "This song!" It's the one I used for my very first optional routine, when I was level seven.

Bobby flaps his knees like his arms. "You like this one?" he asks. "Let's see some moves!"

I've been awkwardly standing here, not sure what to do with my feet in these heels. I obediently bob to the music. "This song—this song was my first optional floor routine," I yell.

"First floor routine?" Bobby asks, dipping closer to me. He has great rhythm. "What does that mean?"

"You know," I say, "do a few flips, dance a little. Ta-da!" I strike a pose. "Gymnastics."

"Let's see it," he says.

"No!" I cry. "Not here. That would be stupid. I'm wearing a dress!"

"Not the flipping part. What kind of moves did you do?"

"I don't remember! It was a long time ago."

"Do you miss it?"

At least I can answer sincerely. "Not really."

Bobby grabs my hand and breaks into an exuberant electric slide. "Come on!"

I follow his lead, sliding to the right, sliding to the left, until we're both gasping with laughter. "You've got the moves, girl!"

I laugh, feeling free and carefree.

It's at that moment that I first see Kristine. She pushes her way through the crowd of dancers and approaches Bobby from behind, reaching out to touch his arm.

"Hey . . . Bobby?"

He starts at her touch. "Hi, Kristine." It might be my imagination—or wishful thinking—but I think his voice lacks enthusiasm.

"Hey," she says, tinkering with the corsage on her wrist.

"The student council did a great job decorating the place," I tell her.

She nods. "We wanted prom to be special. Would you mind if Bobby and I danced?"

Before I can respond, Bobby says, "Right now Charlotte and I are dancing. Maybe you and I can dance later."

"I really miss you."

"Now isn't the time, Kristine. You should get back to your date. I'll find you later."

"Promise?"

"If I get a chance, but I'm here with Charlotte. I'm not going to leave her alone."

Kristine's eyes shine like she's about to cry. My heart wrenches. "Look," I say, grabbing Bobby's sleeve. "I can give you a minute, if you need—"

"Yeah, could you?" Kristine cuts in.

"No," Bobby says firmly. "You don't need to go anywhere, Charlotte." He faces Kristine. "Kristine, we're not getting back together. I keep telling you that."

"Is it because of *her*?" Kristine asks through gritted teeth.

Of course, I'm the "her." I'm a little taken aback by the anger I hear in her voice.

"I am not talking to you about this now," Bobby says harshly.

He grabs my arm, not roughly but firmly enough to pull me into the crowd.

"Sorry," he says when we get to a spot on the floor where the crush of bodies isn't so intense.

"Brandon told me that she wants you to get back together with her. Is that why she put you on the DJ committee?"

He rolls his eyes. "Yes. She keeps finding excuses for us to do things together, but we're not getting back together. Like I told you, she and I aren't a good fit. I'm sorry if she ruined our night."

"Nothing's ruined," I say. "I just feel bad for her. . . ."

"Don't think about her anymore," Bobby says. "Let's just enjoy our night in Paris."

The music changes tempo again. Slower. Really slow. Bobby settles his hands on my waist and pulls me closer.

My pulse picks up, but I wind my arms around his neck, following the lead of the other couples around us. We're friends. This is a friendly slow dance. It's probably good to remind Bobby, too, as his grip tightens on my hips.

"I won't talk about her any more after this," I promise, "but . . . would it help if you tell Kristine we're here as just friends?"

"But what if we don't want to stay just friends?" His voice is a little husky, as though it was difficult for him to toss that thought out there. I squirm a little, and Bobby must feel it, because he rushes on. "I mean, no pressure. If you don't think of me that way—"

"I do," I say quickly. "I mean, I could. I'm trying really hard not to, though, because I have a lot going on, and I don't want a relationship *right now*, but . . ."

I can't believe I said all that. But it's the feeling of the moment, with the dim lights, the smell of his cologne, his breath skimming over my cheek, the warmth of his skin where my arms are draped around his neck. I swallow. "Maybe in a few months."

"I don't want to be nosy, but can you share with me what's keeping you so busy? There's not something bad happening, is there?"

"Oh, no," I assure him. "Nothing bad at all."

I'm so touched that he's worried about me. Maybe I should tell Bobby all about gymnastics tonight, confess about my double life. He would understand, if anyone would. He's a world-class wrestler. He'd know what it takes to be a world-class gymnast.

I start to speak, but at that moment someone shrieks. I hear a scream.

"No skating tonight!" a guy shouts.

"Watch out!" another guy yells almost at the same time.

I turn just in time to see a big guy careening toward me. Bobby grabs me to pull me out of the way, but the guy is moving too fast, and I'm too stunned by his speed to react. He slams into me, one of his heavy Rollerblades clipping my ankle, causing pain to shoot through my foot and calf. My leg buckles—

And I'm falling . . . falling . . . falling.

Chapter Twenty-One

The wooden floor comes up so fast, I don't have time to break my fall. I feel the impact on my shoulder first. Then my head rebounds. Someone's crashing down on top of me. There are legs thrashing in the air over my head, and there is the scrape of rough fabric, the smell of sweat and body odor, the squeak and thud of shoes near my face. Only then do I feel pain reverberating through my ankle.

It must be only seconds, but it feels like I'm on the floor forever. I cover my head instinctively and try to control my breathing, yanking my knees to my chest in a protective fetal position. There's still a body smothering me, heavy shoes pounding around me. The noise of the floor is deafening.

"Charlotte!" It's Bobby's voice. A hand grasps my wrist. Someone's yanking away the guy who's blanketing me.

"Sorry," the guy yells, scrambling up, the wheels of his Rollerblades grinding over the hardwood floor.

"What are you doing, dude? We're dancing tonight, not skating."

I don't know who's talking to him, but I push myself up and back, wanting to avoid coming into contact again with those massive Rollerblades he's wearing.

"It's a skating rink, man," Rollerboy says. "I wanted to dance with skates on."

I'm aware of his feeble protests as a couple of guys and Mr. Alto usher him away.

Bobby gently pulls me to my feet. I wobble. The room tilts. "Are you okay?"

"Charlie!" Josh pushes through the crowd. It seems like half the place has stopped to watch what just happened. The other half has no idea. They're still jumping, hooting, pounding.

"Charlie, what are you doing here?" Josh asks.

I just shake my head. "Don't tell Mom."

"I saw that guy plow into you. Devon Winters is a linebacker. Probably weighs three times what you do. Are you hurt?"

"I don't know."

"We need to get her off the floor, assess the damage," Bobby says. "Make room!" he cries, clearing the way. "She needs to sit down! Are you hurt?"

He wraps an arm around my shoulder. Josh flanks my other side. I take a step, my ankle gives out, and I gasp in pain.

I look up into Josh's face. Even in the dim light I can see that it's drained of color. "Don't panic. Sit down."

One of the chaperones is bustling toward us. "Oh, honey!" She's a mother hen, with her long dress flapping against her legs. "I saw you fall. Are you all right?"

"I don't know," I say, sniffing back tears. "I think I hurt my ankle."

"Crap." Josh's voice is a whisper. "Charlie, no. Don't say that. Let's sit down and see."

"She's okay," Bobby yells at nobody in particular. "Back off!" He swings his arms at the people gathering around, and they scuttle back.

Bobby lifts me into his arms. I cling to his neck, wishing we were in this position for any other reason. He hurries me over to chairs set up against the far wall. Once I've sat down, the chaperone brings me a bag of ice. "How's it looking?" she asks.

I hardly dare to look at it, but the pain is that sharp throb that warns of trouble. "It's my bad ankle," I say. "I broke it a while ago. . . ."

"Oh, honey. Take off that big shoe. Yes, it looks a little swollen."

My stomach churns like I'm about to lose my Italian dinner. *What have I done?* This has to be some kind of nightmare.

I turn to Josh. He's looking back at me, stricken. "I'm so sorry, Charlie."

I force myself to look at my ankle. Face it. Maybe it's not as bad as it seems. But even in low lighting, I can see the swelling, a dark purple bruise running under the skin like a half-moon shadow. "This cannot be happening." My voice sounds strained and hopeless. "This cannot be happening!"

Josh's words are choked. "This is bad, Charl—"

"I know!" I feel my self-control slipping.

"I don't think anything is broken," Bobby says. "A few weeks, and it'll be fine."

"It's not going to be fine," I say. "Nothing is going to be fine."

Chapter Twenty-Two

"I'm going to take her home," Bobby says.

"I'll come with you," Josh says.

"You can't leave your date," I say to him.

He looks around. Then his gaze lands on a girl with dark hair. He holds out his hand, and she comes over. "Morgan, this is my sister, Charlie."

"Hi," she says shyly. "We saw what happened. It looks bad."

"Charlotte!" Zoe cries, rushing toward us. "We just heard about what happened." She takes a step toward me, glances down at my foot, shudders, and steps back. "That looks painful."

The physical pain isn't nearly as bad as the mental anguish. I've totally messed things up. I've ruined everyone's night. I may have ruined my chances to make the Olympic team.

"I'm going to take her home," Bobby repeats. "I'll have the driver bring the limo back for you two."

"Or we can just go with you," Michael offers.

"No!" I shout. "I'm not ruining everyone's prom. Josh,

there's nothing you can do for me at home. You and Morgan should stay and enjoy prom."

"I can explain to Mom and Dad that this wasn't your fault."

I give him a pointed look.

He shrugs. "Maybe it's a little bit your fault, since I have a feeling you weren't supposed to be here. Otherwise I would have known ahead of time that you'd be here."

"You weren't supposed to be here?" Bobby asks.

I shake my head dejectedly. "My mom didn't think it would be a good idea. But I wanted to come. That's why I had you pick me up at Gwen's."

"You got Gwen involved?" Josh asks. "Man, Coach Chris—"

"Josh," I say in a low, threatening voice.

He slams his mouth closed. Clearly confused, everyone darts their gazes between him and me.

"Look, I don't want to mess up everyone's night. I'll call a cab."

"I'm taking you home," Bobby says yet again. "We're paying for the limo whether it's sitting out there or driving around. We might as well use it. I'll come back for Michael and Zoe."

"Okay."

Before I can even move, he lifts me into his arms again.

"I can walk," I insist.

"You can't walk. You can hobble."

This would be truly romantic if my ankle weren't throbbing

and I weren't getting a good deal of unwanted attention. I bury my face in Bobby's shoulder.

"I'm really sorry," I say.

"You should be, for putting the idea into that guy's head that he could skate through a group of dancers."

I jerk my head up. Bobby gives me an ironic smile. "You have nothing to apologize for. It's not your fault this happened."

Bobby finds our limo, settles me onto the seat, and then joins me. Once we're under way, Bobby asks, "Why didn't you tell me that you weren't supposed to go to prom?"

"Because it had nothing to do with you, and I didn't want you to think it did."

"What did it have to do with?"

I shake my head. "Mom just didn't think it would be a good idea."

"Why was your brother making a big deal about Gwen and some coach?"

I grimace. So he heard that. I wish I'd cut Josh off sooner.

"Gwen is an elite gymnast. Coach Chris trains her. He wants her to stay focused."

He studies me intently. "I'm not stupid, Charlotte. There's more to it than that. Your ankle is messed up, and Josh is panicking like it's the end of the world."

I sigh with resignation. "Coach Chris is also my gymnastics coach."

"I didn't think you competed anymore," Bobby says, clearly confused.

"I—I still do. It's complicated."

"Why didn't you just tell me that? I'm going on about watching what I eat. You must do the same."

"Because I don't talk about it."

"Why not?"

"Because I don't want people to know."

He shakes his head. "I don't understand. Why not? Being a competitive gymnast is incredibly cool."

Trying to explain this to Bobby, who is also an athlete, makes me feel foolish. "I need someplace where I can just be Charlotte. Where I don't have the pressure of people having expectations about me making the Olympic team."

"Wait." He pauses like he can't register what I just said. "You're hoping to go to the Olympics?"

I don't blame him for being surprised, for sounding almost doubtful. "Yeah. The Olympic trials are next weekend. That's why my mom didn't want me going to prom. She wanted me to stay focused on my goals."

"And that's the reason Josh was freaking out. Because you're hurt."

I blow out a puff of air. "Pretty much."

"You're *that* good?" he asks.

"I'm going to find out in another week." If my ankle isn't totally messed up. It's throbbing with pain right now.

He looks out the window. "I still don't understand why you didn't tell me."

"To be honest, I don't know either."

He moves across to the other seat so that he's facing me squarely. "You didn't trust me."

"It's not that." But even as I say the words, I know it couldn't have been anything else. I didn't trust him not to be different around me. But I don't tell him that, because I know he'd be insulted. He has every right to feel that way.

"I thought we had something," he says quietly.

"Bobby—"

The limo pulls to a stop.

"I don't know what to say to all this, Charlotte."

"'Charlie,'" I say sadly. "Charlie is the real me. I didn't go by 'Charlotte' until I started back at public school. I just wanted my school life to be separate from my gymnastics life."

"I told you 'Charlie' suited you better."

"So maybe I wasn't able to hide everything from you."

"You hid enough. And Josh wasn't being an irritating older brother when he called you 'Charlie.' You lied about that. I have the feeling there hasn't been a lot of honesty on your part."

The door opens. Bobby gets out and assists me, providing support as I climb out and try not to put any weight on my foot.

The front door opens. Mom and Dad rush out.

"Charlie?" Mom calls out. "What's going on?"

I'm hopping a little, trying to balance on one foot.

Suddenly Bobby sweeps me up into his arms, but it's not all nice and warm like it was before. There is a stiffness to the way he's holding me. I can't blame him. I've basically been lying to him about the biggest part of my life since we met.

"We went to prom," Bobby says as he approaches my parents. "She got hurt."

"You went to prom?" Mom says. "Even after I told you that you couldn't go?"

"How do you get hurt at prom?" Dad asks.

Before I can answer, Bobby says, "I need to get her inside."

He carries on, with my parents rushing after us. When he crosses the threshold, I say, "You can put me down now."

"I'm putting you in a chair, off your feet. Otherwise there is no point in carrying you. Where should I go?"

I hear the repressed anger in his voice.

"To your left. Through that doorway."

He carries me into the front sitting room and gently sets me down on the sofa. He turns, stops. The wall is covered with photos of me at various ages in different leotards. Sometimes I'm holding a ribbon, or a medal, or a trophy. Sometimes I'm posed like I'm about to begin or have just ended a routine. Slowly he approaches the wall, studies the photos.

"We need an explanation," Mom says as she dashes into the room.

"The prom was at a skating rink," I say. "Some guy decided to go skating, and he clipped me." I pull up the hem of my gown.

Mom gasps and covers her mouth. "Oh, Charlie." Kneeling beside me, she tenderly lifts my leg to examine it. "We have to get you to Dr. Kwan tonight."

He specializes in treating athletes and has taken care of me whenever my ankle has acted up.

"We appreciate your bringing Charlie home," Dad says to Bobby.

Bobby faces him. "No problem, but I need to scoot. I'm sharing the limo with some other people." He heads for the doorway.

"Thanks for everything, Bobby," I call out.

He stops, glances back over his shoulder at me. He looks as sad as I feel. "Good-bye, Charlotte."

Then he's gone. And I have a feeling that his good-bye was a good-bye forever.

Chapter Twenty-Three

"What were you thinking?" Mom asks.

"You told me to embrace my crazy, and going to prom seemed like a crazy thing to do. Plus I really wanted to go. It was just one night. I couldn't see that it would do any harm."

Mom glares at me, her mouth in a straight line of disapproval. "You went behind our backs."

Anger flares up in me, but I remind myself that I deserve this. Mom is right. She has every right to be angry.

"I'm sorry, Mom."

"Sorry isn't good enough, Charlie." She paces around the living room, clearly agitated. "So your spending the night with Gwen . . . was that a complete lie?"

"No, I was going to spend the night at her house."

"She was in on this?"

I don't want to get Gwen into trouble. "She didn't know everything."

"No more rides or hanging out with Gwen." She points a finger at me. "Or anyone else, for that matter. You are as grounded as we can make you with trials coming up."

I look over at Dad. He's wearing his solidarity face. He won't contradict Mom. "We're disappointed in you, Charlie," he says quietly.

Mom picks up the phone. "You've taken this secret-life thing too far, Charlie. When you start lying to your parents, *that's too far*. It's time for you to come out, all of you, in front of everybody."

"I told Bobby," I mumble. "I don't think he's ever going to talk to me again."

Mom is quiet for a moment. "I think you have more important things to worry about."

She's right. I still have to face Coach Chris and Gwen, not to mention everyone else who believed in me as a gymnast. All my coaches in Texas, for instance. My Facebook and Team Charlie followers. "Mom, do you think I've ruined my chances to make the Olympic team?"

Mom's expression is flat as she starts dialing. "We'll see what Dr. Kwan says."

While she's talking to him, I take out my phone and text Gwen.

I won't be coming back tonight. I got busted. Long story. I'll call you tomorrow.

Now I just have to hope that I haven't ruined things for Gwen, too.

• • •

Long after midnight I'm lying on my bed with my foot wrapped in a compression bandage and elevated on a pillow to reduce the swelling. Dr. Kwan was willing to see his "little Olympian" in an emergency situation late on a Saturday night. After much poking and prodding, he made his diagnosis: nothing torn, just stretched tendons. I'm so lucky, although I'm not really feeling that way. I took some pain relievers to reduce the ache still throbbing through my foot, but the medication doesn't ease the hurt I've caused for others tonight. My parents are still upset with me and disappointed in my deception. I don't blame them. It was so easy to justify before getting caught, but now I just feel guilty.

Then there's Bobby. I'm staring at my phone wishing he'd text and wondering if I should text him to let him know what Dr. Kwan said. But a part of me is afraid that he won't answer, that he won't care.

A knock sounds on my door, and it opens. Josh steps into my room, closes the door, and leans against it. "How's the ankle?"

"Swollen, hurting. Dr. Kwan says I need to stay off it as much as possible." I point to the crutches resting against the foot of my bed. "But that's not much of an option. I'll test it Monday at practice."

"Can't you give it more time to heal?"

Regretfully I shake my head. "I have to be at a hundred percent by next weekend. If my ankle can't support me, Coach Chris needs to know."

"Either way he's not going to be happy."

"Tell me about it." There's a chance that even if my ankle can take the strain of being jolted and landed on, Coach Chris won't be willing to risk the possibility of my injuring myself further—to the extent that I'll have to have one or more surgeries or that I won't be able to recover in time for the Olympics in August. I don't want to think about how messed up everything is. "How was the rest of prom?"

"Too crowded. Morgan and I left to grab a burger. I got the third degree just now when I got home. Mom and Dad thought I knew something about you sneaking off, but I had no idea." He walks over, moves the crutches aside, and sits on the foot of my bed. "So thanks for keeping me in the dark on that."

He sounds a little hurt. I feel like I didn't do a single thing right in relation to prom.

"What were you thinking?" he asks.

"That I wanted to go to prom. But now I'm paying for it."

Josh stares at me. "Why shouldn't you be able to go to prom, though? It doesn't make any sense."

"Because I have my priorities mixed up," I say, tears springing into my eyes. "I'm going to the Olympic trials, Josh, and here I was stumbling around in high heels. I mean, how did I think that was a good idea? When I saw that guy headed for me, I couldn't move quickly, I couldn't get out of the way. Maybe I deserve to be out of the trials. After this, when the coaches find out I'm injured, I probably will be out."

"They're not going to sideline you for an injury. Not a sprained ankle. People sprain their ankles all the time and still compete."

"Maybe if I got hurt during practice or a competition. But I lied to everyone and went to prom."

"Are you serious? After all the sacrifices you've made? After everything?"

I shrug. "I messed up, Josh. It's a harsh world."

"So you're giving up?"

I have to pause to consider my answer. Am I giving up? Am I giving in to the pain, resigning myself to losing my dream? Or do I have it in me to still fight? Fight through the pain and see what happens.

"No, I'm not giving up."

Josh shifts on the bed. "And what does wearing heels have to do with anything? It was the idiot on the skates who sideswiped you."

"But I shouldn't have been there to begin with."

"Then he would have sideswiped someone else. You actually saved someone tonight, Charlie."

I release a bubble of laughter—the last thing I expected to do anytime soon. "That seems like a stretch, Josh."

"So is thinking that you should be punished for going to prom. Who doesn't want to go to prom?" He plucks at a thread on my comforter. "I'm sorry you didn't feel like you could confide in me, let me help you pull this off."

"You're just sorry that you didn't get a chance to buddy up to Bobby."

He grins. "That, too. I like the guy."

"Would you like him if he weren't famous at our school for his wrestling prowess?"

He actually considers it for a minute. "Yeah, I think so."

I toss a pillow at him. With a laugh, he sets it aside and gets up. "To be honest, I can understand why he wouldn't want to hang around with me. I was acting like an idiot, trying to get in close to him just because he was spending time with you."

"I think he would want to hang around with you if you didn't try so hard to impress him. Actually, the way you acted around him . . . that's part of the reason why I didn't tell people about my gymnastics life. I thought they would try to be friends with me because of my 'star' power. Not because of who I am. Although, I realize that makes me sound a little conceited, to think I'm a star."

"You are a star. Or you will be after the Olympics."

"If I can make the team."

The next afternoon my phone vibrates against the desk. I'm sitting in my room with my foot in ice water.

"Hey, Charlotte." Zoe's voice sounds strained.

"Hey."

"How're you doing? How's the ankle?"

I swallow. "It's swollen."

"Have you been to the doctor?"

"Yep. It's just sprained."

"Not the best prom night, huh?"

I'm not going to lie. It was a disastrous prom night. But there's always a bright side. There has to be. "I had fun until skating boy happened upon the scene." I force out a laugh.

"I feel so bad. I should have left when you did."

"No, you shouldn't have," I say. "Then I would have felt worse than I feel now. How was prom after I left?"

"Wonderful. Which makes me feel guilty, because it wasn't wonderful for you."

"You shouldn't feel guilty," I insist.

"Michael kissed me."

I release a little squeal. "How was it?"

"Nice. Really nice."

"You guys make a cute couple."

"If you hadn't gotten hurt, it would have been the best night ever."

"It's all right, Zoe, if for you it was the best night ever."

"It can't be when my bestest friend gets hurt. Devon Winters is such a doofus. Who wears skates to a prom? Kristine was so mad at him for getting kicked out."

"Why would she be mad?"

"Because he was her date. Did you not know?"

No. She failed to mention that when she was talking to Bobby. "Zoe, how do you keep up with all this stuff?"

"I follow just about everyone on Facebook and Instagram."

"It must take you hours to go through your timelines."

"Sometimes, but I love it. It's like reading a gossip magazine."

Maybe I'll have Zoe handle my social media if I make the Olympic team.

"I should probably get back to studying," I tell her.

"Me too. I'm glad it's just a sprain."

I lift my foot up out of the ice. "I think the swelling is going down. I'll be as good as new tomorrow." A little lie, but there's no point in bringing her down.

"Great! I'll see you at school."

We hang up, and I lower my foot back into the ice. Then I stare at my phone, wishing that Bobby would call.

Chapter Twenty-Four

Monday morning, with my ankle still in a compress wrap, I use my crutches to hobble down the hallways through school. Mom called Coach Chris and told him that I needed to skip my morning workout, but not why. She's going to tell him this afternoon. I'm dreading it.

After third period, as I'm heading to my locker before lunch, I notice the whispering and the odd looks that people are giving me, but I shrug them off, figuring there's gossip about the Rollerblading incident at prom. People must be looking and pointing because I'm the girl who got knocked off her feet.

It doesn't occur to me to think it's anything else, until Kristine stops in front of me in the hallway, plants her hands on her hips, and gives me a steely once-over.

"Is it true?" She slides her tongue into her cheek, like she's trying not to laugh.

"What? That your date knocked me over at prom?"

"If what they're saying is true, you should have been able to leap out of his way."

"What are you talking about?"

"Gymnastics! Woo-woo!" Kristine flaps her arms around. "It's not true, right? It's just coincidence that you have similar names."

My insides freeze. "I don't know what you're talking about." The lie comes out automatically.

"Exactly." Kristine stalks away.

I barely notice anything around me as I make my way to my locker. I see Zoe at her locker. I'm surprised she doesn't rush over. Instead she's watching me like she doesn't know who I am. I stuff my book-filled backpack into my locker and then hobble over to her.

"Hey," I say to her. "I just had the weirdest conversation with Kristine."

"I bet. Do you want to hear something really funny? It's crazy. Totally nuts."

"Sure." I need something to distract me from Kristine's weirdness. Did Bobby say something to Kristine? Did he catch up with her at the prom after her date was thrown out? He's the only one who knows. . . .

"I posted the selfie from prom on Instagram, and I tagged you. And then Morgan Whitcomb tagged it, but with a different name—Charlie Ryland—that linked to a gymnast. She posted a comment that she went to prom with the gymnast's brother."

Oh no. No, no, no.

"Zoe—"

"I followed the link. Imagine my surprise when I discovered that my bestest friend is famous."

"I'm not famous."

She scoffs. "You're an Olympic hopeful, and you didn't even tell me. I feel so stupid, Charlotte." Tears well in her eyes. "Oh, I mean, *Charlie*. People are asking me what it's like to be the friend of a famous person—"

"I'm not famous," I repeat. Not like celebrity, paparazzi-followed famous.

"You will be."

"Not if I don't make the team."

"There were photos of you at a training ranch in Texas. You lied to me about that. I asked for pictures of cowboys. There's a photo of you on the cover of some gymnastics magazine. You have this whole other life, and I knew nothing about it. Why didn't you tell me?"

I shake my head. "I don't know," I answer honestly. "I guess I thought things between us would change."

"Like what? You think that I'm shallow and would only want to be with you because you're famous?"

It sounds so bad. "I'm sorry. I should have told you."

"Yeah, you should have. But you're right. Things between us did change." She slings her backpack over her shoulder and heads down the hallway.

"Charlie?"

I turn to find a girl looking at me hesitantly. I have no idea who she is, but she suddenly grins broadly. "Charlie Ryland. It is you. I can't believe you go to my school and I didn't know it. I train at another gym, nowhere near good enough to make the Olympic team, but I'm hoping for a college scholarship. Will you sign this for me?"

She holds out a notebook, turned to a blank page, and a pen. I'm reeling, trying to make sense of all this. "Sure."

I take the pen while she steadies the notebook. "My name is Malia," she says.

Good luck, Malia! I write, and then sign *Charlie Ryland* with a flourish.

"Thanks," she says, hugging the notebook to her chest.

"Keep working toward your dream," I say automatically.

When she walks off, I fumble my phone out of my pocket and bite my lip as I pull up Instagram. I scroll through the photos, and horror sinks into my lungs, restricting my breath, into my stomach, making it plunge. Not only is the selfie that Zoe took there, but there is a photo of me sprawled on the floor and Bobby kneeling beside me and one of him carrying me. "Oh no . . ."

I stare at the screen. It feels like all the blood is draining to my feet. The photo of me sprawled on the floor has more than 10,000 likes and 654 shares.

Charlie Ryland Gymnast on Facebook has 450,000 followers. And all it took was one tag for all the people who know me in one life to get linked to the other life. I think of Coach Rachel. This isn't nearly as bad as what she went through, but it still hurts, and my mind is filling with thoughts of the various ways that this could play out badly.

I get a text from Josh. *We need to talk.*

I'm at my locker.

Wait there.

I make my way over to my locker and lean against it. The hallway empties out somewhat as the other students head to the cafeteria. Then I spot Kristine talking with Bobby at the far end, where one hallway intersects with another. She's running her hand up and down his arm, like she's testing his muscles.

Then she sees me, points, and laughs. Bobby glances over his shoulder, says something to her. I try not to wonder if they got back together at prom after I was hurt. His date was no longer there, and neither was hers. At the very least she probably got her dance with Bobby.

Leaving her behind, Bobby approaches me. He doesn't give me his enticing grin. The dimple doesn't show.

"How's the ankle?" he asks with very little emotion.

"The doctor said it was just a sprain. I'll find out during practice this afternoon if it can withstand the impact."

"Shouldn't you give it a few days?"

"I can't. Trials are this Saturday, and I have to know. My coaches have to know. This is it for me. If I miss trials, all my dedication and years of practice were for nothing."

"Really?" He wrinkles his brow. "What about all the friendships you made, everything you've achieved up until now. Doesn't any of that count for anything?"

I don't know what to say. "Of course it does," I finally manage. "But I want to go to trials. I will go to trials." No matter how much my foot hurts.

"Good luck. I mean it, Charlotte. I hope—"

"Are you and Kristine back together?" I point as much as I'm able while holding on to the crutches. "She's waiting for you."

"We're not back together. We're just going to lunch."

I nod. "I guess you've heard that my secret is out."

"Yeah, but I didn't have anything to do with it."

"I know."

"Bobby?" Kristine calls out, her voice echoing along the now-empty hallway.

"I need to go." He starts to leave, looks back over his shoulder. "Good luck at the trials."

Luck isn't going to be enough. It never is.

Watching them walk away, I'm feeling sad and alone. I want to feel relieved when Josh appears. Instead I feel betrayed.

"You told Morgan that I'm Charlie Ryland?" I ask when he's near enough to hear me.

He looks guilty. "Yeah. I guess you already know about her tagging you on Instagram and posting photos on Facebook."

"Why? Why did you tell her?"

"I freaked out Saturday. You know that. When I saw your foot bruising . . . She wanted to know why I was so upset. Even after you left, I was worried and she was comforting . . . and everything spilled out. But it was just like you told me it would be. Suddenly she was impressed that she was at prom with the brother of an Olympian. Even though you're not yet an Olympian. She wanted to know if she could go to Montreal with us. Were we rich? Were we going to be on TV? It was like she thought we were the Kardashians or something. Anyway, when she saw Zoe's picture, she wanted to feel special, wanted everyone to know she knew a big secret. So she tagged you. She just told me after class. She wants your autograph."

"You're kidding."

He shakes his head. "Apparently she has a thing for celebrities. So, uh, I'm not going to see her anymore."

"You don't have to not see her because of me."

"Nah, it's gotten weird. I finally understand why you didn't want people to know. I'm just sorry I told her and ruined things for you."

"It's okay, Josh. If the trade-off for making the Olympics is that everyone will know, then I guess I'm hoping that everyone finds out. Want to grab lunch with me?"

His eyes widen in surprise. "We've never had lunch together."

"I know, but you might be the only friend I have left."

"That's sad, Charlie. I'm sorry for my part in this."

"I brought it all on myself. I should have been honest with everyone from the beginning. So, lunch?"

"Sure."

As we head for the cafeteria, a couple of girls give me shiny smiles as they walk past me. Which would be fine if they'd ever given me shiny smiles before. It is so strange to be getting all this attention. I have to wonder if it's the end of normal as I know it.

Chapter Twenty-Five

When I arrive at practice, Gwen is at the entrance to the locker room sipping water.

"Hi, Gwen," I say when I reach her.

She's streaked with dust from bars and still wears her grips. "Hey."

From the locker room entry, I see Mom crossing the gym floor to talk to Coach Chris.

"So, what did you find out?" Gwen's normally exuberant voice is wooden.

"It's a sprain. Dr. Kwan says I can practice if I feel comfortable."

She nods before moving over to her locker. "Good."

I heave a sigh, glancing across the floor at my mom and my coach. They're deep in conversation. Mom looks over at me, and our eyes meet. Coach Chris, in his usual way, is focused intently on what she's saying. I step all the way into the room, set the crutches against my locker, and slide my jacket off.

"As far as my mom knows, I was only sleeping at your

place. You weren't really involved," I whisper, carefully placing my foot on the floor and adding a little weight. The pain is bearable.

"Really?" she asks incredulously, causing me to glance up to watch her. She pitches her grips into her locker. They land with a hollow thud. "Because your mom called my mom, and I'm grounded until after trials."

"No!" Without thinking, I take a step toward her, putting all my weight on my bad ankle. With a gasp I jerk back, letting my foot hang a few inches above the floor.

"That's not good," Gwen says.

"I just have to pay attention to how much weight I place on it." I put my hand on her arm. "Gwen, I'm so sorry. I didn't mean for you to get into trouble. Does Coach Chris know?"

"I don't think so. But don't ask me for any more favors. I've been a nervous wreck, wondering if I'll get into even more trouble. Coach Chris has been yelling at me all day because I can't get my head in the game."

"I'm really and truly sorry."

"I have to focus," Gwen says in a low voice. "I have one dream—to go to the Olympics. I just have to focus on that."

She strides out of the locker room. I don't blame her for being upset. She was trying to help me out, and now she's in trouble too. I don't want her to lose her chance to make the Olympic team.

• • •

I'm expecting practice to pretty much suck, but, on the bright side, at least Coach Chris lets me practice.

First he chews me out in his quiet, deadly way. It's mostly him talking. I answer his questions with as few words as possible and as much respect as I can muster. He ends with, "I don't know, Charlie." He presses his palm against his forehead. "This might be the end of your road. Now I've got to get back to people who really want to be here." He drops his hand and slaps it against his thigh.

I know he'll have a conversation with Claudia Inverso, the head of the national team. She probably already knows that I hurt myself. Will she still want me at trials? Either way, I've got to practice today like I'm still going.

I warm up alone, holding back tears of frustration as my feet pound the mat and pain shoots through my bad ankle. I've been here before, dealing with the agony. I can't ignore it. I know that. It's my body's warning system. But I can adjust how I land on my foot, how much weight I put on it.

Gwen is finishing up with some bar drills when I finally make it over. I swing through a few cast-handstands, but Coach Rachel calls out, "Point your toes, Charlie."

I nod, but I find it impossible to point the toes on my injured foot, because of how tightly I've bound the tape.

"Let's go, Charlie!" Coach Chris shouts. "Pound out that routine. Drop on your landing. I don't want you injuring yourself any worse."

I don't want that either. But the question remains: Do I still believe in myself after everything I've done wrong? I've made so many mistakes, misjudged so many things. I didn't trust Zoe or Bobby to hold my secret. Now I have to wonder if I can trust myself to do everything I have to in order to make the team.

I power through a few giants, release my hold on the bar, and drop gently to the mats, putting as much weight as possible on my good leg.

"As soon as you're warmed up, hit routines," Coach Chris says. "I'm heading over to floor with Gwen, but I'll be watching. How does it feel?"

"I feel okay." But my stomach is knotted. That full twisting double back dismount, the skill I haven't quite mastered yet, is waiting for me. I anticipate the pain that's going to rip through my ankle when I land.

And that's only working on the bars, the event that's easiest on my ankle. If ever I needed a tight mind, it's now.

I suck in a deep, shuddering breath, counting slowly to release my brain from the panic that seizes me. I need to take my mind off my ankle, off my mom, off Dr. Kwan, off Coach Chris. Even off Coach Rachel, who watches me now with her eagle eyes, as if she's waiting for me to mess up, to lose it, to not be mentally strong enough. And with my injured ankle, maybe to not even be physically strong enough.

"Come on, Charlie," Coach Rachel calls. "Let's see it."

I slide the springboard into place and fly into my routine. When I land, pain shoots through my foot, up my leg, and I stumble. I bite down on my lower lip to stop myself from crying out. I can't show any vulnerability or lose my confidence now. Not after everything I've sacrificed and everything my family has given up.

Coach Rachel wanders over. "It looks like that hurt."

"I can work through the pain."

"That's what we do, isn't it? But sometimes it's not enough."

"It'll be enough."

She gives me an understanding smile. "So I hear there was a boy after all. You couldn't have waited a few more months?"

"You didn't." I slap my hand over my mouth. "I'm sorry."

She angles her head thoughtfully. "Nooo, I didn't. I was seventeen and wanted it all. I ended up with nothing."

"Do you regret it?"

"My life is different from what it might have been, but you can't hold on to bad decisions. Let it all go, Charlie. Focus on the now. Not the past, not the future. Just the now. Do the routine again. Try to stick the landing without coming down on that foot too hard. Don't punish it for the mistakes you made this weekend."

I nod. "Thanks, Coach. I appreciate the support and the advice."

"You're good enough to make the team, Charlie. Your

injury will make it more challenging, but it doesn't make it impossible. Just be sure to listen to your body."

"I will."

I get into position, run through the routine. My landing isn't perfect. But it's better. Still, I know I'm a long way from making the Olympic team.

Chapter Twenty-Six

"How was practice?" Dad asks that night when we're almost finished with dinner, as if everything is normal, as if I don't have my ankle stuck in a bucket of ice water beneath the table. We talked about normal stuff at the beginning of dinner. Questions like, how were our classes? Do Josh and I have any special projects coming due as we near the end of the school year? Was Dad able to work out the schematics for his new and improved spark plug idea? How did it go with Mom's client meeting this morning? Boring, normal questions that felt great to talk about. Because they helped me to forget for a few minutes the lousy mess I've made of things.

"It was okay," I say, stirring my macaroni soup. "I'm still struggling with my bars dismount, but I'm closer." I don't know if I'm close enough to have it polished before trials. Coach Chris hasn't called it off yet, though, so there's still a sliver of hope. Without that dismount, I don't feel like I can compete. I saw what the other girls were working on at camp, and everyone is ratcheting their skill level up a notch.

"Did your ankle feel all right?" Mom asks.

"Yeah," I say. "I mean, it hurts, but I always have problems with this ankle, so . . . I'll stay off it as much as I can except during practice."

"Maybe I should get you excused from school for the time remaining before you leave for trials. It would give you a chance to stay off the foot. You could do your assignments at home, take any tests when you get back from Detroit."

It would be nice to check out of school. I could work at home in the quiet, and probably get a lot more done. I'd miss my last student council meeting on Wednesday.

But . . . there are only three more days before I leave for Detroit on Thursday. And I've never been a quitter at anything. I shake my head. "No. People will think I'm hiding."

"Why would they think that?" Mom asks.

"Because Charlie Ryland was outed," I announce.

"It's my fault," Josh says.

"No, it's not," I reply quickly.

"Care to explain yourself, Son?" Dad asks.

Josh explains about Zoe posting the photo and Morgan tagging it with the Charlie Ryland Gymnast handle. Josh runs through why he told her who I was.

"So practically everyone at school knows," I tell them. "And I don't want them to think I'm ashamed or running, so not going to school isn't an option for me."

Mom is quiet for a moment. "It was about to happen anyway, right?"

THE FLIP SIDE · 239

"Absolutely," I say. "After this weekend, when I make the team, everyone is going to know." Even if the way it happened wasn't exactly how I envisioned it. Fame comes with a price I'm willing to pay.

The next morning I have just finished breakfast and am setting my bowl in the sink when Mom's phone rings. "Just a sec," she whispers as she accepts the call. "Get your shoes on, and I'll meet you in the car."

It takes Mom forever to make it out to the car. I'm checking my phone for the time, stressing that I'm going to be late to school. Our morning routine is a little out of whack because Coach Chris instructed me not to come in for morning practice, to take it easy and give my ankle a small chance to recover from yesterday's workout. Mom finally opens the door and slides into the driver's seat.

"That call was from a newspaper," she says, fumbling with her seat belt. She's so flustered, I have to help her buckle it. "They've run a story about you in this morning's paper, and they're trying to do a follow-up for tomorrow."

"What?"

"I guess they tried to call me last night after I had my phone off."

"A story about me? About—okay, I think I know." It hurts to swallow. Mom wouldn't be flustered if it were a good article. "Is it really bad?"

Mom starts the car. "Honey, you're famous now. Instantly

famous. 'Olympic Hopeful Involved in Skating Mishap at Jefferson Prom.' Banner headline. It might make for a rough day at school. If you want, I'll call the principal and tell him you're sick today."

"I can do it," I say. "You always taught me to finish strong, even when it was hard."

Mom nods. "Okay, then. Off we go."

As I'm lumbering on crutches down the hallway to my locker, I'm very aware of the whispers, the pointing, and the stares. I hear an occasional giggle and spot the wide, curious eyes.

"Hey, Charlie!" a girl I don't know calls out. She gives me a big smile and waves her hand frantically as she walks by—like she wants everyone to think we're friends. I give a halfhearted wave.

I'm almost to my locker when two girls suddenly jump in front of me. I jerk back, nearly lose my balance.

"Can we get a selfie with you?" one of them asks.

I tell myself that this is no different from when I'm at a competition and someone wants to have a picture taken with me—but it still feels very strange and very different. I'm not used to being Charlie Ryland within these walls.

I force myself to smile. "Sure."

One of the girls bends her knees so she can place her head close to mine, holds up her phone, and takes a picture. Then her friend moves in and does the same.

"Good luck, Charlie! We're counting on you!" they shout as they rush down the hallway.

Counting on me when I'm not sure I can count on my ankle 100 percent.

I notice some people looking at me oddly. I guess not everyone got the memo about who I am. I feel a little awkward because I don't know if I should announce my truth or try to explain why a couple of girls wanted to take a picture with me. I decide the best thing to do is just carry on. Eventually everyone will know and no explanations will be necessary.

When I get to my locker, I stagger to a stop and my heart sinks. The cover of *Gymnastics NOW!* is taped to my locker door. Someone used a black Sharpie to draw a mustache above my lip and circles around my eyes. Scrawled across the bottom in large letters is *GYMNAST OR FREAK?*

I pull the cover down and wad it into a ball, glancing around me to see if anyone's looking suspicious. But nobody makes eye contact. A couple of people shuffle away quickly. I can just imagine the anger or disgust that's reflected on my face.

What a roller-coaster ride. Enthusiasts wanting selfies. Haters mocking my achievements with childish artwork. I'm not going to let unkind jerks unsettle me. I'm going to focus on those who think that what I do, what I'm aiming for, is as cool as I do.

I try not to think about the fact that Zoe is nowhere around, that she hasn't come up to me to ask how I'm doing.

I keep darting a glance toward her locker, searching for her, but I don't see her. I miss her bubbling over with excitement about some gossip, or sharing her dreams. She never gave up on going to prom or having a boyfriend.

I can't give up on earning a place on the Olympic team.

When I walk into my government class, I spot Zoe already sitting in her seat. Our gazes clash for a heartbeat, before she buries her face in her textbook. No smile, no wave, no indication that she's glad to see me. I know I hurt her feelings by not telling her who I am.

I take my seat beside hers. "Hey."

"Hi," she says without looking at me.

"How are you doing?" I ask.

"Okay."

"Zoe, can we talk after class?"

She turns a page in her book. "I have to get somewhere right after class."

"I know you're mad."

"I'm not mad." She looks at me then, and I see such sadness that my chest tightens. "I'm hurt. And I don't want to talk about it."

"I'm sorry that I didn't tell you."

Shrugging her shoulders like she's shrugging off my apology, she goes back to studying her book. I may have lost her friendship forever, and that hurts worse than my ankle.

The girl who sits in front of me turns around, studies me. "So you're some big-deal gymnast?"

I shake my head. "I'm not a big deal." Not yet. Not as big a deal as I might be.

"You're going to the Olympics," the guy behind me says.

"Maybe," I admit. "It depends on my ankle and how well I do my routines."

"Kristine says that's why Mr. Alto let you be on the student council," the girl says. "Because he thinks you're special."

"I was doing it for extra credit to get my grades up," I admit.

"So he's cutting you some slack on your grades?" she asks. "That's not fair."

"I asked for an extra project to bring up my grades. I had to do the work. He didn't *give* me anything."

Just as the bell rings, Mr. Alto bustles in. "Have you all seen the newspaper?" he asks excitedly. "Someone you may know is in there." He holds up the *Columbus Courant* and taps the front page. "Miss Charlotte Ryland. How does it feel to be famous?"

I manage a weak smile as students shift at their desks to get a better look at me. I'm tired of telling people that I'm not famous. The truth is that in some gymnastics circles I'm a little famous. Earning medals at the World Championships will do that for you. "Weird."

"How's the ankle?" he asks.

From where I'm sitting I can't see everyone in the class

without turning around, but I can feel all the stares. Or at least I think I can. Maybe I'm just being paranoid. "It's getting better. Thanks for asking." I want him to talk about something else.

"It's a good photo." Mr. Alto studies the picture intently. "It's the same one as on the cover of that magazine. You should be proud of your success, Charlotte. Sit up straight and smile. Enjoy yourself."

Instinctively I straighten. But I can't force a smile anymore. Zoe has twisted slightly so her back is to me. Usually she turns around and at least sympathizes when Mr. Alto goes on one of his cheerful rampages. But she's madly scribbling something in her notebook.

"Olympic trials are coming up this weekend," Mr. Alto continues. "You should all watch and cheer for Charlie. Is it okay for me to call you Charlie?"

"I guess so. If you want." Because Charlie is the real me. And I'm getting the distinct impression that as my façade fades, everyone can see straight inside me for the first time. It makes me want to cover up and hide.

But no. Being out in the open, being exposed, being a curiosity, is part of what I asked for when I went elite, when I accepted the invitation to the national team. Charlie isn't my secret identity double anymore—Charlie is the total of who I really am. She's always been the gymnast. And now she's the student at Jefferson High. She's the real me.

I just wish I felt more comfortable with her.

Chapter Twenty-Seven

After the final bell rings, I make as quick a stop at my locker as possible, considering I'm still maneuvering on crutches, before heading out to the pickup zone in front of the school. Students waiting to be picked up are mingling along the sidewalk. I comb my gaze over the steady line of cars meandering along the circular drive, searching for Mom. She's usually at the front of the line waiting for me, but I don't see her. I check my phone to see if she might have texted me that she's running late.

"Charlie Ryland?" I turn to see a stranger hurrying from the opposite end of the parking lot. She wears a suit, heels, and a wide smile. "You're Charlie Ryland, right?"

"Yeah."

A couple of students near me go still, watching as the woman teeters to a stop in front of me.

"Hi, Charlie." She extends her hand as though she's going to shake mine, but then seems to realize that I'm not letting go of my crutches. "It's so nice to meet you. I'm Bonnie Thatcher from the *Columbus Courant*. I was hoping to run into you."

A reporter? I tighten my hold on the crutches and swing my gaze back toward the line of cars. It's shorter now. There are still students waiting to be picked up. A few ease closer to me like they're curious. "My mom's on her way. I have practice."

"Can I ask you a few questions while you wait?" Her smile is blindingly brilliant.

"I guess."

She holds her phone out, like it's a microphone. "I see you're on crutches. Is your ankle going to be fully recovered by the time you go to trials?"

"I hope so. I'm trying to keep as much pressure off it as possible."

"What does your coach have to say about your accident?"

"Uhh . . ." I check the surroundings for Mom again. Why is she so late? "He was upset, of course. But now we've both put it behind us and are ready to work hard again."

"So, your ankle isn't preventing you from practicing?"

I try to ignore the students who are standing around staring at us. This information really isn't something that I want to share, especially if it's going to show up on the front page of the paper. "I've worked through pain before."

"That's amazing," the reporter says. "Good for you."

A Network Four News van screeches to a stop beyond the parking lot, in a no-parking zone.

"Are you feeling confident to perform at Olympic trials this weekend?" Bonnie Thatcher asks.

"I'll do my best. That's all I could do anyway."

I watch two people leap from the van. A guy yanks the doors open and pulls out a huge camera. A woman holding a microphone starts racing toward the school. The guy quickly follows. My stomach tightens into a painful knot. I have a feeling they're here for me. I don't want my face plastered all over tonight's news.

"My mom's going to be here any minute." I start edging closer to the pickup zone.

"Well, we'll just keep going until she gets here," Bonnie says, matching my steps. "Now tell me a little about the accident."

I squirm. "It wasn't really an 'accident.' Just a little fall."

"Can you describe exactly what happened?"

"I'd rather not. I don't like to replay negative things. It's not good for my concentration."

"Sure," she says. "Well, how about this? You went to prom with a guy, and your best friend and her date. How was that? Was it your first time to prom?"

"We had fun. It was a really good evening until I fell down."

"Witnesses say that a guy wearing Rollerblades crashed into you. Was it intentional? Do you think there's someone at Jefferson who doesn't want you to compete at the Olympic Games?"

"Charlie Ryland!" the woman from the van yells just before stepping in front of the other reporter. "I'm Edwina Huang from Network Four News."

The camera guy balances the camera on his shoulder.

"We're in the middle of an interview," Bonnie says, providing the distraction I need. I pull away from them, scan the pickup zone for Mom. Only a few cars remain. Parents are getting out to watch the circus.

Edwina Huang shoves her microphone into my face. "Wait, Charlie. I have just a few questions. I promise not to take up much of your time." I hear her hiss in the camera guy's direction, "Roll tape!"

I make a beeline for the flagpole. Where is Mom? Why is she late on the one day I desperately need her?

"What's your favorite event, Charlie?" Edwina throws the words at me while she and the cameraman follow, hot on my heels.

I stop walking. Because it's pointless. With crutches I can't outrun them, and even if I could, there's nobody to pick me up. "Beam. Always."

"That's right," Edwina says. "You were beam champ at the World Championships both last year and this year. Do you think you'll be able to compete at the same level for trials?"

I don't know. With my ankle compromised I know that competing at all is going to be touch and go, but I can't admit that—not to a reporter, not to the world, and most of all not to myself. "I hope so. I'm going to give it a hundred and ten percent."

"Even with your ankle?" Edwina pushes.

Why can't she leave it alone? Why do reporters have to focus on the negative? Why do they have to keep throwing it in my face that physically I'm not at 100 percent? I have to provide a positive spin. "I won't let my ankle slow me down."

"Charlie!" I'm startled to see Josh jogging toward me.

"Are you ready?" he asks, steering me toward his car. The pickup lane is wide enough for vehicles to go around each other. He stopped his car near the flagpole and is now blocking anyone in line behind him from pulling around.

I can hear the TV news crew trundling behind us. "Are you Josh Ryland? How does it feel to have a famous sister?"

To my surprise, Josh casts a quick glance back but doesn't answer. He guides me toward his car, his arm protectively around my shoulders. He opens the passenger door and helps me climb in, takes the crutches, and tosses them into the back.

"Charlie, are you going to sue the guy who crashed into you at prom?" Edwina asks.

I stare at her.

"Don't answer that," Josh says as he slams the door shut. Then he runs around to the driver's side and slides in.

"Thank you for your time, Charlie!" Edwina calls out as Josh pulls away. I hazard a wave in her direction.

"Your first paparazzi! That was exciting." Josh grins at me.

"It was a newspaper reporter and a TV news crew. I'm not sure that counts."

"You probably need to get used to it," Josh says. "There will probably be a lot of microphones and cameras shoved into your face when you go to the Olympics."

"If I go."

Josh darts a quick glance in my direction. "Why wouldn't you go?"

"My ankle isn't getting better, Josh."

"It just needs a little more time."

I nod and look out the window. Unfortunately, time is something I don't have.

Chapter Twenty-Eight

I held it together for that reporter, the TV news crew, and Josh, but once I'm in the familiar locker room that's more my home than my home is, all my pent-up frustration and anger over my situation is released, like opening the sluice gates on a dam.

I bawl ugly, snotty tears. A few other girls wander in, stand around me, and pet my shoulder, my hair. "You're going to be okay, Charlie." I'm not sure who's even talking most of the time. Someone hands me a tissue, and I wipe my eyes.

Through my blurred vision I spot Gwen standing at her locker door. Uncertainty plays across her face. Finally she walks over and sits on the bench beside me. "Tough day?" she asks.

Which only makes me start to cry again, harder. "Everything is so messed up."

"I saw the article in the paper. Thanks for keeping my name out of it."

I release a strangled laugh and take a swipe at my tears. "I didn't have anything to do with that. They didn't interview me. But if they had, I wouldn't have said anything. I just don't get why everyone is making such a big deal out of this. You're the one they should be talking to. You're the one most likely to make the Olympic team."

"But your story is more interesting. You've got scandal, a wounded gymnast, a secret revealed. They'll probably make a movie about you."

"I hope not."

"Come on, girls." Coach Rachel's voice rings from the locker room entrance. "Five minutes!"

Gwen stands up. The other girls step back. I look up at everyone, grateful that here at least I have people who understand me—who *get* me. "Thanks, guys. Sorry I fell apart there."

"If you can't fall apart with us," Gwen says, "where can you fall apart?"

They all leave. I grab the leo from my bag and limp to the changing room, scraping my hair up into a ponytail as I go.

Once I'm out on the floor, Coach Chris swiftly approaches me. "What's up?" he asks, looking deeply into my puffy eyes. Splashing cold water onto them didn't really help. "Are you going to be with me today?"

"Yes, Coach."

"If I get one hundred and ten percent from you today, we're good. If I don't, there will be problems."

"I know." I'm longing to ask him if Claudia Inverso had

anything to say about me, if I'm still welcome at trials, but he doesn't offer the information, and I don't ask.

"Okay." He nods abruptly. "Let's go!"

"I don't want any reporters in the building today!" Coach Chris yells to Coach Rachel as a group of people with cameras presses up against the window of the viewing room. I've never heard him be so loud before. "You tell them I'm calling the police if they don't get off gym property!"

Coach Rachel gives him a thumbs-up and scurries away to take care of dispersing the reporters.

His forbidding them to be on gym property saves me, actually, because they're waiting across the street when I leave the building. Lights flare, camera shutters chatter. There's not an army of them, but a few. Enough.

Mom's waiting for me in a parking spot near the entrance. The crutches slow me down as I get into the car. I slam the door in frustration. I've decided to retire the crutches when I get home. Time to start letting my foot get used to constant weight again. I won't put my full weight on it, but I can put some weight on it.

"Well!" Mom's face is pale under the dome lights. "Good news. This day is over!"

I laugh. Despite everything, I had a fairly good practice. I blocked everything out and performed. My ankle killed me every single step of the way, and my bars dismount wasn't flawless, but my drive was there. Maybe Gwen was right. I was too distracted before, pulled in too many directions. But now that I haven't heard a word from Bobby, I can let him go.

Which sounds so easy when I'm in the gym, focusing on gymnastics. Now that I'm in the car, the evening twilight embracing me, the radio tuned to Mom's favorite classic rock station, her phone turned over in the console, on silent, gently vibrating, there's room for thinking. And as I'm thinking, I identify a dull ache in my chest. It's the empty space where I used to hold all the hopes that there might be something more than friendship between Bobby and me. I'm not sure that I even admitted to myself that I wanted more—until I couldn't have it. But I've ripped out all possibilities for something between us, and it hurts.

"Have you had a quiet day," Mom asks, "or have the reporters been all over you, too?"

I guess she hasn't had a chance to talk with Josh. I tell her about the after-school fiasco.

"Sorry I couldn't get there," she says. "I was in a meeting with a client, and it turned out to be more complicated than I expected. I just couldn't get away."

"It's okay. It was good practice for what I might have to face before we leave for trials in two days. And Josh really came through."

I don't check my phone. I don't want to know if any reporters have my phone number, or if anyone's tried to text me.

Everything can wait. One more day of school, and then I'll escape all this. In Detroit the Olympic trials will be the news, not "Local Girl Loses Dream."

When we walk through the door half an hour later, Dad and Josh are watching TV. Dad clicks it off as soon as he sees us. He rises quickly from the couch and comes toward us to plant a kiss on Mom's lips and then on my head. "Eventful day, huh?"

"Looks like you got rid of the reporters who were trying to camp out on the front lawn," Mom says.

There were reporters trying to camp out? This is insane!

"Yeah," Dad says. "I warned them that I was president of the homeowners association, that we don't appreciate them being in our neighborhood, and that we won't hesitate to call the police."

"Good job, sweetheart," Mom says. "They were near the gym, too, and Charlie says a couple of reporters came up to her after school."

"We're on the news, Charlie," Josh says from the couch. "You should watch it. Apparently they didn't give up after we left. They interviewed Zoe." Josh doesn't make eye contact with me. "And Kristine."

"Kristine?"

"And then they've got us speeding away, as if we're bank robbers or something." Josh chuckles.

"It's not funny, Josh," Mom says.

"No. Honestly, Mom, I don't care," I say. Because I don't. My heart's already ripped up. Josh laughing at the news story about me is kind of a relief, actually. It breaks the tension. "What did Zoe say?"

"Watch it yourself." Josh points at the screen. "Dad DVRed it."

Mom drops her purse onto the bench by the door. "We've been trying to avoid—"

"No, I want to watch it." I also want to hear what Zoe says, and what Kristine says, and what Josh and I look like speeding away in the car. But I won't admit any of that out loud. I'm morbidly curious.

"But, Charlie—" Mom protests.

"She's tough," Dad says. "Let her watch it."

I settle on the sofa. Mom edges in next to me. Neither of us lean back. We hold hands, our backs straight, as if we're ready to spring off the couch at the first sign of danger. The curtains are already closed. Dad flips off the porch lights and locks the front door.

Josh starts the playback of the news. An anchorwoman's face fills the screen. "Edwina Huang caught up with gymnast and Olympic hopeful Charlie Ryland at her school in Columbus today. Reports reached our newsroom that Charlie has been—get this—*living a double life* to protect her identity at school. Edwina, tell us more."

There's Edwina, walking next to my high school, holding

her microphone. The lapel on her suit jacket ripples in a faint breeze. "Thanks, Trudy. Charlie's secret was violently exposed on Saturday when she sprained her ankle at Jefferson's prom and pictures on the Internet went viral. Charlie wasn't too keen on talking to us on camera, but I caught up with some of her best friends at school to hear their side of the story. . . ."

The shot flips to Zoe standing beside the flagpole. There's a crowd around her, hooting and jumping, jostling her. The Network Four News microphone is shoved into her face. "Oh my gosh, well, I actually never knew that Charlotte was an Olympic gymnast, even though we were best friends. I really, really hope she gets healed up quickly and can go win the Olympics."

I catch that Zoe says we *were* best friends, instead of that we *are* best friends. My heart sinks, even though I'm grateful that she's rooting for me.

"So she didn't tell you, her best friend, who she really was? Why do you think she kept her true identity a secret?"

Zoe furrows her brow, shakes her head. "I don't know. Maybe she was afraid it would get all weird, because it has kinda gotten weird around here."

"How so?"

"All you reporters hanging around, for one thing."

I want to reach through the TV and hug Zoe.

"Are people treating her differently?" Edwina asks from off camera.

"I don't know." Zoe squirms, looks guilty. "I guess."

"Can you give us a play-by-play of that night at prom? You were there, correct?"

"Yeah, I was there." Zoe looks like she wishes she were somewhere else. I don't blame her. "I didn't see her *fall*. I heard the screams and shouts, so I went to see what was going on. She was sprawled on the floor, and her date was trying to help her."

My stomach tightens as the events of that night rush through my mind. I know it's not possible, but it feels like my ankle aches more, like it's remembering too.

The shot changes, and Kristine's face fills the screen. She squints under the lights. Behind her Tasha bobs her head as if she's trying to get into the shot. Jane stands stalwartly at Kristine's shoulder, smiling into the lens. "Yeah, it was pretty shocking," Kristine says, flipping her hair over her shoulder. Next to her, Jane nods in agreement. "I mean, you think you know someone, and then you find out they have this double life. Like, I can't imagine that she's actually that good at gymnastics—"

Edwina Huang interrupts her from off camera. "She's won two World Championship gold medals on beam. She's one of our nation's best."

"Yeah, but you'd never know that by looking at her," Kristine says. "She doesn't *look* like an athlete. She doesn't *act* like an athlete. I know. I play soccer. You've got to have focus.

I doubt she has what it takes. I mean, if she were taking gymnastics seriously, she should not have gone to prom."

Beside her, Jane holds a hand over her mouth to cover her laughter. Then she leans toward Edwina and the microphone, blocking the view of Kristine. "Prom was disastrous for Charlotte," Jane says snidely. "Let's just be honest."

"Hmm, yes, indeed," Edwina says, turning to the camera. "It seems like Jefferson High School, even among her friends, is split about whether to support Charlie Ryland as she pursues her Olympic dream. We'd like to know what she was doing at prom with a gymnastics event of this magnitude right around the corner, but Charlie was unwilling to comment. Chris Betts, her celebrated two-time Olympic coach, also declined to speak with us. USA Gymnastics said they have a press release forthcoming."

"Oh no!" I say hoarsely. I turn to Mom. "Is that true? Have you heard anything?"

She shakes her head. "No one has told me about any plans for a press release, but I'm sure they are going to be supportive. If anything, they'll just want to let people know that you are still able to compete."

"Here I am, saving the day," Josh interjects gleefully, obviously pleased with the spotlight. He can have all of it, as far as I'm concerned.

I jerk my attention back to the TV in time to see Josh shepherding me into his car and then driving us away. As we pass the camera, I'm covering my face like a criminal being led to jail. "Back to you, Trudy and David."

"Thank you, Edwina," says Trudy, shuffling papers.

"What an interesting turn of events for that young lady," says the male news anchor, David, who happens to have painfully sideswiped hair. "I wonder why she felt like she had to keep her gymnastics career a secret."

"Friends say she's a private person." Trudy smiles. "We'll see how she does under Olympic pressure. But we wish her the very best in her endeavors. It would be wonderful to have a local Olympic athlete to root for."

"And now," David says, "another sports story that's a lot less perplexing and a whole lot more inspiring. Let's visit the Columbus Dog Show and meet Mitsy, a very special poodle with a whole lot of attitude. . . ."

I bury my face in a sofa pillow and groan.

Chapter Twenty-Nine

It's three days before I'll know if I made the Olympic team, and my last day at school for a while. My last day *ever* as fill-in for student council secretary. I carry a carefully piled stack of papers, separated neatly with paper clips. I'm going to earn my A in U.S. government class, even if it means being awkward with Kristine and resisting the urge to punch her in the face.

I've given a lot of thought to my last day before I head out for trials, my last student council meeting. I have something in mind that I want to accomplish. I even did some research on parliamentary procedure so I'd know what to say to make things go the right way.

Mr. Alto looks up from his desk when I limp into the room without my crutches. As long as I'm mindful of how much weight I'm putting on my bad ankle, it's not giving me too much trouble.

"Charlotte, when am I going to get an autograph from you," he says. "And I want an Olympic T-shirt with your name on it. Can you make that happen?"

"Sure," I say halfheartedly.

The only empty seat in the circle is between Brandon and Alex. Bobby's eyes dart over to me just long enough for me to know he's aware that I'm here. His arms are crossed over his chest. He looks wonderful, as always. And at least he's not sitting by Kristine.

I've caught glimpses of them in the hallway together, have wondered if they're going out again.

Out of the corner of my eye, I'm aware of Kristine whispering to Jane and Tasha. I busy myself with walking around and passing out the packets I made. The perfect secretary.

"Mr. Alto," I say as I hand him his packet. "Just to avoid any confusion, I need to make sure that you know this will be my last student council meeting, because I'll be out of town for the next couple of weeks."

Mr. Alto takes the packet and looks it over. "Very nice job here, Charlie."

"I'm sorry I can't finish out the year."

"Oh no, that's all right." He rubs his nose with the back of his hand. "You've done a terrific job filling in for Mandy. We're winding down the year anyway. I think you've earned that extra credit."

"Thank you, Mr. Alto."

"No, no," he says. "You have a nice time in Detroit. And you go to Montreal and win us a gold medal, you hear?"

"I'll try."

Kristine raps her desk. "I'm calling this meeting to order."
I take my seat.

"Okay, where is the agenda?" She flips through the papers I handed her. "Where are the minutes from last week?"

"The minutes are on top," I say. "The agenda is beneath that."

"By now you should know I prefer the agenda on top. I guess maybe you were just distracted trying to be an Olympic gymnast."

"At least I'm not distracted by being interviewed on the evening news."

"The people deserve to know the truth," she says, flipping her hair back over her shoulder. "I was doing my civic responsibility. Now please call the roll."

I could argue with her, but there is nothing to be gained, so I call the roll. Everyone is here. I turn to a blank page in my notebook. My chest feels tight, but I breathe to control it. Twenty more minutes, and I'm out of here, forever. I'm surprised by how much I'll miss being part of this group. I won't miss the Kristine aspect, but I will miss working toward accomplishing something. In spite of everything, I feel a sense of satisfaction that I had a role in helping with prom.

Kristine reports on prom, claiming it as a huge success for the student council. I have to agree. Except for my little accident, it was a wonderful night. Then a couple of action items are discussed. Finally she says, "If there is no further business to come before the assembly—"

The moment I've been waiting for and dreading just a little. I raise my hand. "Actually, there is. I have something to say."

"Are you presenting a motion?"

"Yield me the floor."

She glances around, and I know she doesn't want to. She has no idea what I'm going to say. She clears her throat. "You really should have talked with me about this before the meeting."

"Actually, that really is not a requirement. Yield me the floor."

"She's correct, Kristine. Yield her the floor," Mr. Alto says. If looks could kill, I'd be drawing my last breath.

"The chair recognizes *Charlie* Ryland," Kristine says.

"Thank you." I stand up, balancing carefully on my good foot. "As you all know, it was recently revealed that I'm an elite athlete with Olympic aspirations. I know some people feel betrayed because I kept my hopes and dreams a secret. Some people are judging me because of it. But they don't have all the facts. So . . ."

Everyone, even Bobby, is looking at me. I see curiosity on their faces. I clear my throat. Performing in front of a crowd of thousands is one thing. Talking to a group of twelve is more unnerving.

"Charlie Ryland has four hundred fifty thousand followers on Facebook. Charlotte Ryland has thirty. Some people adore Charlie, and some people hate her. She can come away with the gold, and there are people who will still find fault with her performance, her dismount, the position of her feet, the color of her leotard. That's fine. Everyone has an opinion. But I have to look at their opinions only when I go to Facebook."

A couple of people nod as though they can relate to getting criticized on social media.

"I used to be homeschooled. And I missed sitting in a room with people. I missed laughing with someone or groaning because the teacher announced a pop quiz. The only people I ever interacted with were other gymnasts. And they were all girls. They were all ambitious, determined, and talented. They all had the same dream that I had. But I was getting a skewed perspective on the world. Because not everyone thinks it's normal to want to spend seven hours a day in a gym flying through the air and landing on your back more times than you land on your feet.

"So I decided to go back to public school. I wanted to have friends who weren't gymnasts and who had experiences different from mine. But I didn't want their opinions of me to be based on my gymnastics talent. I didn't want them to say to my face what I was reading on Facebook. I didn't want to find things like this"—I pull out the marked-up cover of *Gymnastics NOW!*—"taped to my locker. So I decided to become Charlotte Ryland, who no one had ever heard of."

I release a self-mocking laugh. "And that kind of backfired, as you all know. But that's okay. You see, Charlie Ryland wouldn't have had to serve on the student council to bring up her grade. She would have been given a quick and easy project. But Charlotte Ryland had to figure out how government worked, so she had to serve on the student council. I enjoyed it a lot more than I thought I would. It gave me the opportunity to get to know all of you a little bit and to work to give those who went to prom a night to remember. And no matter what else happens, I'm glad for that."

This whole time I have avoided looking at Bobby. But it's time now. His gaze is on me. I look into his brown eyes. After all, this little speech of mine—it's actually for him. "I'm really sorry, Bobby, that I didn't tell you the truth about me. I regret more than you'll ever know that I was stupid and careless with our friendship. I'm really truly sorry. You deserved better."

I look over at Kristine. "And with that, Madam President, I yield the floor back to you."

I sit down. No one says a word. Kristine clears her throat, shifts in her chair. "Uh, is there any further business? No? Then we're adjourned."

"I knew who you were," Brandon says as he grabs his backpack and stands.

I stare at him in amazement. "What?"

He grins. "Yeah, my sister's in gymnastics. I've seen you at some meets. You're going to kill them in Montreal."

I'm so touched. Tears sting my eyes. I smile. "Thanks, Brandon."

He shrugs and gives me a teasing grin. "But I'd like you more if you'd voted for the Prom Wars theme."

Laughing, I reach down for my backpack, and realize that Bobby has already picked it up and is holding it out to me.

"Thanks," I say.

"I still don't understand why you couldn't have just told me all that before."

"I should have when I realized how much I was beginning to like you. But then there never seemed a good way to say it so that it made sense. So much of my life is about getting scores for how I perform that I guess I think people are scoring me on everything."

The room has cleared out. Only Mr. Alto is left in the corner, studying his phone.

"I misjudged Kristine when we were going out," Bobby continues. "I thought I'd done the same thing with you. Wrestling is part of who I am. It's not something I can separate from. For you to be at the level you are, that means gymnastics is part of you. After I discovered you had this double life, I just felt like I didn't really know you."

"Charlotte and Charlie aren't that different. Not really. I finally figured that out. It's actually a lot easier just being Charlie. More challenging in some ways, but still easier. Which makes no sense."

"I think I get what you mean."

I hope he does. "I guess we'd better get to class," I say.

"See you around, Charlie Ryland."

I watch him walk out. I'm glad he's at least talking to me again, but I can't imagine that he'll want to hang out with me anymore.

I'm nearly to my locker when I see what appears to be a gaggle of girls gathered in front of it, apparently doing something to it. Defacing it, no doubt. If I didn't need one of the books in it for class, I'd just walk on.

One of the girls turns slightly, her eyes widen, and she begins shoving on the other girls and pointing at me. They turn and start hopping up and down. People stare at them, stare at me.

"Charlie Ryland!" a girl with short blond hair shouts. "We had no idea you were at our school. But then, we're just freshmen and so beneath you, but when we saw the news last night . . . OhmyGod! OhmyGod! Charlie Ryland at our school."

A girl with long black hair pulled back into a ponytail steps forward. "Can I carry your backpack for you?"

I blink at her. "What?"

"You don't need the extra weight, not with your ankle trying to heal. I wish I'd realized sooner that you were at Jefferson. I would have totally carried your backpack for you all week."

I guess Zoe doesn't Friend the freshmen on Facebook, or they don't Friend her.

"Thanks. That's okay. I've got it," I say. "But I do need to get to my locker."

"Oh, sure. Absolutely."

The girls part like the Red Sea, and that's when I see what they've done to my locker. Tears sting my eyes. My chest tightens. There are starbursts and glittered signs taped to the door.

GO, CHARLIE!

WE BELIEVE!

CHARLIE ROCKS!

YOU CAN DO IT!

A string of balloons has been tied to the handle. They've decorated my locker like the cheerleaders decorate the lockers of the football and basketball players before a game.

"We just think you're amazing," the blonde says.

"Totally amazing," the dark-haired girl says.

I figure they are the voice for the group. There has to be at least eight girls, smiling at me.

"Thanks so much for doing this," I say, waving my hand over my locker, like Vanna White revealing a puzzle on *Wheel of Fortune*. I imagine them working on the signs, gluing and glittering. "It means more to me than I can say."

"Oh, totally," another of the girls says.

I get my book out of my locker and close the door. I can't help but smile at all the enthusiasm taped to it.

"I've got to get to class," I say, regretting that I don't have more time to get to know them.

"Oh, we do too," the blonde says. "But we'll be watching the trials on TV."

"And rooting for you," one of the other girls says.

"Thanks."

I'm still smiling as I head to class. This fame thing is a mixed bag. They reminded me that it's not all bad, that I can bring excitement to others' lives, that all I've been working for isn't just for me. It's for anyone who has ever had a dream.

I have one more thing that I need to do before I leave school today, before I head into the most important weekend of my life so far. I have to talk to Zoe.

She's been incredibly skilled at avoiding me in the hallways and at our lockers. But she can't escape me in Mr. Alto's class, because he has us in assigned seats. When I walk into government, I'm glad to see Zoe hunched over her desk, scribbling in her notebook. That's been her usual posture in this class since Monday.

I hobble over to my desk, take my seat, remove my book from my backpack, and then slide the backpack beneath my injured foot so that I can keep my ankle elevated as much as possible. The swelling is way down, but my ankle is still tender.

The seats around us are empty. I lean over slightly toward Zoe. "I saw you on the news last night. You handled the interview really well."

Without looking at me, she lifts a shoulder, drops it back down, keeps scribbling.

"It means a lot to me that you still want me to go to the

THE FLIP SIDE · 271

Olympics," I say. "I wish I'd told you the truth about me, that I'd had your support all along."

With her head still ducked, she peers over at me. "Why didn't you tell me? I tell you *everything*."

"I just felt like I needed to keep my two lives separate. My life is so totally crazy right now. I wanted someplace that was gymnastics-free." Which isn't the entire truth, and I know I have to be completely honest with her if I want to regain her friendship. "Plus I was afraid things might change between us."

Straightening, she twists around to face me squarely. "Like how?"

"I don't know." The bell is about to ring. Students are rushing in. Desks scrape across the floor as people throw themselves into the seats around us. "Can we talk after class?"

She glances around, sees that we've lost our privacy, and nods.

The bell rings. Mr. Alto strides in and announces a pop quiz. I groan. Maybe I'm not going to have an A in this class after all. I've barely studied over the past two nights.

He gives a stack of quizzes to the first person in each row, and the sheets are sent back. I take one and pass the remaining pages to the person behind me. I read the first question. *Name the three branches of government.* Easy enough.

I'm starting to write out my answer, when Mr. Alto is suddenly taking the paper from my desk. I look up at him.

He winks. "You're exempt, Charlie."

I shake my head. "I don't want to be exempt."

"You've earned your grade with the extra credit you did by serving on the student council. You need to be focusing on this weekend now, your upcoming trials."

I can feel a couple of the students' gazes boring into me.

"I don't want to be treated differently, Mr. Alto." I hold out my hand. "I need the quiz paper back, please."

"But you are different, Charlie."

"Not in school. Please, can I take the quiz?"

He chuckles but sets the paper back on my desk. "I've never had anyone ask to take a quiz. Good luck, Charlie."

I don't know if he's talking about the quiz or the Olympic trials, but it doesn't matter. For right now I have to concentrate on this one hour, this quiz, one question at a time. I finish just as the bell rings. I'm actually feeling pretty good about my answers as I limp to the front of the class and drop off my paper.

"Good luck, Charlie," Mr. Alto says again.

"Thanks."

When I walk out into the hallway, Zoe is waiting for me. I can't describe the relief that washes over me.

"That was weird," she says as we start walking toward our lockers.

"I know. It gets worse. He wants me to get him a Charlie Ryland T-shirt."

She staggers to a stop and stares me at me. "You're kidding?"

I bite back a huge smile as I shake my head.

She rolls her eyes. "Okay, so maybe everyone didn't need to know you're Charlie Ryland, World Championship gymnast—but I should have known."

"I know, Zoe. I'm so sorry. I didn't mean to hurt you, but I can see that I did. We don't have to be best friends, but I hope we can at least be sort-of friends."

"Sort-of friends don't want to punch Kristine. Only best friends want to do that. I couldn't believe the things she was saying during the interview yesterday."

"She has an issue with Bobby taking me to prom."

"She has issues period."

"So are we friends again?"

She skews up her mouth like she's thinking. "Depends. Will you get me a T-shirt too?"

I laugh. I want to hug her, but I don't know if we're totally there yet. "Absolutely."

Growing serious, she looks down at my wrapped foot. "Are you going to be able to compete well enough to make the team?"

I tell her the truth, because she deserves it and because I'm going to tell her only the truth from now on. "I don't know, Zoe. I honestly don't know."

Chapter Thirty

I have a sprained ankle, and I'm not sure what's going to happen with my bars dismount, but I'm going to Olympic trials anyway. I carefully fold my new leotard, shimmering purple with pink-swirled sleeves, and place it in my carry-on. I don't trust it to checked luggage.

Things between Zoe and me aren't perfect, but they are on the mend.

I also have to give some serious thought as to whether or not I'm going to public school next year. Mom said I would find normal boring. I can categorically say after the past few days that my life is anything but normal. It's bordering on weird, with some people embracing who I am and others resenting it. I don't know if I want to deal with the roller-coaster ride that school could become after the Olympics. If I make the team. And if I don't, I'm not sure I want to deal with people like Kristine saying that I didn't have what it takes to be an Olympian.

A familiar tap sounds on my door. Mom pokes her head in. "Are you ready?"

"I'm as ready as I'll ever be."

"You've got your toothbrush, your leo, extra athletic tape?" she asks.

The list has always been the same, to every meet, for forever. There's comfort in knowing what I need to pack.

"And all my hair stuff. We'll just have to get more hair spray when we get there."

"Got it," Mom says. "I'm getting my shoes on."

I hoist my duffel bag onto my shoulder. I'm heading down the stairs when a text comes in from Josh, who wasn't excused from going to school today. He's sent me a picture of the marquee that stands outside the front of the school. The lettering reads: GOOD LUCK, CHARLIE!

I text him back. *Thanks for sharing!*

Dad is already in the car with the motor running, anxious to make sure that Mom and I get to the airport on time. He and Josh will drive up after dinner tomorrow. Because Coach works to keep us focused on our goals, I probably won't get a chance to visit with them until the competition is over. Another text comes in as I'm opening the car door.

I glance down, and my heart trips. It's Bobby.

Hey. Safe travels. You got this.

I smile. "You got this" is my inside joke with Gwen. Funny how it makes me feel that maybe everything will be all right.

Normally when we fly, Gwen and I sit together. We share

snacks, talk about boys, and share earbuds. But as I walk to the check-in counter, I realize that this trip might be different, because Gwen is so totally focused on this weekend. She comforted me during my blubber-fest after I got cornered by the reporters at school, but other than that she has stayed pretty much to herself. I'm not sure she has quite forgiven me for involving her in my prom plot, which resulted in her being grounded.

I don't see her until I'm at the gate. As if to confirm my fears, Gwen turns away when she sees me, chatting with her mom, who flew in from Georgia last night. Her dad, brother, and little sister are all flying together straight to Detroit. Gwen rests her head on her mom's shoulder. And ignores me.

There's an open seat next to her. I sit down and pull my duffel bag onto my lap.

"Well, hello, Charlie," Mrs. Edwards says. "How's the ankle?"

"It could be worse."

Mrs. Edwards nods. "Well, I was very sorry to hear about your accident. I'm glad you're on the mend. Although, I wasn't too pleased when I learned about the mischief you and Gwen got into."

"It was totally my fault, Mrs. Edwards. Gwen never thought it was a good idea, but she went along with it because I wanted to go to prom so badly. But now I'm not sure I even want to go to public school next year. I think I want to do an online program, like Gwen."

Gwen stares at me. "Why? The Olympics will be over."

"It's weird enough at school now. It'll be even weirder next year. Besides, I've got to get my priorities straight."

Gwen shifts in her seat. "Seriously?"

"That's funny," Mrs. Edwards says, "because Gwen was just talking to me about going to public school next fall after the Olympics in August. You know, she's done online school since first grade. How is this child going to handle a strict schedule of classes and homework assignments?"

"Mom!" Gwen whispers, jabbing her.

"No, I understand," her mom continues. "You see your friend here doing all these high school things. You think you're missing out on something big. Well, honey, let me tell you . . . No, better yet, let Charlie tell you. Is there anything special about high school that Gwen will miss out on if she doesn't go? I've told her she's missing out on a whole lot of nothing and heartache."

I mentally go through a checklist of my public school experiences. "It has its moments. I've met other people, other friends. There are extracurricular activities that can be surprisingly fun. If I do stay at Jefferson, I might run for the student council."

"I thought student council was a lot of work," Gwen says.

"It was. The good kind."

"See, Mom?" Gwen says. "Plus it'll be my senior year. What if I just want to *experience* it?"

"That's fine," Mrs. Edwards says. "But you've got to realize that your gymnastics might suffer. Here you've been going so strong for so long. It would be a pity to mess all that up."

Gwen slouches miserably. "But it'll be four years before the next Olympics. I'll be in college by then. It just seems like at some point in my life I should go to a public school before I head to college."

"And if you go to public school, you might get a text like this." I hold out Bobby's latest for Gwen to see.

She leans forward in her seat. "Bobby told you, 'You got this'!"

We both laugh, because he unintentionally tapped into our private joke.

"Oh, wow, I hope that's not a prophecy or anything!" Gwen cries. "I mean, are you totally going to bite it on your Amanar?"

As long as my ankle can withstand the impact of my landing on the mat, I'm pretty confident that my vault is not going to totally bite. "I better not! I'm struggling enough with other stuff as it is. At least give me a decent vault!"

Our laughter dwindles. Talking about my struggles probably reminds us both about my injury and how I got it.

"I'm really sorry, Gwen," I whisper. "I shouldn't have gotten you involved in my drama."

Gwen leans toward me now, away from her mom. "Truthfully, it was kind of exciting. I was so afraid we were going to get caught. But I wanted to be there with you for the whole night."

"I wish you could have been. I'm so sorry that you got grounded because of me."

The corners of her mouth turn up slightly. "It's only for another couple of days, but you do owe me now."

"I'll pay up anytime."

Gwen's eyes soften. "Like I told you before, I was a little jealous. You manage all this stuff all the time, and I can manage only one thing. Okay, two things—gymnastics and school—and you've got a whole social life and a boyfriend and—"

"Bobby's not my boyfriend," I say.

"But he *wants* to be your boyfriend."

"Not anymore."

"What happened?"

I fill her in on all the details about prom night and the Facebook debacle.

Gwen's eyes narrow. "But he sent you the text."

"He was just being nice."

"What did you text back?" Gwen asks.

"Nothing."

"You didn't text him back?" Gwen cries. "You need to text him!"

"We talked yesterday. I apologized. It's over."

Gwen tips her head. "You really like him, don't you?"

I shift down in my seat, fighting off the disappointment about things ending between Bobby and me. I liked him a lot, but I'm not sure there is any point in admitting it. "I don't know. It doesn't matter anyway."

Gwen wraps her arms around me. "Since when have you been a quitter?"

"This is different. I'm facing reality."

"He wants you," Gwen says. "I saw how he was looking at you when he picked you up for prom."

I lean my head on Gwen's shoulder. "I'll worry about it after trials."

"No, you will not. You're going to text him now."

"What do I even say?"

"Tell him he's hot. Tell him he's your bae."

I jab her in the ribs. "I'm not telling him that!"

"Okay, then tell him your friend Gwen has a huge crush on him."

"Do you really?"

"No." She giggles. "He's cute, looked really good in that tuxedo, but I don't know him. I'm just trying to get the conversation started for you two. Although, I wouldn't mind if you ask if he has a friend who is in need of a girlfriend."

I can't blame her for the interest in guys. With online schooling, she has had very few in her life. "But what do I say? I don't want to seem desperate."

"Say 'thanks,'" Gwen says. "He wished you luck the only way he knew how. You say 'thanks.'"

"Okay." I pull out my phone and type grudgingly. *Thanks.*

"Put a smiley face."

I add a smiley face.

"Put those big lips."

"No!"

Gwen laughs. "Just kidding."

I press send.

"There," Gwen says. "Was that so hard?"

"I'm not getting my hopes up. I really think I blew it."

Gwen shakes her head. "You're impossible! Just relax, okay? See if he texts back."

"Okay." I lay my phone in my lap. Gwen and I both stare at it.

"I hope he texts soon," Gwen says after a few long moments.

"He's probably in class."

"We've got to tighten up our minds," Gwen says. "Focus on what's ahead. Podium training."

I nod. "Podium training." For large meets all the apparatuses are placed on podiums so that the audience has a better view of the events. We'll get a chance to work on the equipment before the official competition starts, so that we have an opportunity to get used to the way it feels.

"What would you text back if someone just said 'thanks' to you?" Gwen asks.

"Uh, I don't know."

"Exactly. You need to text more."

"What else do I say?"

"What does he like to do?" Gwen asks. "Ask him a question. Then he has to answer."

How's wrestling going? I type. "How's that?"

"He's a wrestler?"

"A really good one."

Gwen gapes at me. "Girl! Why did you not tell me that?"

"He's too perfect. I am so dead."

"It's going to be okay." Gwen grips my shoulder. "You asked him a good question. He's going to text back soon."

We slump back into our seats. I set my phone on my knee. We stare at it.

"Look up there," Gwen's mom says, pointing at the television screen mounted to the wall. "Y'all are famous."

"Is that the *Today* show?" Gwen cries. "Whoa. This is big-time!"

Our smiling faces flash across the screen. They used our national team photos and the spreads from *Gymnastics NOW!* Closed-captioning scrolls below the images. It's a mess of typos, not to mention time-delayed, but Gwen reads it out loud. "'What a contrast between these two young athletes. Best friends. Competitors. One who leaves her family to fly across the country to join a coach who can take her to her Olympic dreams, the other who leads a double life, hiding her true' . . ." Gwen's voice trails off. "That's mean," she mutters.

I avert my eyes just as Coach Chris bounds over to us.

"We've got to stay focused, girls," he says, squatting in front of us. "You're going to see a lot, you're going to hear a lot. You're going to have reporters crawling all over you from now on. You keep cool, you keep smiling, you let me and USA Gymnastics take care of it. You'll get official word if you're going to be part of an interview, if you're going to talk to anyone publicly about anything, all right?"

Gwen and I nod in unison.

Coach hops to his feet. "All right, then. It's time to board."

"Did they call our seats?" Mrs. Edwards asks, scrambling to collect her things. "I didn't hear."

"Our seats weren't called, but we're boarding anyway. I talked to the flight attendant. I want to get these girls in a safe, closed environment where they won't be bombarded by the news." He heads off to take care of things.

"That's smart." Mrs. Edwards stands and throws her satchel-like purse over her shoulder. "I like that Coach Chris. Always thinking."

I don't mean to glance at the screen, but I do. It's a picture someone took at prom. Bobby is looking up at me from where he's crouching on one knee. I'm looking down at him, my face tight with pain but a slight smile playing on my lips as I try to be brave. Under the photo scrolls the text, *The question remains: What was Charlie Ryland thinking? Has she sabotaged her gymnastics career?*

"Come on, honey." Mom tugs me to my feet, the skin around her eyes wrinkled with concern. "Time to go."

But that question keeps rolling through my mind. Have I sabotaged my gymnastics career?

Chapter Thirty-One

"How does that feel?" Coach Rachel asks, patting my bound ankle.

It's Saturday evening, and we're in the arena locker room. The do-or-die moment is rapidly approaching. "Tight," I tell her.

"Exactly what it should feel like," she says. "Let's see you point."

I obediently point my toes.

"All right. You're set. You get 'em today, okay?"

I nod. It's hard to find words. Only routines are playing through my mind. Last night I had a difficult time falling asleep, because my mind was working, going over and over my passes, rehearsing every move, every pivot, every flip and pirouette. It didn't want to rest, didn't want to sleep. But I knew I needed sleep more than anything else.

After warm-up I stand shoulder to shoulder with Gwen, ready to march into the auditorium. She reaches for my hand and squeezes. We don't speak. There aren't any words for this moment. Everything we could say has fallen away.

When the girls in front of us move forward, we follow, striding in perfect tempo into the huge auditorium. The lights are brilliant, the crowd loud. Flags wave. I slow my heartbeat with my breaths. I breathe the pain in through my injured ankle, which I refuse to limp on, and out again through the same ankle, letting it go.

Tight mind, I remind myself. *This is it. Everything comes down to this.*

"U-S-A! U-S-A!" The chant fills the high ceiling, reverberates around us, echoing and repeating. The stands are a blur of faces.

We're introduced. We wave to the crowd. Camera shutters buzz like cicadas.

I see Coach Chris standing off the floor with Rachel, clapping along with the crowd. He catches my eye and gives me a brief nod and a rare smile of encouragement. Tonight is the finals. Everything we've worked for comes down to the next couple of hours. Our scores will be combined. First place has an automatic "in" on the Olympic team. Apart from that guaranteed spot, the Olympic committee will handpick the rest of the team, looking for those who stand out, both all around and in individual events.

Behind Coach Chris, in the stands, I catch a glimpse of Mrs. Edwards waving an American flag, with a garland of red, white, and blue carnations around her neck. I wonder if my parents are nearby.

Focus. Breathe.

This is just like any other competition. Except it's not.

Gwen and I are assigned the same rotation, beginning on vault. She's ahead of me in the lineup. Our teammate from nationals, Cora, goes first.

She points and flexes her toes as she waits for the call from the judges. When it comes, she gracefully raises her arms and arches her back, a perfect line from her toes to her fingertips, presenting herself to the judges before taking her position at the top of the vault run. I half-watch, but my brain is focused on my own vault. I'm attempting my Amanar today. I desperately need its level of difficulty to get an Olympic placement.

"Come on, Cora!" I shout, my voice ringing along with the voices from the crowd. "Come on, girl!" But I'm not focused on her. I'm mentally rehearsing my own routine so thoroughly, I don't notice Cora's vault until I hear the cry of alarm from the crowd, followed by a shocked hush. When my eyes focus, I see that she's flat on her back on the mat on the other side of the vault. It's clear that she's not injured. She just had a crummy landing. We all have them at one point or another. It was just bad timing for hers to happen tonight.

Gwen and I exchange glances, but we don't speak. We don't want to jinx ourselves.

Cora rises shakily and hurries over to her coach. He presses his hands into her shoulders, his head wagging as he speaks.

Once again she finds her spot at the top of the vault run, shaking off her nerves, focusing on the end result—a perfect landing.

But even perfection can't do much for her now, because her first fall will give her an unimpressive score that can't be overcome when the two are averaged.

I'm not going to ask Gwen if she thinks Cora still has a chance. We both know the answer is, *Not without absolute perfection on everything that remains.*

Gwen raises one leg forward in her signature pre-vault stance. "Gwen!" I yell. "Do it, Gwen! Stick it!"

She strikes the springboard and hurtles through the air. She steps out of her landing, but brings her feet together quickly and presents herself with arms raised, back slightly arched.

I let out a breath. One more vault. "Come on, Gwen," I whisper.

Her second vault is solid, though she takes two hops on her landing. Still, she throws up her arms, straight and grace- ful, and smiles. Relief. I know the feeling. One event done.

Gwen's scores flash up on the huge display board above our heads. Gwen Edwards. First vault, a solid 15.5. The sec- ond is scored slightly lower at 15.2.

Now it's my turn.

I sweep my arms in circles, keeping my eyes on the vault. *Run. Spring. Arms tight. Stick.*

"Charlie Ryland," the head judge announces.

I present with back arched, arms high over my head, fingers straight, my body in perfect alignment, before stepping to my place on the runway.

I take a deep breath, let it out, narrow my focus until it's just me, the runway, the board, the vault, the mat. There's no crowd, no other competitors. It's just me and this apparatus that if used properly will make me fly.

I take off running as fast as I can. With arms swinging, legs churning, I gather speed, round off to hit the vault with all my power, and spin through the air. *Smack!* My feet hit the mat in unison, my tightly wrapped ankle smarting with the impact.

I throw up my arms. The cheers of the crowd roar in my ears.

Coach Chris congratulates me as I pass him. "Keep it high, Charlie. I need more power, more flight."

I nod. My second vault rushes by faster. I feel the hiss of wind against my ears as I spin. The ground comes up fast, and I wobble sideways as I land, but manage to hold my ground. Because my ankle rolled slightly during the wobble, pain is shooting up the side of my shin.

I hide my grimace behind a smile, present, and jog off the mat. Coach Chris meets me with a hug. "Nice job, Charlie. Keep it up."

Then Gwen wraps her arms around me. "That was amazing," she says.

"You too," I say.

"I stepped out and hopped. You held on to that last one."

Just barely. I shake my head slightly. I'm not going to mention how that landing ripped up my ankle. I adjust the sleeves of my leo and reach for my water bottle. My eyes flit over the crowd for a moment, hoping I'll spot Mom and Dad, but there is a sea of faces, none of them recognizable.

My scores flash onto the screen. A 14.9 and 15.4. My first vault wasn't high enough to give me the best score, but I corrected the second. My average score is only slightly lower than Gwen's.

I follow Gwen over to the bars, noticing the thin gold ribbons her mom braided into her hair.

I know everyone is waiting for Gwen's bars. "You know what they've nicknamed you, don't you?" Coach Chris asked before the competition started. He reached out and tweaked her ear. "The Flash."

Gwen laughed. "Why?"

"Because you're fast and powerful on those bars."

And it's true. Gwen swings into action. Her legs are perfectly straight, her toes pointed, her body a straight line as she swings up into a handstand and pirouettes. Even though I've watched her routine a thousand times, I still hold my breath. She swings into a giant—her body fully extended as she rotates 360 degrees around the bar—picking up momentum for her famous Kovacs.

Silence ripples through the auditorium. The bars creak as she comes around one more time, rotating her wrists on the bars so that her giant is inverted, and then—bam! She lets go, flips once, twice, above the bar, and grabs hold with a jolt that would throw a normal person off center. But not Gwen. She sails into a kip, rises up into another giant series, and dismounts—a full twisting double. Her feet strike the mat, her hands fly up. She turns her beaming face to me.

After she dashes off the mat, we give each other a quick hug, then keep our eyes on the board, awaiting her score. I'm aware of the cameras pointed at us. Coach Chris stands behind her, hands gripping her shoulders.

When the score comes up a 16.050, the noise in the auditorium is deafening. I long to scream along with them, but I'm already pacing myself through my own routine. I don't have a Kovacs, but my new dismount should add to my difficulty level enough to keep me in the running.

As I head to the bars, Coach Chris keeps pace with me. "How's the ankle?"

"It's holding up."

"Are you sure?"

"Yes." I'm not going to tell him how it felt on vault, how it's still pulsing with discomfort beneath the wrapping.

"You can go to the simpler dismount," he says. "You've practiced it a thousand times. You can pull it off and make it clean."

"I need the new dismount," I say. "If I have any hope at all of making the team. We both know it. I didn't come this far to give up now."

"You're limping, Charlie."

"No, I'm not!" I straighten up, force myself to step on my foot as if it doesn't hurt.

"Okay," Coach Chris says. "But you've got beam and floor coming up. I need you at your best."

"I will be at my best," I say firmly.

"Show me what you've got," he says, slapping my shoulder as I cross to position the springboard.

I take off, and everything passes by in what seems like merely a second. I'm on autopilot, going through the moves, feeling everything lining up. What I end up with is a pretty clean routine on bars, close to the best I've ever done . . . and a landing that makes me grind my back teeth to keep from screaming in pain.

I have to limp off the floor. No amount of bravado can cover this up. But I did it. I nailed my full twisting double back. Against all odds.

Coach Chris claps me on the back. I'm grateful that he doesn't mention my limp. He knows what that routine cost me. "That was solid," he says. "You pulled it off."

My score proves that I did pull it off. A 15.85. It's just a touch lower than Gwen's, even with her Kovacs.

"Are you okay?" Gwen asks. "It looks like your ankle is giving you trouble."

"I'm fine."

Coach Rachel thrusts an ice pack at me. "Ice it while you wait. You've got some time before beam."

I take the ice gratefully and sink into a nearby seat. A cameraman closes in on me, but I don't pay any attention. We're not expected to. My thoughts need to be on beam now, my next event, not worrying about news footage.

I close my eyes. I wish, just wish I could look up into the stands and catch a glimpse of Mom and Dad. That would give me the lift I need right now.

I raise my eyes, scan the crowd. One of my other teammates from nationals, Anna, is doing her floor routine. Her music blares over the sound system. She flips a triple pike, lands with a step out into a side straddle jump.

And then I see them. Mom holds an American flag high and dances to the pulsing floor music. A large purple flower glows in her hair. It's the same shade of purple as my leo. Dad is wearing his CHARLIE'S DAD sweatshirt. Josh is beside him, looking down at his phone. With an obvious laugh, he elbows the person next to him and points to the screen on his phone.

My heart freezes as that person leans over to see what Josh is trying to show him. It can't be. I must be hallucinating. But no.

It's Bobby. I'd know his build anywhere, not to mention his hair. *What is he doing here?*

"How's the ankle feeling?" Coach Rachel asks, crouching next to me.

"Oh—um—I hardly notice it anymore."

"You looked like you were in a lot of pain after that dismount. Do you want the doc to look at it?"

"No, I'll be fine."

"Okay," she says. "If you're sure."

Anna finishes her routine with a flourish, chin tipped back, hands crisscrossed over her head. The crowd goes wild. Mom bounces with her American flag. Dad leans around Josh and says something to Bobby. It looks like he laughs in response. He lifts his phone, possibly snapping a few pictures. With it, he scans the auditorium . . . and seems to pause when he reaches me.

He waves.

I wave.

Mom, Dad, and Josh wave.

Then I notice who is sitting in front of them, because Zoe jumps up and starts to wave wildly. Beside her, Michael is a little less enthusiastic but still waving.

Focus, Charlie, focus!

But I'm doing well. I'm second in the standings after Gwen, even with my bad ankle. And I have beam and floor coming up, my best events.

Mom blows me a kiss. I blow one back.

Enjoy the ride, Mom always says. *Embrace your crazy.*

Can I embrace the fact that Bobby drove a little more than three hours to watch me compete at trials? I long to tell Gwen, but she's staring at the floor with her headphones on. She's doing what she's supposed to be doing—staying in the zone—while I wave and smile and stress about Bobby being here.

Coach Rachel leans close to my ear. "They're calling us over to beam."

Chapter Thirty-Two

Gwen's beam scores aren't her highest ever, but she's still holding firmly to first place, thanks to her unbelievable performance on bars.

When it's my turn, I mount the beam using a springboard, careful to land on my good foot. I slide through my first dance sequence, spinning into my leg-up double turn. During my leap sequence, my ankle twists as I'm coming down from my switch-ring. I wobble, but hold it. That'll cost me a few tenths.

My dismount crunches my ankle again, but I still manage to nail my landing.

Coach Rachel crosses to hug me as I step off the mat, and ends up having to help me hop to a seat. I cringe as I sit down.

"We're getting the doc to look at this," she says.

"No, please! I have one more event. Then I'll rest it and ice it and do everything I need to!"

"Charlie . . ." Her voice is firm.

"I know what I'm doing. I know how to listen to my body.

I've lived with this injury for more than seven years. Dr. Kwan confirmed that it's just a sprain."

"You're doing fine in the standings. You go easy out there."

"There's no such thing as going easy," I say to remind her and myself. "I'm going for the Olympics. If I go easy, someone else is going to take my spot. Floor is one of my best events. I can do this."

Coach Rachel stares me down. "You won't be able to *walk* if you severely injure your ankle and keep competing on it. Then you might not be able to compete at the Olympics at all."

"I know I'm not pushing it too far. It's tender, yes, but the pain isn't bad. I promise that I'm not taking a risk I shouldn't. If the pain gets bad, and I know that I can't push through it without causing serious harm, I'll stop. But I can't give up now, when I know there's no reason to. Not yet. I came here to get onto the Olympic team. I can't walk away without giving it my best."

Gwen performs amazingly during her floor routine. Her only big mistake is a step outside the boundary lines during one of her back passes, which will cost her. It's an uncharacteristic miscalculation for her—she usually sticks her landings and knows exactly where she's sticking them. But she still comes off the floor with radiant joy. Her 14.55 holds her first-place spot.

I find my starting position on the floor. Strike my beginning pose.

The music charges forward. I run, leap, straddle, only to have my ankle give out in my landing. I stumble sideways but catch myself before I fall completely. There's an audible gasp from the crowd.

I collect my wits, but my brain is scrambling.

Breathe, I remind myself. It's not the first time in my life that I've stumbled. It's not the first time I haven't stuck something. I can do this routine in my sleep. I have to keep believing in myself, keep moving. If I quit now, there will be no Olympics, ever.

I plant myself in the corner of the floor and prepare for my next pass. But even as I begin running, I can feel that something is off. My first front tuck is too high, the spin too great. I rebound into my second and feel myself sprawling.

Tight!

My brain screams the word. It's what every good gymnastics coach I've ever had, since I was a little kid, has always reminded me—*Tighten up, Charlie. Tighten up!*

I tighten up now, hit the floor with my one good foot, and rebound into a split leap.

The music courses through me. I dance with abandon, throwing back my head, flinging away the pain.

My last tumbling pass.

My hands form tight fists, and I grit my teeth in a tense-lipped smile. No turning back.

I lengthen my body into a twisting layout, followed by two

whips and a full twisting double. And land it firmly on my safe foot. But when I step back, my ankle rolls, loose like jelly.

I fling my weight forward, sidestepping into the final moments of my dance.

I kneel, bend back, my ponytail swinging against the soles of my feet, my arms outstretched to the auditorium ceiling, and . . .

I've done it. I finished the routine without any major mistakes, without my ankle giving out on me, without any huge blunders. But I still don't know if it was enough to make the team. What I do know is that, for today, it was my best.

"You're a fighter," Coach Chris says into my ear, patting my back.

I don't want to see the scoreboard. My routine was riddled with tiny flaws that are likely to affect my score. But I did it. I gave it everything I had—110 percent, like I promised I would.

"I'm proud of you," he says. "Whatever happens."

"Thanks," I whisper.

Gwen hugs me. Neither of us can speak. We've reached the part of the journey where all the striving, at least for the time being, is behind us. Glory or bitter disappointment is ahead. It's a moment that allows only silence.

We cling to each other as we wait for my score. I check the seats for my parents and find them quickly now, in the first row behind the railing. Mom is sitting, her hands clasped in front of her like she's praying, the American flag folded on her lap.

Dad and Bobby are talking, their eyes on the scoreboard.

What is taking so long?

Every second that ticks past feels like an hour. I bite my lip, feel the lenses of a hundred cameras, which translate into thousands of eyes, staring at me.

"Come on, come on," Gwen says under her breath.

I feel that same urgency. If I'm clearly out with this score, then I'm out. I mean, there's always a chance I could go to the Olympics just to compete in beam, but Team USA has plenty of other girls who are solid on beam, and in everything else, too.

Coach Rachel brings me more ice for my ankle and settles down next to me and Gwen to wait for my scores.

Coach Chris paces.

The scoreboard changes. *Charlie Ryland*, it reads. *Floor:* *14.85.*

I take a deep breath.

My floor score puts me in fourth place all around.

I'm not sure it's enough, because more than the scores are factored into the final decision regarding who makes the team.

Gwen holds on to first, which means she's an automatic in for the Olympic team. I scream and am the first to embrace her. "Yes! You did it!" I shout as the other girls from Gold Star gather around to congratulate her.

"I can't believe it!" She places her hands over her mouth

to hide her huge smile. She's made the Olympic team, while the rest of us are still in limbo.

"Enjoy the moment," I tell her.

She nods. "I want all of you to make it."

But we know that all of us won't. There are only five spots on the team, and the competition area is filled with Olympic hopefuls.

As we head off the floor to the room where we'll wait with the rest of the gymnasts for the Olympic committee's decision and the official introduction of the women's U.S. Olympic team, I know Gwen is trying not to smile too brightly.

"You have to make it too," she whispers. "You just have to."

"Gwen, I'm so happy for you."

"I'm afraid to believe it, Charlie."

"Don't be. You earned it." I give her arm a squeeze. If my ankle weren't throbbing, I'd be doing cartwheels down the hallway to celebrate that my best friend made the Olympic team.

Gwen looks over at me. "I'm proud of you. You fought for what you wanted."

I'm proud of myself too. But mostly I'm proud of my friend. "I'm going to be your biggest cheerleader at the Olympic Games, no matter what."

As soon as we step into the room where we're supposed to wait, Gwen pulls me into a hug. Other girls join us, crowding around, until we're a large knot of group huggers, a mass of white USA Gymnastics warm-up suits, swaying quietly, proud of each other for being there.

"We're all winners," Gwen says. "Every one of us."

Which makes us all tear up. So, there we are—sniffling, wiping our eyes, clinging to one another—when the head of the Olympic committee arrives.

"We've come to an agreement," she says. "Before we return to the auditorium to formally and publicly introduce the Team USA women's artistic gymnastics team for the Montreal Olympics, I'd like to announce the five team members, as well as name the three alternates."

A heavy silence falls over the room.

The woman flips a paper on her clipboard. "Without further ado, here is the women's Olympic team. Please hold your applause until the end."

I'm not breathing. But my heart is thundering. I can practically hear the blood rushing in my ears. There's nothing else I can do. I've done everything that I can, but I don't know if it was enough. I close my eyes and wait as the names are called.

"Gwendolyn Edwards from Gold Star Gymnastics, Columbus, Ohio."

Deep inside I release another screech for Gwen. I'm so incredibly happy for her.

"Anna Zhang from Burtinelli's, Manchester, New Hampshire.

"Fatima Akbar from Twisters West, Palo Alto, California.

"Genevieve Patel from White Cliff Gymnastics, Dallas, Texas.

"And Charlie Ryland from Gold Star Gymnastics, Columbus, Ohio."

She names off the alternates, but I'm barely listening. I can't believe it. I did it. I actually did it. I want to do back-flips. Not that I have any room to maneuver. Gwen grips me so hard, I might lose feeling in my arms, and my ankle is pulsing with pain. But none of that matters, because I'm going to the Olympics.

"We did it!" we both cry out at the same time. We hug each other, rock side to side.

"I'm so proud of us, Gwen."

All the hard work, long hours, sacrifices, and pushing through the pain has paid off.

I'm going to be an Olympian.

The march out onto the floor, the presentation of the U.S. women's Olympic team, are a blur. My heart feels like it's beating somewhere outside my body, and all I can concentrate on is gripping the flowers they handed me at the door before I walked out here. My ears ring from the cheering coming from the moving, churning crowd. I clutch the medal at my chest.

I hear my name announced and lift my arm to wave. I search for my family. I want them here with me. They deserve to be up here on this podium, taking all this praise along with me.

After the presentation we're swept back into the anteroom, where our coaches are waiting to congratulate us. There are tears and hugs, and I'm whimpering my thanks into Coach Chris's chest when my parents find me.

Mom's mascara is running down her face, and she blots her eyes with a tissue. Dad's sweatshirt is crooked, like it's been yanked and pulled from many directions. I can imagine Mom gripping his shirt when my name was called, shouting, jumping up and down. They're hugging me so tight that I can't breathe.

They release me, and Mom turns to Josh and shrieks, "She's going to Montreal!"

"I know, Mom," Josh says. "Duh. I was in the stands watching."

"Come here, you!" I order, spreading my arms wide. Josh isn't big into hugging, but he suffers through it, even hugging me back.

"I'm proud of you, Sis."

I release my hold on him, step back. "Thanks, Josh."

"You're a hero," Dad says. "I never saw anyone fight like you fought out there. Great job, kiddo."

"We've got to get that ankle checked out again, pronto," Mom says. "How's it feeling now, hon?"

"I'm barely aware that I have any feet at all," I say, which is the truth. In my present state of euphoria, my leg could have been bitten off by a great white shark and I probably wouldn't have noticed yet. "I feel like I'm flying. There's some slight pain, but it's going to be okay."

Then I notice Bobby standing by the wall, watching me, only me.

I pull away from my family. "Bobby!" I limp toward him. Yes, limp, because my leg won't do anything else, apparently. "What are you doing here?"

"Josh invited me to drive up here with him and your dad. We didn't get in until late last night, too late to see you." He smiles. "And today you were a little busy."

"Yeah, Coach Chris keeps us pretty isolated on the day of an event so we can stay focused. And Mom didn't say anything."

"She probably didn't want to give you any distractions. Hope it didn't bother you when you saw me in the stands."

I shake my head. "Not at all." I grimace, because from now on I intend to be completely honest with him. "Okay, maybe for a couple of minutes. But in a good way. It means a lot to me that you came."

"You were totally amazing."

At his compliment I feel the heat warming my cheeks. "Thanks."

"I saw you limping after a couple of the routines. I was worried that you weren't going to make it."

I shrug. "My ankle has bothered me since I broke it when I was eight. I'm used to having discomfort now and then. I just concentrate and push through it."

"Charlotte!" Spinning around, I see Zoe and Michael striding toward us.

"I can't believe you're here!" I give her a great big hug.

"Your dad drove us," Zoe says, hugging me back. "I couldn't miss watching my bestest friend compete for a place on the Olympic team."

Tears sting my eyes as I push back and study her. "Am I, Zoe? Are we best friends again?"

She rolls her eyes. "Of course we are. Even if you don't get me a T-shirt."

I laugh. "I'll get you a T-shirt." I spot Gwen. "Gwen! Come over. Look who's here."

Gwen prances over. "It's so great that you all came to root for Charlie."

"We were rooting for you, too," Zoe says. "You were awesome!"

"Oh, thanks."

"I mean, when you did that double backflip . . ."

As they start talking about Gwen's routine, I know they're going to become fast friends. I can see us doing so much together in the future.

I turn back to Bobby. "It's really special that you're here."

"I have something for you." He holds out his balled fist and slowly unfurls his fingers to reveal a cardboard badge that reads, I SURVIVED PROM.

Laughing, I take it and press it against my chest, near

the medal dangling from the ribbon around my neck. "Prom wasn't *that* bad. Actually, it was pretty wonderful, except for the Rollerblading *incident*."

"Maybe we'll give it another shot next year."

My heart kicks against my ribs. I don't think I'm going to do homeschooling. "The good news is that I won't be preparing for Olympic trials."

"So, what's next?" he asks.

"I've got to go directly to training camp. Since the school year is basically over, I won't be going back to finish out the classes. I'll just take my finals and be done."

He nods, gives me a small grin. "I'd like to come to Montreal and watch you compete there. Unless you think I'll be a distraction."

I think of all the warnings from Coach Rachel, my mom, even Gwen. I slowly shake my head. "Not one bit."

"How about a kiss? Would that be a distraction?"

"Absolutely, but it's the kind of distraction I'd like. I think. I've never been kissed."

"We can fix that easily enough."

He lowers his head until his lips touch mine. I wrap my arms around his neck and close my eyes. Definitely a distraction. A very warm, pleasant, lovely distraction.

When he draws back, I smile. "Remember when you took me stargazing and I told you my wish?"

"Yes."

"That wasn't really my wish. I said one silently first. I wished you'd kiss me."

A corner of his mouth curls up. "Funny. I wished for the same thing."

"We have the power to make our wish come true."

"We absolutely do."

And he kisses me again.

"Charlie, Gwen," says the woman in the blue suit coat. She holds the microphone in between us, to catch both our voices. "How are you feeling at this moment? Best friends, heading to the Olympics together."

"It's surreal," Gwen says, flashing her brilliant smile. "To have all these friends and family and fans here to cheer us on. It's amazing."

I nod my head in total agreement.

"Gwen, you beat out everyone for the only guaranteed place on the women's Olympic gymnastics team. How does that feel?"

"Oh, well, it feels great, but I couldn't have done what I did today without all these other girls, especially Charlie. I mean, all of us, we've all trained so hard together. It's great to see our hard work paying off."

"And, Charlie?" The woman turns the microphone toward me. "The question we've all been wondering . . . how's the ankle? And do you think you'll be recovered enough to perform at your best at the Olympic Games in August?"

"I worked through the pain today," I say. "I'm certain I can keep doing whatever it takes to be in top form for Montreal. Just, no more school dances for a while."

The reporter laughs along with me.

"Who needs school dances when you've got a guy like Bobby in the stands watching you and cheering you on?" whispers Gwen after the interview as we're weaving our way to the doorway. Our families are waiting outside. "Can you believe he came?"

"No, I cannot. Not at all."

"It's all going to be okay, isn't it?" Gwen asks, slipping her hand into mine. "I mean, we're really making it."

"We're official Olympians now." I give her hand a squeeze. "No turning back."

The stands are filled with red, white, and blue. The chant of "U-S-A! U-S-A!" rises into the huge domed ceiling above my head.

I adjust the sleeves on my leo, a rich raspberry color, adorned with rhinestones that sparkle in the overhead lights. I'm wearing the uniform of Team USA and going for gold.

I hear my name, present to the judges, and then step out onto the spongy floor.

My eye is on the vault platform at the end of the runway. I'm going to take that springboard with a bang and go higher and faster than I ever have before. I'm going to make that two-and-a-half twisting layout look easy.

Watch me.

ABOUT THE AUTHOR

SHAWN JOHNSON has accomplished a lifetime of achievements that include winning four Olympic medals, writing a *New York Times* bestselling memoir, starting her own business, and establishing a career in broadcasting. Johnson is a 2007 World Champion gymnast, a 2008 Olympic women's gymnastics gold and silver medalist, and a 2006, 2007, and 2008 gymnastics National Champion—all titles she attained by the time she turned sixteen. At the age of seventeen, she became the youngest-ever contestant on ABC's eighth season of *Dancing with the Stars*, and in May 2009 she was crowned champion. *The Flip Side* is Shawn Johnson's debut YA novel. Find out more at ShawnJohnson.com.